River's Bend

JoAnn Ross

Praise for JoAnn Ross's books

1

"THE BID IS fifteen hundred and sixty dollars. Do we have fifteen-seventy? Seventy-five? Who'll give me fifteen-eighty?"

Rachel Hathaway stood silently at the back of the wainscoted room, her gray eyes resolutely dry as she watched the past fourteen years of her life being sold off piece by piece. The thick cloud of perfume hovering overhead was beginning to give her a headache.

When she was a little girl growing up on an Iowa farm, her parents had encouraged her to believe in fairy tales. An obedient child, Rachel willingly complied. After graduating with an advertising degree from Iowa State University, she went off to New York City, where she got a job working as a copywriter for a prince of a man named Alan Hathaway.

On their first date, she and Alan decided they wanted to have children together. On their second, Alan proposed and Rachel moved into his one-bedroom castle in Brooklyn. As the years went by, Alan's business grew by leaps and bounds, allowing them to move into a larger palace in Connecticut where Scott—heir to the Hathaway Advertising throne—was born.

The only problem with fairy tales, Rachel had discovered, was that they didn't warn you that the prince could die of a perforated ulcer, the creditors could end up with the castle, and it could be back to the ashes for Cinderella.

"Ladies and gentlemen," the dapper auctioneer cajoled winningly, "may I remind you that this table is in excellent condition. Even without the matching chairs, it could be considered a steal at two thousand."

Remembering the years of celebratory dinners shared around the elegant dining room set, Rachel wondered how anyone could put a price on love. She'd worked the floral needlepoint covers for the chairs herself that long-ago winter when she'd been pregnant with Scotty.

Flushed with the glow of impending fatherhood and concerned for her health, Alan had insisted she quit working. Bored nearly out of her mind, she'd taught herself needlework to pass the long hours spent waiting for her husband's return from his Madison Avenue advertising agency.

"Fifteen-seventy-five," the auctioneer conceded when his efforts were met by a stony wall of silence. "Going once, twice, gone to the lady in the red hat.

"The next item going up for bid is a superb-quality Sheraton revival satinwood bookcase."

"You look as if you could use a break," Janet Morrison murmured as the workmen carried the dining room set from the dais.

"I'm fine," Rachel insisted, her gaze directed toward the bookcase.

She and Alan had discovered it in a little out-of-the-way shop in London the summer Scott had turned two. They'd justified the hefty purchase price by telling each other that the bookcase would become a family heirloom. Something their son would pass on to his children.

"Well, I'm in desperate need of a cigarette," Janet said. "Come keep me company."

Taking Rachel by the arm, she practically dragged her out of the library, down the long terrazzo hallway and out onto the back terrace.

"I thought the doctor warned you to give those things up if you wanted a speedy recovery," Rachel reminded her long time friend and neighbor.

"I still have a few weeks until surgery." Janet lit the cigarette with a gold monogrammed lighter. "Besides, everyone I know gains at least ten pounds when they quit smoking. I'm attempting to forestall the inevitable as long as possible."

At forty-eight, Janet was fourteen years older than Rachel. Her honeyed complexion was nearly flawless, save for the small network of lines fanning outward from her eyes and the slight bracketing around her russet-tinted lips. Like so many other women in the neighborhood, she was resolutely fit, tanned, and blond.

Cursed with fair skin that refused to tan and rain-straight black hair, Rachel had, on more than one occasion, envied her best friend.

"I still don't understand why you feel you need a face-lift," she said honestly. "I think you look great."

"Easy for you to say," Janet retorted. "Your husband didn't just hire a new secretary who looks as if she should be turning cartwheels and leading cheers for the high school football team." She groaned the moment the words left her mouth. "Oh, damn, honey. I'm sorry. It just slipped out."

Rachel could feel her lips smiling, but inside she remained numb, as she had for the past eighteen months. "Don't worry about it. I'm fine. Really."

It was Janet's turn to submit Rachel to a lengthy examination. "No," she said finally, "you're not. Oh, you've been putting on a good show, but anyone who truly knows you could see that you've just been going through the motions. Although it's no wonder, considering the mess Alan left behind."

Rachel didn't immediately answer. Instead, from her vantage point atop the hill, she looked out over the acres of serene, unspoiled woodland, realizing that this would be the last time she'd be able to enjoy the view. The trees were still a deep, leafy green, but in another few weeks they'd be ablaze in their autumnal coats of red, gold, and bronze, and she'd miss seeing the free-flowing stream cutting through the brilliantly colored forest.

Come winter the stream would freeze solid, but for the moment it tumbled merrily over moss-covered rocks, oblivious of its fate. The same way she'd been before Alan's death.

"Do you remember when I began volunteering one day a week helping people who visited the food bank fill out SNAP applications?" she asked suddenly.

"Of course. I didn't really believe that there were any food stamp recipients in Connecticut."

"I know. You asked me to bring a few extra stamps home for pâté and caviar."

"We were having a party that weekend, and every little bit helps. Is this trip down memory lane leading anywhere?"

Rachel dragged her hand through her hair. Her simple

gold wedding band—one of the few pieces of jewelry she hadn't sold—gleamed in the afternoon sun. "I met so many women there, women who'd led lives of convenience and comfort, who were suddenly forced into dire financial straits due to divorce or their husband's death.

"They weren't underprivileged. They were intelligent and well educated. Yet each had made the mistake of allowing her husband to make all the decisions, to handle the money without her knowledge or consent. I felt sorry for them, but inside, I couldn't help feeling a little smug, you know? Because Alan and I always shared everything." She sighed heavily. "At least I thought we did."

"How could you have known the recession had put Alan's business into such a slump? He was only trying to protect you."

That was the same thing Rachel had been telling herself over and over again these past months as she'd struggled to pay off the debts incurred by her late husband. Unfortunately, she hadn't reaped any financial rewards by understanding Alan's motivation.

"I know. I just wish he'd trusted me enough to come to me with his problems."

Janet put her hand on Rachel's arm. "And what could you have done?"

Looking down at her friend's perfectly manicured fingernails, it occurred to Rachel that her own nails were ragged and unpolished.

"The same thing I've done," she answered without hesitation. "Sell the Manhattan apartment, the house, the furniture, the jewelry, take Scotty out of private school, and return to work full time."

"That's not the life Alan wanted for you."

"Well, like it or not, it's the life I ended up with. If he'd only bothered to ask, I would have told him that I'd rather go back to our first apartment than continue living in Connecticut without him."

"He undoubtedly believed he could turn the business around."

Rachel exhaled a soft, rippling little sigh. "I know." And he would have. If it hadn't killed him first.

Both women remained silent for a time, gazing out over the rolling expanse of lawn. The tennis court needed work. The red clay was badly scuffed and covered with debris. Dead leaves floated on the swimming pool she kept forgetting to cover.

"So, how's Scotty taking the move?"

"I thought he'd be upset about changing schools for the second time in eighteen months and leaving all his friends behind, but all he talks about is moving to the Wild West. In fact, not only have cowboys replaced the Yankees in his nine-year-old hierarchy, I haven't had to listen to a Spiderman or Masters of the Universe plot for six weeks."

"Kids are resilient."

"Isn't that the truth? Although it was tough in the beginning, now you'd never know that his world had been turned upside down." Rachel was grateful for her son's apparent ability to bounce back from what had been a disastrous eighteen months.

"How about you? How are you holding up?"

Rachel took her time in answering as a covey of quail bobbed across the lawn. Drawing in a breath, she leaned her head against one of five white wooden posts supporting the slate roof. The post bore the inscription Alan

Loves Rachel. Her husband had carved the romantic declaration the weekend they'd moved into the house nine years ago.

"I'm fine. Really," she said as her friend gave her a long, judicious look.

"You're still too thin, but I think you're beginning to look a little less tense. And either you've discovered some miracle cosmetic cover-up I don't know about, or the circles beneath your eyes are finally beginning to fade."

"I've been sleeping better lately." Ever since she'd made the decision to move to Oregon. "Sometimes all through the night."

"Well, that's something. Did you finally break down and take my advice?"

"Advice?"

"About seeing Larry Newman."

Dr. Lawrence Newman was president of the country club and on the board of directors of several hospitals, as well as being a leading psychiatrist. There were probably very few people in Rachel's circle whom he hadn't seen on a professional basis, causing Alan to have once suggested that if the good doctor ever decided to write his memoirs, the book would probably sell out in Greenwich within minutes.

"I had one appointment."

"Really? How did it go?"

Rachel shrugged. "It didn't. I didn't go back."

"If it's the money, I can lend you Larry's fee."

They both knew it would be useless to offer Rachel the funds outright. While the rest of her life may be in tatters, Rachel's pride had remained formidable. Ignoring legal advice to declare bankruptcy to get out from under the burden of her husband's business responsibilities, she'd insisted on paying off every last dollar, at considerable personal sacrifice.

"It's not the money." Rachel felt her cheeks burn as she remembered the look of pity on the psychiatrist's handsome face. After the pity had come the pass.

"Larry hit on you, didn't he?"

"You don't sound surprised."

"Rachel, practically every woman at the club has had an affair with the guy."

"You're kidding."

"Not at all. Don't tell me you never noticed? Ever since he moved to town, there's been enough hanky-panky to generate a new Sex in the Suburbs series that would make Peyton Place look tame by comparison."

"I never knew." Rachel wondered if Janet had participated in any of the alleged hanky-panky.

"How could you, since whenever you and Alan showed up at any functions, you couldn't keep your eyes—or your hands—off each other." Janet shook her head. "Didn't anyone ever tell you wide-eyed innocents that lust is supposed to die by the first anniversary?"

"And love? When does that die?"

"By the fifth. At least."

"I never stopped loving Alan."

"Nor he you. That's what made the rest of us jealous as hell." She stubbed the cigarette out on the stone terrace with the toe of her Christian Louboutin pump. "I do wish you'd spend tonight with us instead of staying at some dreary motel."

"It's not dreary." Just not the Four Seasons Alan would have booked. "And I truly appreciate the offer, but

I really want to spend our last night in town alone with Scotty. In case he gets depressed about leaving the only home he's ever known and wants to talk about it. Also, because of delays cataloging everything by the auction house, instead of moving last month, as I'd hoped, it's already mid-September. Oregon schools started earlier than here and I don't want him too far behind."

"He's a bright kid. He shouldn't have any trouble catching up," Janet assured her. "Look, I understand why you want to open your own restaurant. You've gone to cooking school, you've catered every party around here for the past five years, even before you took my advice and started charging, and everyone loves your food. But what in the hell made you decide on that Last Chance Café in Oregon? What's wrong with Connecticut? Or even Manhattan?"

"It's the New Chance," Rachel corrected. "In the first place, I could never afford to open a restaurant in Manhattan and Connecticut isn't that much less expensive. For what six month's rent would cost here, I was able to buy the café outright. And have enough left over to rent a house."

"Both sight unseen," Janet reminded her.

"There were photos on the internet." The real estate agent had sent the link after Rachel had responded to a classified listing in Restaurant Magazine.

"Blurry photos. And what you could see isn't going to win you any Michelin stars."

"I'll admit it looks as if it could use a little work. But it's rather . . . unique." In a rustic, Oregon ranching country way.

"Unique." Janet sniffed. "That sounds like real estate

jargon for a dump. Along the lines of a 'Honeymoon Special.' Or 'Handyman Fix-up.' For heaven's sake, Rachel, just because Alan died doesn't mean you have to banish yourself to the wilderness."

"I'm not banishing myself," Rachel repeated what she'd been saying since she'd come up with the plan. "I'm starting a new life." In a new town and a new house where every room she went into didn't remind her of her husband, forcing her to face all the years they'd never have together.

"So, start a new life here," Janet insisted. "Expand your catering company or open a small restaurant, begin dating again, enjoy yourself for a change."

"I tried dating, remember?" Her one-time excursion into the singles world, with the agent who'd listed the Manhattan apartment Alan used whenever he stayed in the city, had turned out to be an unqualified disaster.

Janet shrugged. "So, Bernie was a bust. There are a lot more fish in the sea."

"That's probably true enough. But I'm not into angling these days."

"I'm really going to miss you." Janet threw her arms around Rachel.

Moisture stung her eyelids as Rachel returned the hug. "And I'm going to miss you."

"I'll come visit," Janet promised as they parted.

"By next summer I should have the café running well enough to take a few days off," Rachel said. "We'll drive over to the beach. The scenery's supposed to be magnificent, and Chef Madeline Durand has opened a restaurant and cooking school on the coast."

"I'll bet her restaurant's not in a log cabin," Janet said.

"You'd win that bet. But it is in the Shelter Bay farm-house she grew up in."

"How quaint." Janet shook her head. "Sorry. I really don't mean to sound so negative. I just don't want to lose my BFF. I'll fly out there next summer," she confirmed.

Rachel wished Janet wasn't making it sound as if she were planning a trip on a Conestoga wagon to the wild and wooly western wilderness country.

Her decision hadn't been entirely impulsive. Using due diligence, she had, after all, searched out River's Bend's website and discovered that the town that billed itself as "Oregon's Most Western Town—where spurs have a job to do and cowboy hats aren't a fashion accessory," had a year-round population of three thousand, eight-hundred and thirty-six citizens. The top two industries were ranching and tourism, the second due to its outdoor lifestyle, proliferation of dude ranches, and the number of western movies that had been filmed there.

"It's a date," she said.

Both women's smiles were forced. As they walked back into the house, Rachel knew that in spite of all best intentions and promises, their lives, which had been entwined for so many years, were inexorably drifting apart.

2

THE NEW CHANCE Café was a wreck. Which wasn't all that surprising, Cooper Murphy considered as he stepped over the heavy fire hoses and sloshed through three inches of blackened water. Fire had a way of making things downright messy. Although the flames had been extinguished, a thick cloud of acrid smoke hung heavily over the interior of the restaurant, stinging his eyes and scorching his throat.

He found three members of the volunteer fire department in what remained of the kitchen, drinking coffee. Amazingly, the enormous stainless-steel urn had escaped unharmed.

"Hey, Coop." Cal Potter greeted him with a grin that appeared broad and white in his blackened face. "You're just in time for the cleanup."

Cooper waded through the grimy water to the urn, wishing he'd worn his weekend work boots. Wet soot had already darkened the silver lizard skin of his Tony Lamas to a muddy gray.

"My timing's always been terrific," he said as he poured coffee into a chipped white mug.

"Speaking of timing, what do you think Mitzi's gonna

do when she finds out about this?" Fred Wiley asked. The fireman's face was as dark and streaked as his partner's.

"Mitzi?" Cooper tasted the coffee and understood why the urn had escaped destruction. If it could hold the battery acid that Johnny Mott called coffee, it had to be lined with whatever they'd used on the outside of the space shuttle.

"Do you think she's going to notify that woman?" Fred asked.

"What woman?"

"You know, the Easterner who bought this place."

"Name's Rachel Hathaway," Dan Murphy, former River County sheriff and Cooper's father, said.

"Oh, her." Cooper shrugged. "I supposed it'd only be the right thing to do, considering." His gaze swept the room, taking in the destruction.

Water was everywhere—on the floor, the counters, and six-burner stove. The ancient wood countertop was already beginning to swell. By tomorrow it would be warped beyond repair.

The commercial oven hood, designed to handle a reasonable amount of smoke, had been completely blackened, and the prison green paint on the walls was badly blistered.

"Where's Johnny?"

"Al drove him to the hospital in Klamath Falls. We were worried all this smoke might bring on an attack of his emphysema," Dan said.

"Is he in bad shape?"

Cooper's father shrugged. "Didn't seem much worse than usual. I suspect he's mostly stressed out about the possibility of the sale falling through."

"Mitzi should call that buyer," Cal Potter put in his two cents' worth. "Especially her being a widow lady and all. Finding this mess waiting for her would be bad enough if she had a man to help her get the place put back together again."

"Yep, Mitzi's gonna have to call her," Wiley agreed with a nod of his grizzled gray head. "Even if it does mean losing her commission."

"She can't," Dan said.

"She already spent the money?"

"It's got nothing to do with the money," Dan said. "The reason Mitzi can't call the Hathaway woman is that she's on the road and apparently somewhere out of cell range. She should be arriving today."

For the past six months Dan Murphy had, in the local vernacular, been keeping company with Mitzi Patterson, River's Bend's sole real estate agent. Mitzi was also the River's Bend Register's social reporter, which put Cooper's father in a position to know more than he wanted to about the town's goings-on.

Cal Potter and Fred Wiley whistled in unison. "Wouldn't want to be the one who's got to tell the little lady that she bought herself a pig in a poke," Wiley muttered.

"Me neither," Potter agreed.

Dan remained silent and looked grim.

Cooper was looking out the front window as a green Volvo station wagon with Connecticut plates towing a small rental trailer pulled up in front of the café.

"Looks as if somebody's going to have to break the news," he said.

Three pairs of eyes followed his to the parking lot.

Silence settled over the ravaged kitchen.

"I think Coop should be the one," Potter said finally.

"Me, too," Wiley seconded the motion.

Cooper had served for eight years in the Marines; six of those years in the military police, deployed to both Iraq and Afghanistan. After returning to civilian life, he'd signed on with the Portland Police Bureau, working in high crime districts, which often hadn't seemed all that different from the war zones he'd left behind. In all those years working in risky situations, he'd never—not once—considered himself a coward.

Until now.

"Why me?"

"Seems reasonable," Dan drawled. "Seein' as how you're the sheriff."

Damn. Keeping law and order in River County was one thing. Telling a widow who'd driven all the way across the country that her dream had just gone up in smoke was quite another.

Cooper took another fortifying drink of coffee and wished to hell it were something stronger. Not that anything short of toxic waste was stronger than Johnny Mott's sorry excuse for coffee.

"I don't suppose I have any choice."

"Don't suppose you do," Dan murmured. Although his tone remained noncommittal, a fleeting look of sympathy appeared in his eyes, reminding Cooper of the winter when he was seven and his father had been called away from dinner to tell Mrs. Vance that her husband wouldn't be coming home for Christmas. Ed Vance's logging truck had hit a patch of black ice and skidded out of control on one of the mountain switchbacks.

Then there'd been the time Billy Duncan had drowned in Potter's Pond. According to Ethel MacGregor—River's Bend's answer to Paul Revere when it came to spreading the news—Cooper's father had held a hysterical Karen Duncan in his arms, rocking her like a child, murmuring words of comfort until the woman had run out of tears.

There had been other such occasions during Daniel Patrick Murphy's twenty-five year tenure as sheriff. None of which could have been easy. All of which had probably stayed with his father like some of the stuff Cooper had witnessed while deployed lingered in his mind.

"Guess it comes with the territory," he said unenthusiastically.

"Yeah. It does," Dan agreed.

This time it was pride Cooper viewed in his father's eyes. Pride and empathy.

He drew in a deep breath and put the chipped mug down on the muddy counter. "Well, here goes nothing."

3

RACHEL CLENCHED THE steering wheel as she stared out the window at the New Chance Café. The scene that greeted her was not the least bit encouraging.

"Well, you'd certainly never see anything like this in Connecticut," she said with feigned cheer as she took in the log building sitting in the middle of a gravel parking lot where a white pickup, a red fire truck, and a black Jeep Grand Cherokee painted with River County Sheriff's Department on the side, were parked.

"The cow's neat," her nine-year-old son offered.

Despite her best intentions to remain positive, Rachel cringed as she raised her eyes to the life-size statue of a brown cow standing on top of the roof. A cow the photographs posted on Mitzi Patterson's real estate website had failed to reveal.

"It's unique, at any rate."

"Wait 'til Jimmy finds out we own a log cabin restaurant with a cow on the roof," Scotty said. "He'll never believe it! Can I call him tonight, Mom? And tell him about the cow?"

"I suppose so," Rachel murmured, staring up at the

cow. Could it be any larger?

"Let's check out the inside," she suggested. "We'll have a nice brunch and take a tour of the kitchen before going to Ms. Patterson's real estate office to pick up the key to our house."

"Do you think the house will have a cow on the roof, too?"

"I fervently hope not."

"Maybe it'll have a horse," Scotty suggested. "Wouldn't that be sweet?"

"Sweet," Rachel agreed absently.

She'd just left the car and was headed toward the café when a man came out the scarred wooden door, causing her to come to an abrupt halt.

He was, in a word, perfect. Impossibly, magnificently perfect. His tanned complexion revealed a lot of time spent outdoors, his jaw was firm, his chin square and marked with a deep and delicious cleft. His nose was straight, and his eyes, beneath the brim of a fawn-colored cowboy hat, were a remarkable green so bright that were the rest of him not so flawless, she might have suspected he was wearing tinted contacts.

He was wearing a blue chambray shirt with jeans, wedged-heeled boots and a pistol worn gunslinger style on his hip. It was as if that iconic Marlboro man had suddenly sprung to life and walked off a billboard.

"Ms. Hathaway?" he asked.

His voice was a lush, deep baritone that was as impossibly sexy as his rugged good looks. For a fleeting moment, Rachel imagined showing up with this man at the country club back home. The women would all go wild; it would be like throwing him into a bucket with a school of starving piranha.

That image had her smiling for the first time in a very long while.

"Are you a cowboy?" Scotty asked, staring up at the hat.

"Not really," he said.

Disappointment moved across her son's freckled face.

"But I am sheriff of River County." He reached into a shirt pocket and pulled out a metal badge.

Scotty beamed. "A real live sheriff. Holy cow! Wait'll Jimmy hears about this!"

"Jimmy is Scotty's best friend," Rachel explained. "Back home in Connecticut."

Not that Connecticut was her home any longer, she reminded herself. This was home now. This restaurant with the enormous brown cow on the roof.

Up close, the cow appeared even more gargantuan. Rachel blinked, hoping that when she looked again, the enormous animal would prove to be merely a mirage, brought on by exhaustion and too many hours staring at the seemingly endless miles of asphalt crossing the country.

No such luck. When she opened her eyes again, the cow was still there in all its bovine glory.

"I figured as much." When he took off his hat, revealing thick sun-streaked chestnut hair, Rachel decided that it was unfair for a man to be gifted with such physical beauty. "I'm Cooper Murphy."

"It's a pleasure to meet you, Sheriff. This is my son, Scotty."

"Mom," Scotty complained. "I keep telling you, you have to call me Scott. I'm the man of the house, now," he explained to Cooper. "Scotty's a little kid's name."

The sheriff held out a broad dark hand to her son. "Hi, Scott. I never would've taken you for a little kid. Welcome to River's Bend."

"Me and my mom came to Oregon to start a new life," Scotty—Scott—revealed.

"My mom and I," Rachel corrected.

Her son shrugged off the murmured grammatical correction. "Anyway, my mom and I bought this restaurant because she's the best cook in the whole world. Everyone thinks so. Not just me. Wait 'til you taste her braised short ribs. They even got written about in the newspaper."

"It was a very small review," Rachel said, remembering how excited she'd been to see Rachel's Home Catering in print. Even if it had only been a weekly local paper.

"I'm looking forward to trying them," the sheriff said.

"Dad always said they were even better than Grandma's."

"If your dad said so, it must be true."

"It is. Grandma died. So did my Grandma and Grandpa Field who lived far away in Iowa. They were my mom's mom and dad. But that was a long time ago, when I was just a baby. But I've seen them on the DVDs Mom kept in the old bookcase we had to sell after my dad died, too. So we're all alone now, but we still have each other. Right, Mom?"

"Right," she said absently.

Dragging her gaze from where it had drifted back up to the roof again, Rachel decided to call a halt to this conversation before Scott proceeded to reveal her entire life story.

"Well, as nice as it's been meeting you, I'd like to inspect my café."

"Sure. Come on in and I'll show you around."

"I appreciate the offer, Sheriff Murphy, but you needn't bother. Surely giving restaurant tours isn't part of your job."

"The name's Cooper," he corrected, taking her elbow as he shepherded her toward the front door. "And as for this being part of the job, Ms. Hathaway, I'm afraid that it is."

4

THIS WAS THE widow lady? Cooper couldn't quite believe that this woman in the sharply creased jeans and white silk shirt was the one the guys had been talking about only minutes earlier.

An educated guess put her age somewhere in her early thirties. Her hair, tied at the nape of her long, slender neck, was smooth ebony that gleamed like polished obsidian. As he opened the heavy wooden door, Cooper hoped that the willowy Rachel Hathaway was a helluva lot tougher than she looked because the widow lady was going to need every bit of strength she possessed.

And then some.

"Oh, no!" Mist gray eyes widened in a cameo face as she stared in dismay at the wreckage that greeted her entry into the restaurant.

"Geez," Scott said, his eyes wide, dark saucers behind the lenses of his Harry Potter glasses. "It looks even worse than the time Peter Martin's science project exploded inside the microwave."

"I'm afraid the kitchen is in even worse shape." Since her already fair skin had paled to the color of newly driven snow, Cooper watched her carefully for signs that she might be about to faint.

"I find that hard to believe," she murmured. Her gaze swept the room, taking in the smoke-tinged log walls, the blackened ceiling, and the sodden green felt of the pool table in the corner.

"Perhaps you should go back outside in the fresh air and sit down for a moment," he suggested solicitously.

As if shaking off her shock, she squared her slender shoulders. Then lifted her chin. "I'd rather see the kitchen," she said, meeting his concerned look with a determined, level one of her own.

Cooper tipped the brim of his hat back with his thumb, his admiration mixed with concern. "Now it's not that I want to stand in your way, ma'am, but I've got to warn you that it's an unholy mess back there."

Reminding herself that the reason she had come to Oregon, the reason she had dragged her child all the way across the country, was to escape just such solicitude, Rachel stiffened: shoulders, back, resolve.

After what she'd been through, she refused to allow a bit—all right, a great deal more than a bit—of smoke and water to get the best of her.

"I believe you, Sheriff," she said. "But unholy or not, it just happens to be my mess."

With that, she brushed passed him, pushing open the swinging doors that led to the kitchen.

Taking in the destruction that made the dining room look neat and tidy by comparison, Rachel reluctantly admitted, if only to herself, that Sheriff Cooper Murphy definitely couldn't be accused of exaggeration.

The brown linoleum floor was awash with soot and ashes while acrid smoke hung over the kitchen like a funeral pall. Which was appropriate, because the devastation represented the death of a dream that had been keeping her going for weeks. And across all those seemingly endless miles of asphalt.

At the very center of the muck and mire were three men who were all looking at her with varying degrees of interest. One, seeming shocked, bit through his cigar.

"Good morning, gentlemen," she greeted them, forcing a smile that she was a very long way from feeling.

"Morning, ma'am." One of the men yanked off his hat and actually gave her a stilted bow that he might have bestowed on Kate Middleton, were the Duchess of Cambridge ever to pay a royal visit to River's Bend, Oregon.

"Mornin'," the man who'd bit his cigar in two mumbled. He stared down at his boots and plucked bits of tobacco out of his mouth.

"Ms. Hathaway." The third man extended a hand. "I'm Dan Murphy and these two gentlemen are Cal Potter and Fred Wiley, members of River's Bend's Volunteer Fire Department. Along with being fire chief, Cal's also River County's deputy sheriff and Fred—" he gestured toward the cigar biter—"runs Wiley's Feed and Grain.

"It's a real pleasure to meet you, ma'am, although I wish it could have been under more pleasant circumstances." Dan Murphy continued.

"I certainly can't argue with you there," Rachel murmured as her hand disappeared into his much larger one. "Murphy," she said. "Are you—"

"My father," Cooper filled in for her. "And former sheriff of River County."

Eyeing Dan Murphy with renewed interest, Rachel

realized that had she not been so stunned by the devastation of the New Chance Café's kitchen, she would have spotted the resemblance immediately.

The former sheriff's tanned face was older and more weathered by the elements, but there was no mistaking the square jaw, the firm lips, and those incredibly green eyes that had her thinking of sunlight shining on a newly watered lawn. He was remarkably handsome for a man she guessed to be in his early sixties.

"I can see the resemblance," she said.

Dan's answering grin lit up the room. "Lots of folks say that. Which is when I always point out that I'm the good-looking one."

"And modest, too," Cooper murmured.

"Hell, son, no point hiding your light under a bushel. Not when there's a pretty woman around." His laughing gaze paid her a masculine compliment before moving beyond Rachel to her wide-eyed son standing in the doorway.

"You must be Scott. We're pleased as punch to have you in River's Bend. The town's in need of young blood."

"How did you know my name?"

"Mitzi told me. She's been going on and on about you and your mom. There's nothing that woman loves more than helping families settle into new homes."

"Are you a cowboy?" Eyeing the black hat Dan Murphy was wearing, Scott asked the question he'd asked the sheriff.

"Well," Dan drawled, "if owning a few head of mangy, mean old cattle makes a man a cowboy, I suppose I am."

"Wow." Scott breathed appreciatively, looking up at his mother. "A sheriff and a cowboy. All on our first day!

What a great place, huh, Mom?"

"Great," Rachel answered absently. She'd only been vaguely aware of the conversation as she studied the kitchen with the eye of a woman who might be down, but wasn't about to be counted out. Yet.

"How did the fire start?" she asked. "Was it the wiring?"

"Nothing that serious, ma'am," Cal Potter, assuming his fire chief role, said. "You see, Johnny, he's the one who owns the place, is getting on in years."

"So Ms. Patterson told me," Rachel said. "I remember her also saying that he was selling the restaurant so he could move to California to live with his son and daughter-in-law."

"And their five kids," Dan said. "Johnny's had a real hankering to be a live-in granddad ever since John Junior invited his daddy down to Bakersfield to live with them."

He shook his head as he looked around the kitchen. They'd opened the back door, to allow the smoke to drift outdoors, but instead of making the place look better, the bright shaft of autumn sunlight only highlighted the devastation.

"It'd be a crying shame if he doesn't get to make the trip. What with his emphysema and all, no telling how long the poor old guy's got."

The suspicious look Cooper shot his father suggested he was surprised the older man would play an emotional blackmail card. Which was what he appeared to be doing.

"I can imagine." Rachel was determined to remain pleasant, but equally determined not to be bulldozed. "And I sympathize with Mr. Mott and his son and each and every one of his five grandchildren. But you still haven't told me how the fire started."

"Grease trap," Fred Wiley said, finally deciding to speak up. "Damn fool forgot to clean it out last week."

"That's all it was? An overfilled grease trap?"

"That's about it," Cal agreed, shooting Wiley a sharp look seemingly intended to remind him exactly who was the fire department spokesman.

"So, what you're saying is that if Mr. Mott had remembered to clean out the grease trap, this fire wouldn't have occurred."

Cal Potter gave her a look that suggested she'd just won the final round of the Jeopardy championship.

"That's it, exactly. The wiring's fine, ma'am. My brother Hal, who's an electrician over in K. Falls, installed that new stove and hood for Johnny just last winter. He also checked out the rest of the wiring and said it was all shipshape."

"I suppose your brother would know?"

"Yes, ma'am. Hal knows the electrical business better than anyone in this part of the state. The county inspector gave the job a green tag first time out."

Rachel nodded thoughtfully as she reached up and ran her finger along the blackened overhead hood, which several buckets of hot water, Mr. Clean, and some old fashioned elbow grease should return to its gleaming copper glory.

She might have admittedly been living a life of privilege these past years, but deep down, she was still a farmer's daughter, unafraid of hard work. The countertops were beyond repair, but she would have wanted to replace the scarred, less than sanitary wood.

The paint was blistered; the walls would have to be

scraped and sanded, but from what she could tell, the color had been a muddy military green that would have made her feel as if she were cooking in an Army mess kitchen. Or a prison.

"I take it the restaurant is insured."

Cal Potter nervously cleared his throat.

Fred Wiley returned to his previous mute state and took a sudden interest in digging soot from beneath his grime-encrusted fingernails with a pocketknife.

Dan Murphy took off his hat and began finger-combing his wavy silver hair.

The silence was deafening.

"I'm afraid it's not," Dan said finally. "You see, the policy was up for renewal last week and with all the moving preparations, Johnny just—"

"Forgot to pay the renewal premium," Rachel guessed.

"That's about it in a nutshell," Dan admitted. "But if you'd still be willing to buy the New Chance, I'm sure Mitzi could work out some sort of compromise price."

Even as Rachel considered the magnitude of such a challenge, she was faced with a lack of choices. She couldn't go back to Connecticut; her house and all her possessions were gone. She had no family, no ties anywhere else.

The truth was, she'd pinned all her hopes on River's Bend. Unless she could find another affordable restaurant for sale, and quickly, like it or not, right now the New Chance Café was her only chance.

"I don't know." She opened a cupboard and found it filled with heavy white plates. Many of them chipped. "Without insurance . . ."

"River's Bend is a real friendly town, Ms. Hathaway,"

Dan said encouragingly. "We do things here a little differently than you're probably used to back east in the city. I can guarantee that if you decide to stay, we'll all chip in."

"My brother would be glad to donate his services," Cal Potter assured her with an equally encouraging smile. The late morning sun, pouring in through the open door, glinted on his gold front tooth. "And I'm right handy with a hammer and nails."

"I've been promising the wife I'd paint the front room all summer," Fred Wiley mumbled. "I don't suppose it'd make much difference if the job waited a few more months. If you'd like yourself some Navajo white paint."

"I'm an old hand at refinishing wood," Dan said. "Some sanding and linseed oil would get those cabinets back to tip-top condition in no time."

Personally Rachel considered that more than a little optimistic since she doubted that the cabinets had been in tip-top condition for a very long time. Besides, she'd rather have more efficient shelving, so she probably would have taken them down.

"Hank Young, down at Young's Hardware, still owes me from last week's poker game," Cooper entered into the conversation. "He's always had an unfortunate tendency to draw on an inside straight. He'd probably be more than willing to donate some roofing material to pay off his loss."

Rachel could hardly believe her ears. After Alan's death, she'd received innumerable offers of assistance, all prefaced with the words, "If there's anything I can do."

There had been a great deal those well-meaning individuals could have done to ease the burden she'd found herself facing, but when it came to actually requesting specific favors, she'd choked on her damn pride.

This time, however, four men, all virtual strangers, were offering specific solutions to her problems. It was as wonderful as it was incredible.

"Why?" she asked. "Why would you all be willing to help a stranger?"

"If you decide to stay in River's Bend," Dan said simply, "you won't be a stranger."

"That's right," Cal agreed. "You'll be one of us."

"And River's Bend takes care of its own," Wiley put in.

Although Cooper remained silent, perhaps not wanting to pressure her into a quick decision, she could feel him watching her. Meanwhile, Scotty was shifting anxiously from one sneaker clad foot to the other, waiting for her answer.

"I believe I'd like to talk with Ms. Patterson," Rachel decided at length.

"She had to drive up to Eugene," Dan said. "She just sold her own house up there. Took her six months to decide to list it, then damned if it didn't sell the very first weekend. Of course she was upset when the title company insisted on closing today, what with you coming to town. But I promised I'd take care of things."

"I can certainly understand why she had to leave town, but there's the matter of our rental house—"

"Don't worry. She gave me the key this morning before she left."

Potter and Wiley's muffled snorts of laughter drew a warning look from Dan.

"As if people didn't have anything else to talk about, it

seems my personal life has become the favorite topic down at Harry Banks' barber shop these days," he grumbled before turning back to Rachel. "Mitzi asked me to help you and your son get all settled into your rental house. Then you and she can discuss your real-estate deal over dinner out at my place."

"I wouldn't want to put you out." As much as Rachel appreciated the gesture, she was slightly uncomfortable with the gregariousness of the townspeople she'd met so far.

Dan laughed. A deep, robust sound Rachel was certain the absent Mitzi found more than a little appealing. "Hell, Rachel, the day I turn down a chance to spend time with a pretty woman is the day they can start measuring me for a casket. Right, son?"

Cooper returned the smile, but his gaze was directed straight at Rachel. "Right," he answered absently.

As his green eyes took a leisurely tour of her face, Rachel remained still, deciding to humor the man, even as she sought to pretend such masculine appraisal was a common, everyday occurrence.

She'd just prided herself on her success when his eyes settled on her lips. The spontaneous pull his look incited was every bit as unexpected as it was unwanted.

"Well," she said briskly as she glanced one more time around what only the most charitable person could describe as a restaurant kitchen, "I suppose I've seen enough for now."

"We'll get you all settled into your new place in no time." Dan rubbed his hands together with obvious satisfaction. "Cooper, why don't you come along," he suggested. "An extra hand's always good to have on moving day."

"I'd be glad to help."

"That's very nice of you, Sheriff," Rachel said. "But surely you must have more important things to do than carry boxes."

"None that I can think of at the moment, ma'am," Cooper assured her, matching her polite tone. "If you do decide to stay, you'll discover things are pretty peaceful around River's Bend."

"Well, let's get going," Dan said heartily, putting a friendly arm around Scott's shoulders.

As Rachel returned to the Volvo, she considered that despite the fire, despite the fact that the New Chance Café was far from the quaint western eatery Mitzi Patterson had made it out to be, despite the fact that the town's sheriff had her experiencing feelings she had no business even thinking about, despite all that, she just may have found a new home after all.

5

AS SHE DROVE TO their rented house, Rachel realized that River's Bend website hadn't exaggerated its credentials. Having grown up watching western movies with her dad, she wouldn't have been at all surprised to see John Wayne or Clint Eastwood riding their horses down Front Street.

"Wow. It looks a lot like the town of Dirt in *Rango*," Scott said, his eyes as wide Johnny Depp's chameleon character in the animated film as they took in the wooden storefronts. "But all fixed up."

"Which is a definite plus." If she'd found herself in anything resembling the desolate ramshackle buildings in the movie her son had watched more times than she wanted to count, Rachel would have turned right around and headed back east. Still, Scott wasn't far off when he said the street resembled a movie set.

The small bungalow she'd rented, again, sight unseen, was two blocks away on Mountain View Drive and fortunately, proved to be everything the café wasn't. It had been painted a soft cream yellow with white trim. There were flower boxes beneath the windows and a green wooden screen door that opened onto a screen-in front porch. Yellow and orange mums bloomed in planters on the steps and the lawn had been recently mowed.

"It's lovely." She breathed a relieved sigh. It was going to be all right after all. She and Scotty—Scott—would be all right. She turned to her son. "How long has it been since you've seen a picket fence?"

"I've never seen a picket fence," Scott pointed out.

"I guess you haven't," Rachel said vaguely, entranced by what seemed more an enchanted cottage than a proper house. "We had a picket fence around our front yard when I was a girl."

"In Rockwell City?"

"In Rockwell City," she confirmed. The self-proclaimed "Golden Buckle on the Corn Belt" wasn't actually a city, but a small community of two thousand. "I used to walk along the top rail and pretend I was a circus tightrope walker."

"I guess things must've been pretty boring back in Iowa, huh, Mom?"

"I suppose it'd seem so these days, but back then—"

"He's here," Scott interrupted, jumping up and down on the seat as he began fumbling with his seat belt.

"I suppose you're talking about Sheriff Murphy." Rachel glanced into her rearview mirror at the black Jeep Grand Cherokee that had pulled up behind them.

"Yeah. Isn't he neat, Mom? A real sheriff!" He was off, out of the Volvo, racing toward the Jeep.

As Rachel followed her son, Cooper climbed out of the SUV and headed toward her, his long stride exuding strength and power. And an overabundance of testosterone she so didn't need.

"This is really very kind of you, Sheriff Murphy," she said as he approached.

"Would you do me a favor?" he asked.

"What kind of favor?"

"Would you mind calling me Cooper? After twenty-five years of hearing my dad called Sheriff, and before that my grandfather, I'm still having a little trouble getting used to the title."

"But not the duties," Rachel guessed.

His faint smile was echoed in his eyes. "I suppose the work does come more naturally."

She wasn't surprised by his admission. Cooper Murphy possessed an unmistakable aura of confidence that unexpectedly reminded her of Alan. A thought that was immediately followed by a stab of guilt for comparing her late husband to a virtual stranger.

"I've got a call," he apologized as the radio in the Jeep began to crackle. "Be right back."

She and Scott stood on the tree-lined sidewalk, watching him. His conversation on the radio was brief.

"I'm sorry to run out on you like this," Cooper said as he returned. "But I'm afraid duty calls."

"I hope it's nothing serious." River's Bend looked like the peaceful town Mitzi, his father, and the sheriff all had promised. But the unmentioned cow on the roof of her restaurant proved that appearances could be deceiving. Rachel dearly hoped she hadn't dragged Scott all the way across the country only to put him in danger.

"Just one of our good old boys causing a bit of trouble

down at City Hall," he assured her. "I really do apologize for leaving you in the lurch like this."

"Not exactly in the lurch," Rachel pointed out as Dan drove up in the white pickup. Following him was the red pumper truck with Cal at the wheel and Fred Wiley seated beside him.

Cooper gave her a slow, easy smile that was more dangerous than it should have been. "If you give us a chance, Rachel, you'll discover River's Bend can be a real friendly town."

"I'll keep that in mind."

He nodded. "You do that." He was halfway to the Jeep when he turned back to her. "I almost forgot. I'll pick you and Scott up at six for dinner."

"Really, Sheriff—" Rachel objected, ignoring the way Scott was desperately yanking on the back of her blouse in an effort to influence her decision—"that isn't necessary."

"The Bar M is pretty remote, especially for a newcomer," Cooper said. "What kind of sheriff would I be if I let you get lost your first day in River's Bend?"

"But—"

The radio's insistent crackling resumed, cutting her off before she could point out that the Volvo did possess a GPS.

"Gotta go. See you this evening," he said over his shoulder as he began jogging back toward the Jeep.

"Did I hear Cooper say something about this evening?" Dan asked as he strolled toward Rachel on an easy, loose-limbed stride.

"He offered to drive us out to your ranch for dinner,"

Rachel said. "I assured him it wasn't necessary. I did manage to cross several states coming from Connecticut to Oregon without getting lost, so I'm sure I could have found my way. But he insisted."

"Cooper has always been a helpful boy," Dan said.

"Real helpful," Cal Potter agreed as he joined them.

Fred Wiley's choked sound was somewhere between a snort and a laugh.

Deciding to ignore their knowing looks, Rachel turned her attention to her son. "Come on, kiddo. Let's go check out our new home."

6

C ITY HALL WAS on Front Street, across from the town square, located between the sheriff's office and the post office. The bronze plaque on the cornerstone revealed that the red brick building had been dedicated in 1904. In addition to the offices of the city council, it housed various county, state, and federal offices.

As soon as Cooper entered the building, a harried looking man in his fifties, sporting a crew cut and wearing a brown, ill-fitting suit, came marching toward him.

"It's about time you got here," Mel Skinner complained without preamble.

"Nice to see you, too, Mel," Cooper said. "I came as soon as I got the call."

"Well, it wasn't soon enough. You'll never guess what the damn fool's threatening to do this time."

"You know I've never been much for guessing games. Why don't you just calm down and tell me why you felt the need to take me away from helping River's Bend's newest resident settle into her rental house?"

His news stopped Mel Skinner in his tracks. "The widow's staying?"

"She's considering it."

"Does she know about this morning's fire?"

"She does."

"And she didn't take off running?"

"Nope. My guess is that she'll stay."

The older man shook his head. "She's either crazy or a glutton for punishment."

"She didn't seem crazy."

A paradox, perhaps. Her stoic reaction to the disaster that had awaited her had proved her strength. The confusion in her wide eyes as his gaze had involuntarily settled on her lips had hinted at softness Cooper would like to explore further.

"Well, if she does decide to reopen the restaurant, she'll probably make it. Lord knows, she can't be any worse cook than Johnny, and he's always done okay," Skinner decided. "Of course it doesn't hurt that the New Chance is the only restaurant in town."

"That did tend to give Johnny a captive clientele," Cooper agreed. "So, getting back to my reason for leaving a pretty young widow in the lurch—"

"Young?" Skinner interrupted. "Nobody said anything about her being young."

"Well, she is."

"How young?"

"Early to mid thirties, I suppose. About Jake—"

"Good looking?"

Cooper thought back to Rachel's shiny raven hair and mist gray eyes and skin that reminded him of the porcelain dolls his three-times-great-grandmother had insisted on bringing across the country in their covered wagon. The dolls that, against all odds, had survived the journey intact and were now in the River's Bend historical museum.

"Pretty enough, I suppose," he said noncommittally.

He knew that were he to tell the truth about finding her more than a little appealing, not only would he replace his dad as the hot new topic of conversation down at Harry's Barber Shop, the River's Bend grapevine would have him head over heels in love by lunchtime, engaged by dinner, and married before the week was out.

"Now, about Jake," he tried again.

"The damn drunken fool's threatening to take a baseball bat to my computer!" Skinner's Adam's apple bobbed above the turquoise and silver slide of the bolo tie he'd started wearing after a vacation trip to Arizona last winter. "You have to stop him, Cooper. Without that computer, we might as well close up shop and go home."

"Maybe that's what Jake has in mind," Cooper suggested as he walked down the hallway to the Farm Services Agency's offices on the first floor.

It wasn't the first time Jake Buchanan's feud with the government had garnered official attention. Ever since losing his land to foreclosure, Jake had been waging an ongoing, but futile war against the system as the eviction clock ticked down. As much as Cooper felt for Jake, and all the other small landowners who'd gone under in the past few years, as sheriff of River County, it was his job to maintain the peace.

"That computer is the property of the United States Government," Skinner reminded him tartly. "If anything happens to it, I'm going to hold you personally responsible."

The unmistakable sound of Jake's swearing filtered down the hall. "Why me?" Cooper hoped he'd be able to calm the older man down before things got out of hand.

"Because you should have arrested him last week. After he threw that beer bottle at my car when I drove up to his house."

"The bottle was empty. And he missed."

"That's not the point. That just happens to be an official government car. Do you have any idea how many forms I would have had to fill out if he'd put a dent in it? Or even worse, broken a window?"

"Knowing the federal government, probably quite a few," Cooper said.

"I want Buchanan arrested, Cooper. I don't care if he is your father-in-law. That's no excuse for favoritism."

Cooper stopped in his tracks and looked down at the man, a dark storm threatening in his normally friendly eyes. "Favoritism is a serious charge, Mel," he said quietly, folding his arms. "If I were you, I'd be sure of my facts before you began spreading that accusation all over town."

The challenge hummed in the air between the two men.

"Just stop the damn fool from smashing my computer," Skinner said finally.

Cooper nodded. "I'll do my best."

Damn. The scene that greeted Cooper was not encouraging. A covey of secretaries hovered around the open door, staring into the office with a mixture of fascination and dismay. Papers and manila files had been swept off desks, coffee cups along with them, leaving dark brown trails on the industrial carpeting.

In the center of the chaos stood a small, wiry man wearing a green John Deere baseball cap, a red-and-gray plaid wool shirt, jeans, and a pair of scuffed Justin work boots. He was carrying a Louisville Slugger.

"Hey, Jake." Cooper's voice was calm, steady.

From the way Jake Buchanan's eyes narrowed suspiciously, it was obvious that he'd been expecting a harsher greeting. "Coop."

Cooper pulled a bright red pack from his shirt pocket. "Want some gum?"

Buchanan shook his head. His eyes remained watchful. Wary.

"Suit yourself." Taking a stick from the pack, Cooper took a long time unwrapping it. "Nice day, isn't it?" He leaned back against a metal desk and crossed his legs at the ankles, frowning at the smudges of ash that still darkened the toes of his new boots. "Gotta love Indian Summer."

"Sheriff," Skinner interjected impatiently. "Are you going to arrest this man or not?"

Cooper ignored the bristling bureaucrat. "Of course, it's been so warm this year, the folks up at the Modoc Mountain ski bowl are probably biting their fingernails down to the quick, worrying whether they're going to get enough snow for their Thanksgiving weekend opening."

Buchanan didn't answer, but his fingers relaxed imperceptibly on the baseball bat.

"Looks as if you've been busy," Cooper said, glancing around the office.

"I came to get my land back," Jake growled. The sweet, pungent scent of Jack Daniels floated on his breath.

"It isn't your land any longer," Mel Skinner said. "It belongs to the United States Government."

Buchanan's answering oath was brief and harsh.

"Sheriff, I want this man arrested," Skinner insisted. "For disturbing the peace, destruction of official government property, along with assault and battery."

"Hell, I haven't assaulted anyone," Buchanan shot back. "Leastwise not yet."

"And that's just how I'd like to keep it," Cooper said mildly. "You know this isn't the way to handle things, Jake."

"You want to tell me what I should do? This damn squint-eyed little weasel of a bureaucrat steals my land— land that's been in the Buchanan family for four generations—and I'm supposed to just roll over and take it?"

"That's it!" Mel Skinner slapped his hand down onto a desk. "I'm getting damned sick and tired of you telling anyone fool enough to listen to your alcoholic rants that I'm a worse thief than Bad Bill Barkley."

"If the boot fits. You might not rob trains, but you're even more of an outlaw," Jake Buchanan shot back.

"Sheriff, I insist you add libel to the rest of those charges."

"Mel," Cooper drawled, "I came here to do my job. Now if you don't leave this office right now, I'm afraid I'm going to have to haul you in for obstructing justice."

"Obstructing justice?" Skinner asked disbelievingly. "What the hell does that mean?"

"It means you're getting in my way."

"You're also pissing me off," Buchanan said, waving the bat and weaving drunkenly.

Skinner's angry gaze moved from Cooper to Buchanan to Cooper again. "You're going to regret this, come election time."

Amused, Cooper raised a brow. "Is that a threat, Mel?"

"Dammit," Buchanan complained, "if you're going to

arrest me, Coop, would you just do it now and get it over with? I'm tired of holding this damn thing up in the air." He'd begun swaying dangerously.

"You always did have a tendency to choke the bat," Cooper said. "I've tried to tell you that an easy grip makes for a much smoother swing. Helps you hit those long balls."

He held out his hand for the bat.

"And since you brought it up, I suppose I don't have much choice but to take you in, Jake. Until you sober up."

Buchanan's red-rimmed eyes shone with moisture. "He stole my land, Cooper," he complained, dropping the Louisville Slugger to his side. He didn't struggle as Cooper relieved him of the weapon.

"We'll talk about it later," Cooper promised soothingly. "For now, let's get you somewhere you can lie down. Before you fall down."

"He stole my land," Jake Buchanan repeated to the curious crowd gathered outside the office. "I made those payments. Never missed a one . . . Damn bastard stole my ranch."

As the two men walked out to the Jeep together, Cooper's arm around Jake's shoulder to steady him, tongues clucked, and heads wagged.

The confrontation was rapidly showing signs of replacing Mitzi and his father as River Bend's hottest topic of conversation, but Cooper knew that when people found out about the arrival of the enticing widow Hathaway, he and Jake would quickly become yesterday's news.

7

MITZI PATTERSON POSSESSED the type of bubbly personality usually reserved for cheerleaders and Miss America contestants. Petite, blond, and indefatigably good humored, she deftly monopolized dinner conversation with entertaining stories of other real estate disasters she'd encountered over the years.

"When you saw that mess, I'll bet you wanted to make a big old U-turn and go right back to Connecticut," Mitzi said knowingly.

"I considered it." Rachel took a sip of coffee. It was rich, dark and strong.

The meal—a pale pastel swirl of squash soup with red pepper cream, succulent pink slices of grilled American Kobe beef raised on the ranch, and crunchy on the outside, steaming on the inside sweet potato fries—had been superbly prepared.

"This was an amazing dinner," she told Cooper's grandmother who'd prepared the meal. Betty and Mike Murphy lived in a small log cabin next door.

"It's not hard to cook a decent meal when you've got good ingredients," Betty, a lean, gray-haired woman who appeared to be somewhere in her eighties, said. "The Bar

M's got the best beef in the state. Probably even the country, which is why so many fancy restaurants have taken up cooking with it." Her pride in the family ranch was obvious. "Why, that famous New York chef who has a restaurant on the coast even came down here to check us out."

"After tasting Mom's prime rib, she became a regular customer," Dan said.

"Are you talking about Chef Madeline Durand?" Rachel asked.

"None other," Betty answered. "But she's got herself a new husband now. She's going by Chef Chaffee. She's visited a few times. Even worked in my kitchen with me."

There'd been a scandal, Rachel vaguely remembered. Something about Madeline Durand's French chef husband's adulterous sex video going viral. But having been caught up in her own problems at the time, Rachel hadn't paid much attention.

"The Bar M couldn't run without Mom," Dan said.

"Well, the outside would get along well enough," Betty Murphy allowed. "But you'd probably have starved to death after Julie's passing."

"Julie was my mom," Cooper told Rachel.

"She was a fair to middlin' cook herself," Betty allowed. "But throwing a hunk of meat on the grill is about the height of my son's culinary expertise," she said with a cluck of her tongue. "It's a pitiful thing when a grown man can't even feed himself."

While Rachel didn't want to tip her hand regarding her decision regarding the New Chance, she made a mental note to ask Cooper's grandmother if she'd be willing to share her recipe for the soup.

"At least he's never burned water," Mitzi said.

"You didn't burn water," Dan corrected. "Just the kettle you'd put it in."

"I got called out on a listing," Mitzi explained. "And forgot I'd left the kettle on for tea. Fortunately, though it smelled to high heaven after all the water boiled away, it didn't burn the kitchen down."

"Unlike the New Chance's kitchen," Rachel said.

A trio of gold bracelets jangled as Mitzi braced her elbows on the table and observed Rachel over linked fingers. Reflected splinters of light from the wagon-wheel chandelier overhead made her steady gaze appear even more intent.

"Has the fire changed your mind about buying the restaurant, Rachel?" she asked.

Gone was the cheerleader, and in her place was a fifty-something Realtor who could have been pushing mansions in Greenwich or Beverly Hills.

"I still haven't made up my mind."

"Cooper mentioned that you've moved into the house."

"If you call unpacking a few things moving in." Rachel wasn't about to admit that after dropping the trailer off at the local gas station that served double duty as a U-Haul rental business, she'd spent the rest of the day settling in.

"Renting a furnished house isn't that different from leasing a vacation home," she pointed out. "We could be out in an hour if we choose to go back to Connecticut."

"Is that the decision you're leaning toward?" If she were worried about losing a potential sale, Mitzi's friendly tone didn't reveal it.

Rachel took another sip of coffee and chose her words

carefully. She could feel Scott's pleading gaze riveted on her face. Although it was extremely difficult, she managed to ignore him.

"It represents a lot of work. More than just restoring the café to its previous condition. It would have to be completely redecorated," she answered finally.

Mitzi nodded her golden head approvingly. "Of course. With the exception of the new stove and hood, Johnny hasn't redecorated the New Chance since Carter was President. And heaven knows, the seventies weren't exactly the most fashion forward decade of the last century. It's understandable that you'd want to put your personal touches on the decor."

Personally, Rachel thought that referring to the faded linoleum and torn olive green and orange vinyl booths as decor was stretching the point, but opted not to argue. Not when more important things were at stake.

"I'd need to gut the interior entirely and begin with a clean slate."

Mitzi didn't argue. There was no point since it was true. "At least the building has good bones. And the exterior's sound. I made Johnny get a termite inspection before I'd list it."

"Place has stood in the same spot for over a century," Cooper's grandfather, who'd been quiet during the dinner, spoke up. "Going back to the Wild West days. They say Bad Bill Barkley ate there a lot. Between train and stagecoach robberies."

"Bad Bill Barkley?" Scott, who'd been sneaking bits of beef to the Australian shepherd beneath the table, suddenly gained interest in the conversation. Coincidently, Bad Bill was the name of the Gila monster outlaw in

Rango, which along with being her son's favorite movie, was also his most-played video game. She could tell he was looking forward to a tall tale along the lines of the *Gunfight at the O.K. Corral*.

"He was an outlaw from around these parts," Mike Murphy said.

"Dad's got a good point," Dan said. "You'd be buying yourself a heap of history."

"And along with the history," Mitzi said, "you'll also be achieving that new beginning you want so badly."

She reached across the table and placed her hand on Rachel's. "Don't think I don't know how it is. Having to start again. To reinvent yourself. I've been there, Rachel, though in my case, I was coming off a divorce, and it's never easy. But it's worth it. In the long run."

"It would take a great deal of work," Rachel repeated. "Not to mention money." The latter could be a serious problem.

"Sure would," Dan agreed. "But you'd have a volunteer crew of willing workers," he reminded her.

"As for the money," Cooper said, entering the conversation for the first time since it had turned to business, "I'll bet Johnny'd be willing to cut a few thousand off the purchase price. Wouldn't you say so, Mitzi?"

"I'm sure I could convince him to see the wisdom of lowering the price," Mitzi agreed with a bright, professional smile. "Especially since the fire, while accidental, was his fault. Not to mention the little matter of the lack of insurance."

"I've no doubt that when you put your mind to it, you could convince a man to do just about anything," Cooper said approvingly.

"I've always been a firm believer in not giving up, that's for sure." Mitzi's gaze cut quickly to Dan, then back to Rachel. "Johnny's the impatient sort, and he's anxious to move to Bakersfield. I'm certain we can work out a deal agreeable to everyone involved."

"Then there's the matter of the sales commission," Cooper said.

Beneath her expertly applied blush, Mitzi paled every so slightly. "Sales commission?"

"Seeing as how the entire town's willing to help Rachel salvage her restaurant, I figured you'd want to cut your commission in order to give her a bit more operating capital," Cooper said. "If you lower your commission, Johnny would probably be happy to pass the extra savings on to Rachel."

"Him being so eager to move to Bakersfield and all," Dan tacked on.

Mitzi chewed on her bottom lip. Rachel could practically see the wheels turning inside the real-estate woman's blond head.

"I suppose I could live with four percent," she said finally.

Two percent less than the six Rachel knew Johnny had agreed to pay. The additional money could buy new dishes. Rachel gave Cooper an appreciative smile, only to discover he wasn't finished.

"Now, sweetheart," he drawled with a coaxing smile, "everyone in town knows that you expected to be sitting on that listing until Modoc Mountain crumbles to dust. Even at three percent, you'd still come out smelling like a rose."

"Why don't I just donate my entire commission?"

Mitzi suggested dryly.

"That'd be real hospitable of you," Cooper said agreeably. "And I know Rachel would appreciate it. Wouldn't you?"

Entranced by the masculine power of Cooper's smile, Rachel took a moment to answer. "Of course I would, but—"

"Then it's settled." The satisfied look on his handsome face suggested he'd never expected any other outcome.

Rachel still couldn't entirely believe what had just happened. "Surely you didn't mean that? About donating your entire commission?"

Mitzi shrugged her cashmere-clad shoulders. "Shoot, honey, we're in the last quarter of what's been a pretty good year for me. If I make any more money, I'll just have to give a bunch more to the tax man."

It was too much. Rachel blinked hard, hoping that she could keep from embarrassing herself by breaking into tears.

"I've heard about Western hospitality," she said, forcing her words past the lump in her throat. "But don't you think you're taking this a bit too far?"

"Not at all," Dan said. "River's Bend is a family town, Rachel. Always has been. We all know one other, and more importantly, we care, whether we're dancing at our weddings or mourning our dead. We also understand that some people might consider that old-fashioned. Even boring." He shrugged his broad shoulders. "But that's just the way we are."

Rachel didn't consider such behavior at all boring. Old-fashioned, perhaps. But nice. However, she knew that many small towns tended to be standoffish with outsiders and wondered if Dan Murphy might be taking too much for granted.

"I think it's a wonderful way to live," she said. "But don't forget, I'm new here."

"We don't force anyone to live in River's Bend, Rachel," Cooper said quietly. "People move here because they like what the town has to offer. If you choose to stay, you'll be one of us."

She still couldn't quite believe it could be that simple. "But—"

"One of these days you'll come to understand," Cooper's grandfather interjected with a reassuring smile. "But for now, why don't you just relax and enjoy dessert? Betty's chocolate truffle hazelnut cake is famous in River County. You could do worse than serve it at your new restaurant."

Her restaurant.

It was a dream come true. All right, maybe right now her dream was a little sooty and in need of some major renovation. But when the New Chance Café reopened with its inviting new look, she'd be in business.

"Thank you," she said with heartfelt appreciation. "Thank you all so much."

"Does that mean we're staying?" Scott asked.

Rachel turned toward her son, who looked as if he were holding his breath. "Yes. We're staying."

The heavy oak chair clattered to the floor as he jumped to his feet and threw his arms around Rachel's neck. "Everything's going to turn out great, Mom," he promised. "Just you wait and see."

Returning her son's enthusiastic hug, Rachel felt Cooper watching her. Looking up, her wary gaze collided with his.

"We'd better get going," she said as his slow, sexy smile sent unruly hormones ricocheting around like pinballs inside her. "We're enrolling Scott in school tomorrow. He should be getting to bed."

"But Mom," Scott started to complain.

"I'm not hearing a word of argument, young man," Rachel cut him off firmly. Then she turned back to the Murphys and Mitzi. "Thank you for the delicious meal and all your help."

"It was our pleasure," Dan said.

"Sure was," Mitzi agreed. "It'll be nice having a new girlfriend to go shopping with." A sudden thought lit up her eyes. "In fact, if you want, we can drive up to Eugene, and I can introduce you to another friend of mine. Pam's a decorator. You'd love her work."

"I think it's going to be some time before I can afford a decorator."

"I understand that, honey. But I was thinking more about using her professional discount to buy some material to recover those tacky booths. And maybe a few western rugs for the floor."

"I'd appreciate that." Rachel said with a smile. Things were getting better and better, proving that despite the fire and the rooftop cow, she'd made the right decision. She turned back to her son. "Come on, Scott. You've had a busy day and it's getting late."

"It's only eight o'clock," he pointed out. "And I'm not tired."

It was also eleven o'clock eastern time, which he was accustomed to, but Rachel didn't want to get into a drawn-out discussion about time zone changes. "You have school tomorrow."

"I had school in Connecticut, too. And my bedtime was nine o'clock."

"Let's get going, Scott." Cooper rose from his chair. "If you like, you can talk on the police radio on the way home."

Disbelief and hope warred on Scott's freckled face. Hope finally won out. "Really?"

Cooper picked up his hat from the sideboard and plunked it down onto the auburn curls Scott had inherited from his father. "Really."

The brim of the Stetson practically covered her son's eyes. He pushed it back to look up at Cooper with undisguised adoration. "Wow!"

"There is one important police rule."

"What rule?"

"You're not allowed to cuss. It's against regulations."

"I never cuss," Scott said, not quite truthfully. Rachel had overheard him practicing swearing with Jimmy last month.

"I didn't either, at your age," Cooper lied with a laugh. Draping his arm over Scott's shoulder, he led him toward the front door, leaving Rachel to follow.

8

URING THE RIDE back to her rental house, Rachel
was happy to sit in the back seat of the Jeep and
watch her son, who was riding shotgun, practically burst with importance as he called their destination into
the deputy manning the base unit at the sheriff's office.

When Cal Potter didn't seem the least bit surprised to
hear the voice of a nine-year-old coming over the police
airwaves, she wondered if everyone in town knew that
Cooper had driven her out to his father's ranch this
evening and decided that they probably did.

"I suppose Scott and I have been the topic of a great
deal of speculation," she said softly, not wanting to wake
her son, who'd finally crashed and fallen asleep.

Cooper shrugged. "It's all been good, if you're worried."

"I wasn't exactly worried. Not really. It's just that . . ."

Rachel's voice trailed off. She'd driven down from
Portland this morning, had been faced with the devastation at the New Chance, unpacked, cleaned up the house,
went out to dinner, when she would have rather called out
for Chinese or a pizza, which was impossible in River's
Bend, then negotiated a real-estate deal. All in one very

long day. As exhaustion came crashing down on her, she couldn't come up with the words to explain her feelings.

"You're sick and tired of people speculating about your life," Cooper said quietly. "About whether you're not grieving long enough, or too long, or whether this idea of starting your own restaurant is a reasonable, thought-out decision, or merely an overreaction to your situation.

"And you're especially fed up with everyone handing out advice and blithe platitudes, as if they were something that could ease your pain."

The depth of empathy surprised Rachel. Their eyes met in the rearview mirror, and in the muted glow of the dashboard lights, she could see both compassion and understanding in his gaze.

"I suppose, as sheriff, you've witnessed more than your share of pain."

"Too much." He returned his attention to the road. "But the observation came from personal experience, Rachel. Not professional."

She was curious, in spite of herself.

"My wife died," he answered her unspoken question.

The night sky was lush black velvet, studded with diamond bright stars extending as far as the eye could see. They could have been the only two people in the world. And in the dark, swirling quiet, Rachel was sorry she'd brought the subject up.

It was too personal.

Too intimate.

"I'm sorry." Speaking of blithe platitudes . . .

Rachel regretted her words the moment they'd left her lips. It was the same thing people said to her when they learned of Alan's death. Although well meant, the phrase sounded as empty to her now as it had eighteen months ago.

As if able to read her mind, Cooper sent her a reassuring smile in the rearview mirror. "So was I."

Rachel wanted to ask how long ago his wife had died. And how. She would have been young; it must have been an accident. Or worse yet, some painful, lingering disease.

At least Alan's death had been mercifully quick.

She wondered how Cooper had gone about putting his life back together. How he'd overcome the guilt and anger at being the one left behind.

Rachel wanted to know all these things, but she refrained from asking, knowing that it was none of her business.

"It gets better," he said into the darkness.

She managed a slight, answering smile. "I know."

Cooper nodded. "I figured you did."

That was all either one of them said until he pulled up in front of her bungalow. Scott was sprawled on the front seat, the smile on his lips suggesting that he was reliving his moments as River's Bend's assistant deputy sheriff.

"I'll carry him in for you," Cooper offered.

"Thanks, but you don't have to bother. I can do it."

"It's no bother," he insisted quietly. Firmly. Without giving her time to argue, he got out of the Jeep, went around to the passenger door, unfastened Scott's seatbelt, and scooped the sleeping boy into his arms.

Rachel wondered if the man's refusal to hear a word of dissent was a result of his occupation or something in his nature. Whichever, while he seemed well meaning, he was going to have to learn that he couldn't run her life the way he appeared to run River's Bend.

Working like a maniac on speed, she'd already un-packed what few items she'd brought with her. The small house was neat and tidy. The newly washed floor gleamed and lush green plants she'd carefully babied all the way from Connecticut bloomed vigorously atop gleaming tabletops. The air smelled of lemons from the furniture polish.

"You've gotten a lot done."

"I didn't want Scott living out of boxes any longer than necessary. Children need a great deal of stability, though heaven knows the poor kid hasn't had a lot lately."

Realizing that she was in danger of sounding sorry for herself, she blew out a breath. "His bedroom is right down this hall," she said. "It's the second door on the right."

9

COOPER UNDERSTOOD RACHEL'S need for maintaining control. He'd been there, done that, and had kept the T-shirt when he'd accepted the job of sheriff.

The way she'd managed the real estate discussion, along with her brisk manner as she'd pointed out the way to the bedroom, would have left Cooper wondering if he'd imagined that brief softness she'd demonstrated on the drive back from the ranch, had the lingering sadness in her voice not given her away.

He followed her down the hall. She was dressed more formally than the local style, in a rose-colored sweater, a dark gray skirt that fell to mid-calf, and a pair of pewter-gray boots with mid-high heels that contributed to a sexy sway in her walk.

She led him into what was definitely a boy's room. Posters of sports superstars covered the walls. Action figures filled two blue painted shelves beside the window and in contrast to the tidiness of what he'd seen in the front room, comic books describing the exploits of invincible superheroes were already strewn over the floor.

Scott remained dead to the world as Rachel whipped

the Spiderman bedspread away, permitting Cooper to lay the boy down on the mattress.

He stood back in the doorway and watched as she helped her son, who'd roused slightly, out of his jeans and sweatshirt into a pair of pajamas bearing the names and logos of various sports teams, then walked him into the bathroom to brush his teeth.

Motherhood suited her. She was soft and incredibly gentle, but from what he'd witnessed thus far, the lady was definitely no pushover.

Rachel Hathaway was, to borrow from his grandfather Murphy's vernacular, one plucky lady. And Scott was a very fortunate little boy.

"I'd offer you a cup of coffee," she said, once they returned to the living room. "But I'm afraid that's something else I forgot to buy when I went to the market this afternoon."

"That's okay. I should be going. You look as if you could use a good night's sleep."

She lifted a hand to her hair. No longer tied back with this morning's clip, it fell in a sleek dark curtain that skimmed her shoulders. "That bad, huh?" The fleeting glimpse of vulnerability in her eyes tugged at something inside Cooper.

"Not at all." He smiled, restraining the impulse to touch her face to find out if that fair flesh covering her high cheekbones was as soft as it looked. "Actually, I've been wanting to tell you all evening how lovely you looked, but I was afraid you'd get spooked and bolt."

With apparent calm, Rachel met his gaze. "I'm not that easily spooked."

"I've already figured that much out." They were face-to-face, their bodies close. "So, how about if I tell you that you smell terrific?"

"Since that body lotion is the single remaining indulgence I allow myself these days, I'd say thank you."

"You're welcome." When the urge to touch became irresistible, Cooper jammed his hands into his front pockets to keep them out of trouble. "You know," he said, looking around the room, "from all the work you've put into the place already, it's obvious that you'd decided to stay in River's Bend before I picked you and Scott up this evening."

"It wasn't as if I had many other options."

"Nevertheless, now that I know you intended all along to stay, I'm doubly impressed with how you handled Mitzi. Inside her cotton candy exterior dwells the predatory instincts of an old-time robber baron. You must be a natural-born businesswoman, to be able to bluff as well as you did."

"Hardly." Her tone was dry. "When it comes to business, eighteen months ago I was a mere babe in the woods."

Eighteen months was a long time, but Cooper knew that time was relative when it came to grief. When she'd first asked about his marriage, he'd waited for the pain and had been relieved when it hadn't come. He'd thought himself over Ellen's death, as much as anyone could be, but there was something about the widow Hathaway, something about the feelings she inspired that had him uncharacteristically unsure of anything.

"Sounds as if fate provided you with a crash course," he said.

"That's one way of putting it."

"Well, you obviously passed with flying colors." The mantle clock chimed, reminding Cooper that Rachel had already had a very long and difficult day. "I'd better get going," he said. "Hummer, he's my dog, starts eating the couch if I leave him alone too long."

He stopped and turned toward her as she walked him to the door. "Oh, by the way, Rachel, in case you're concerned about the success of your restaurant, you can stop worrying. It's going to be a smash."

"Says the man who hasn't tasted anything I've cooked."

"Don't have to. After having watched you in action since you hit town this morning, I've figured out that you don't do anything halfway."

It was her hesitant, but enticing, smile that did it. Unable to resist any longer, he ran a finger along her jaw. It was just as he'd expected . . . ivory satin.

"I'm glad you've decided to stay, Rachel."

"I'm glad, too," she said even as she backed away and put a little distance between them. "Thank you for all your help."

Cooper saw the emotions swirling in eyes that bore soft shadows of fatigue beneath them. There was desire, unwilling though it might be. And an unmistakable wariness that told him if he moved too fast he'd only end up chasing her away.

"No problem," he said with a careless shrug. "After all, it's—"

"Part of the job."

She sounded disappointed. Not wanting her to think he was laughing at her, Cooper held back the smile her regretful tone encouraged. It would take time. And patience. But eventually, he'd win her over.

"Not at all," he corrected amiably. "Actually, in your case, Rachel, it was definitely one of the perks."

He said good night, then left the house, strolling unhurriedly out to the Jeep. Although she'd closed the door, he could see her, standing in the window, still watching as he pulled away from the curb.

Once he'd turned the corner, Cooper realized, that for the first time since he'd headed up the search party that had found Ellen's body, he could remember how it felt to be truly alive.

10

"YOU DON'T HAVE to worry, Mom," Scott assured Rachel as she drove him to the Sacajawea Elementary School the next morning. "This isn't the first time I've changed schools since Dad died. I've got it figured out. It'll be fine."

"Of course it will be," she said. Hoped.

"And those cookies will be a big help. No one can resist your chocolate chip cookies."

She'd baked them last night after Cooper had left. Because though she'd been weary to the bone, the day's unexpected events had left her wired, even before his butterfly soft touch on her face had set her body to humming.

Since cooking had always proven an antidote for stress, she'd gone to work in the kitchen, baking Scott cookies to take to school. Not exactly to bribe the other kids.

Oh hell, whom was she kidding? As Rachel drove him to school, she admitted they were intended as both icebreaker and bribe.

Which apparently hadn't been needed at all. From what he'd told her over dinner that night, as he'd regaled her with tales of life in the third grade, he'd already made new friends before he'd pulled out his Spiderman lunchbox filled with a thermos of chicken noodle soup, half a tuna sandwich, and all those sweet, chewy cookies.

Even beginning the renovation of the café turned out to be less of a problem than she'd feared. True to their word, Cal Potter, his electrician brother Hal, Fred Wiley, and Dan Murphy had shown up at nine that morning and worked through the day, stopping only for the sandwiches and cookies Rachel had insisted on bringing from home.

Cal's assertion about being handy with a hammer and nails proved an understatement.

The first glitch came the second day when she decided to tear down a wall to increase the size of the kitchen and build a second wall with a large open window. Although Alan hadn't wanted her to work full time, Rachel had been happy with her catering business. But whenever they ate out, she'd carefully study what elements she'd want in her fantasy dream restaurant.

She'd always been drawn to an open kitchen. Instead of hiding it away, where waiters would disappear behind swinging doors, then reappear with plates of food, to Rachel's mind, the view of an open flame and mouth-watering aromas of roasting meats and stews bubbling away on the stove created a warm ambiance. Not only were diners' eyes drawn directly to the center of activity the moment they walked in the door, it welcomed them more fully into the restaurant.

"Good idea," Hal said as she sketched out her idea on a yellow legal pad. "I wired one of those over in Medford last year. But since you're deviating from the original plan, which is going to involve a change in electrical and plumbing, you'll need to get approval from the city building department."

In Greenwich that could turn into long-drawn out bureaucratic process, seriously disrupting her schedule. But this was River's Bend. Where everyone had already been so friendly and helpful.

"I'll be back in a few minutes," she said.

Which turned out to be an overly optimistic statement.

The woman behind the counter was as congenial as everyone else she'd met, making Rachel wonder what they were putting in the town's drinking water. She took Hal's more detailed drawing of her sketched out plan, left the room, and returned with what appeared to be the necessary permit, which she put on a desk.

"All done," she said with a smile. "It just needs to be stamped by Hester, who takes care of that final step."

That said, she walked out of the room, leaving Rachel standing there, waiting for Hester, whoever she was, to arrive.

Five minutes later, a forty-something woman wearing black slacks and a yellow and black striped sweater, which brought to mind a bumblebee, walked into the small room carrying a chef salad in a plastic container and a Coke. Sitting down at the desk, she began to eat. Although there was only that black metal desk and white Formica counter between them, Rachel felt as if she'd become invisible.

"Excuse me," she said.

The woman looked up from her salad. "Yes?"

"I believe that's my permit."

The woman glanced over at it. "Are you Rachel Hath-away?"

"Yes. The new owner of the New Chance Café."

"Yeah. I heard you'd arrived in town. It looks all in order."

"That's good news. So, you'll stamp it?"

"Sure," the woman said agreeably. "As soon as my lunch break is over."

"Excuse me?"

"If you'd read the sign on the counter, you'd have seen that we close for an hour lunch break."

Which, Rachel realized, explained the office that had, except for Hester, emptied.

"But the permit's right there on the corner of your desk," she said. Right next to a big official looking stamp thing. "If you could just—"

"Sorry. If I made an exception for you, then pretty soon this place would be filled with people wanting things all day long and none of us would ever get a break."

Since she hadn't seen signs of a building boom, and given River's Bend's population, Rachel highly doubted that possibility but chose not to challenge the point.

"I understand. And, of course you deserve a lunch break. But perhaps, since I'm here alone and no one would know—"

"Sorry," Hester said around a mouthful of lettuce and hardboiled egg. "Rules are rules for a reason. And now, if you don't mind, I'd like to watch my story."

With that, she clicked a button on her computer, bringing up the swelling musical theme of a soap opera.

Debating whether it made sense to return to the café then come back, or just stay until the official lunch time was over, Rachel opted for a middle ground and decided to wait in the park across the street.

She was sitting on a bench beneath a red-leafed maple, shopping for light fixtures online from her phone when Cooper Murphy came out of the sheriff's office next door to the courthouse.

11

"WELL NOW, ISN'T this a lucky coincidence," he said as he crossed the lawn. "I was just headed to the café to talk with you."

"I'm trying to get a permit to make changes to the original plan," Rachel said.

"Which isn't happening because it's the lunch hour."

"How did you know?"

"Because the city offices, all except for mine, close down between one and two every weekday. Always have, probably always will. Tradition," he said with a quirk of his lips, "is a big deal around here."

"The plan's already been approved. I just needed a damn official stamp," she said.

"And you'll get it. One thing you'll also discover is things move a little slower than you're probably used to. So, it's Hester holding you up?"

"I wouldn't want to take her away from her soap opera." A tinge of uncharacteristic sarcasm sharpened Rachel's tone.

"She does love all that drama," he agreed. "But she's always liked me. If you want, I can go in there and see what I can do to speed her up a bit."

"No." She sighed. "You've already done so much. Besides, having been running on warp speed, trying to get everything done since Alan died, I suppose I could work on pacing myself a bit."

If she were to be perfectly honest, she'd have to admit that having managed to get through the bureaucratic red tape required to get her Connecticut catering license, she shouldn't have been surprised. But lulled into complacency by everyone's helpfulness, she'd expected to breeze through the permit process and get back to work.

"Good plan," he agreed. "Which is what I was coming over to talk to you about. How would you and Scott like to go on an outlaw train ride this Sunday?"

"What, exactly, is an outlaw train?"

"It's a tourist thing. A few years ago the town council got the idea to fix up an old logging train that runs on a narrow gauge rail from here up to Modoc Mountain. They feed everyone a box lunch. Now that I think about it, you might want to consider putting in a bid for the lunches when the contract comes up for renewal in January since it could add to your cash flow.

"Along the way, a gang of bad guys board the train and rob it. It's all over-the-top cowboy drama and the money they take from adults, who are in on the gig, goes to the local food pantry. In the end, just like those old cowboy flicks that helped build River's Bend's western reputation, the good guys win.

"And in case you're worried about it being too realistic, the guns are the movie kind, which only shoot blanks, and the guys ham it up even more than they used to. Some parents warn their kids ahead of time that it's all for fun, but I suspect Scott would handle it without any problem."

"He'd love it. But I need to work."

He lifted a brow. "On Sunday?"

"Are you suggesting River's Bend is so peaceful that the sheriff's office closes down on weekends?"

"Touché," he said easily. "Though I could argue there's a slight difference in our situation, but I get your point."

"I may not be responsible for keeping the law, but unlike some people, I don't punch a clock." Rachel shot a dark look toward the courthouse where her nemesis Hester was wasting valuable time by watching TV. "There's so much more I need to do. I'd hoped for a Thanksgiving opening, but now I'll be lucky to open by Christmas."

"It's just as well," he said. "Most people around here tend to eat Thanksgiving at home with family, so it's not as if you'd get much of a crowd. Now, Christmas, that's a more popular day for eating out, though in past years it meant driving to Klamath Falls or Lakeview. Besides, even God took a day off."

"Obviously God didn't need a building permit from Hester to create the world."

"That probably would've added a day or two longer to the creation calendar," he agreed. "But a few hours spent with Scott isn't going to make that much of a difference in the whole scheme of things."

His expression sobered. "We both know that life can be unfairly short, Rachel. That there are no replays nor rewinds, so you'd do well to write some personal time into your daily work schedule. Gram mentioned us losing my mother. What she didn't say was that Mom died of ovarian cancer the same month I graduated from high school."

"That must have been horribly hard on you."

"It wasn't easy. But though we never talked about it all that much, I suspect it was even harder on my younger brothers. But getting back to Sunday, I'm guessing it's been a while since you've allowed yourself some fun. And it could be one of those special memories Scott might look back on when he's a dad. Maybe, if he stays around here, someday he'll take his own son or daughter on the same train."

"You realize that could be considered emotional blackmail."

"Could be. Is it working?"

Telling herself that returning to work Monday fresh and re-energized wasn't such a bad idea, Rachel stood and lifted both arms into the air.

"I surrender, Sheriff."

His answering laugh drew an appreciative look from two women eating lunch on a nearby bench. "And to think I didn't have to even break out my handcuffs," he said.

Because, despite the annoyingly uncooperative Hester, Rachel was actually enjoying herself, she gave a little toss of her hair. "Well, shoot. If I'd given any thought to that idea, I just may have held out a little bit longer."

She could tell by his sharp, cowboy squint as he tried to determine whether her statement had been a suggestion or merely a bit of flirtatious humor, that she'd surprised him.

And he wasn't the only one. The unbidden sexual innuendo was as much of a surprise to Rachel as it was to him.

Cooper studied her for a few humming seconds that

tangled her nerves.

It was time to leave. Now.

"I'd better see if Hester's finished her lunch and her soap opera and will stamp my permit," she said, stepping back into the skin of that briskly efficient woman who'd managed to pay off creditors, sell most of her possessions, buy a business, then drive her child and a trailer filled with houseplants all the way across the country.

"Good luck with that," he said. "I'll pick you and Scott up at ten."

She was about to tell him that she was perfectly capable of finding the train station herself, then remembered what a kick Scott had gotten riding in the sheriff's department Jeep.

"Sunday mornings I make pancakes. If you'd like to drop by closer to nine, you're invited to breakfast."

"That sounds right tasty." His slow, laconic cowboy smile managed to blur her brain and cause her pulse to skip. "Mitzi told me you were a high-powered private chef back east."

"I don't know how high-powered I was. But I did have a catering business. I served food at weddings, anniversary parties, political banquets, events like that."

"And I'll bet you were really good at your job. I don't suppose you'd happen to have one of those tight pink dresses with your name embroidered in white script?"

"No." She folded her arms again when his gaze drifted down to right above her breast, where that name would be embroidered. "I don't."

He shrugged. "I didn't figure you did. But a guy can always hope."

"I'm talking about making you pancakes, Sheriff. Not

helping you act out some kinky nineteen-fifties diner fantasy."

"We all have our fantasy worlds," he said easily. Then jingled the metal handcuffs hanging from his leather belt, to remind her that she'd alluded to an entirely different fantasy kink. "But homemade pancakes are pretty high on my list, too. Johnny's were like hockey pucks. You'd risked breakin' a tooth biting into them."

Even when he was joking, which surely he must be, Cooper Murphy exuded testosterone like the expensive cologne worn by the men from her social circle back in Connecticut. Worse yet, by the light in his impossibly green eyes, he knew it.

"Nine o'clock," she repeated. "You can leave your handcuffs at home."

He touched his fingers to the tip of that macho cowboy hat. "Yes, ma'am."

Rachel wasn't used to being teased. She wasn't even sure she liked it. But she couldn't deny as she returned to the courthouse, that River's Bend's sheriff had awakened something in her that she'd thought had died with her husband.

12

OOPER ARRIVED AT nine on the dot, carrying a square Stetson box, which he handed to Scott. "I brought you a little something," he said.

"Wow!" Rachel's son looked stunned as he lifted out a smaller version of Cooper's hat. "Is this really for me?"

"If you're going to live in cowboy country, you've got to dress the part." Cooper plunked the hat on Scott's head, rocked back on his heels and studied the look.

"It fits. So now we need to shape it." He turned to Rachel. "Do you have a tea kettle?"

"Of course."

While they waited for the water in the kettle to boil, Scott raced to the bathroom to check himself out in the mirror while Rachel continued mixing pancake batter. "That was an incredibly nice thing to do."

"Around these parts, a boy's first cowboy hat is a big deal," he said, thanking her as she handed him a mug of coffee. "Figured you might not have run across that during all your research, so I picked one up at the Stockman's Shop yesterday."

"I wouldn't have thought of it," she admitted. "So, thank you."

"You're welcome. It was my pleasure, believe me."

The kettle whistled just as Scott returned to the kitchen.

"Good timing," Cooper said as he plucked the hat from Scott's head. "Now, when you get a new hat you've got to shape it." He held the hat with the stiffly turned up sides up to the steam coming out of the kettle. "First thing is to flatten it out."

Which he proceeded to do, each side at a time, then the front and back until the brim of the hat rested flat as a pancake on the kitchen table.

"But yours turns up," Scott said, frowning he took in the seemingly ruined hat.

"We're gettin' to that." Cooper returned to the kettle, used steam to dampen one side, and began to curl it back up. "Now, everyone's got a different idea of how high to turn the sides up to suit their personal style, but this is how I usually like mine." He held the hat toward Scott. "What do you think?"

"It's perfect!"

Of course it was. Rachel didn't think there was anything Cooper Murphy could do that her son wouldn't find absolutely perfect.

With deft hands and a skill that suggested he'd done this several times over the years, he shaped the other side, then tilted the front down, with a bit deeper downturn to the back, then set it back on Scott's head.

"Go check this out."

Scott returned to the bathroom and was back within seconds. "I look like a real cowboy!"

"You sure do," Cooper agreed.

"If I didn't know you were my son, I'd think for certain you were a cowboy," Rachel said, enjoying the pleasure beaming on her son's face.

"I need to go show Warren." The nine-year-old class-mate who lived next door had become what Scott described as his "second-best" friend. Cooper, unsurprisingly, occupied top position.

"Later," she said. "After we get home this afternoon. Breakfast is ready, and you don't want to be late for the train."

"Another thing you should know," Cooper said as Scott began to sit down at the table. "Hats usually come off indoors. And definitely while you're eating. Though if you're sitting at a lunch counter, the rules can slide.

"Here at home you can hang it on the rack by the front door, but if you ever need to set it down, put it with the crown down. Otherwise, it'll flatten again. There are different ways of taking a hat off, but personally, I like lifting mine from the crown."

"Me, too," Scott said, doing exactly that. When he ran off to hang his new hat next to Cooper's on the rack in the entryway, Rachel's vision momentarily blurred.

"Something wrong?"

The man never missed a thing. Rachel guessed that came from all the years of being in law enforcement. She shook her head and blinked away the moisture that had risen in her eyes.

"Nothing. It's just been so long since I've seen him so . . ."

She waved her hand as the words stuck in her throat. "Don't pay any attention to me. I'm usually not so emotional."

"We all have emotions," Cooper said mildly. "No

shame in showing them from time to time. And hey, if it makes you feel better, Scott's seemed like a pretty happy kid before I showed up with the hat. You just need to be easier on yourself."

It was the same thing Janet had told her for months. It was also easier said than done.

Rachel was surprised at how natural having Cooper sitting at her kitchen table felt. She'd never cooked for any other man but her husband, yet Cooper proved so easy going, answering Scott's seemingly non-stop questions about local old-time outlaws, by the time the sheriff declared her spiced pumpkin pancakes topped with cinnamon brown butter and maple syrup the best breakfast he'd ever eaten, she began to relax, her earlier embarrassment at revealing emotions dissipated.

Then he'd surprised her yet again by insisting on helping clear the table. Although it seemed a bit strange, watching him load the dishwasher while she cleaned off the counter, she felt comfortable with him being in what had always been her sole domain.

Scott continued to chatter away on the drive to the station.

"Look, Mom," he said as they approached the ticket window. "Wanted posters!"

"They seem to be." Studying the black and white pictures on the wall next to the ticket window, she noticed that were it not for the oversized bushy mustache, one of the wanted men bore a striking resemblance to Cal Potter.

"So, buckaroo, your hat suggests you'd be a cowboy," the ticket seller said to Scott as Cooper bought the tickets.

"I'm not, really," Scott admitted reluctantly. "I got this hat from the sheriff. But my mom has a restaurant with a cow on the roof."

"That's close enough." He handed Cooper the tickets, then rubbed his chin. "You think you could help the sheriff handle some outlaws if any were to show up on the way to Modoc Mountain?"

Scott squared his thin shoulders. "You bet!"

"I figured as much . . . See, here's the deal. I've heard rumors some desperadoes are planning to rob this train."

"Really?" Scott shot a glance at Rachel. Rather than look worried by that news, he appeared even more excited than when he'd first seen that damn cow.

"Now, I can't say if it's true or not," the man drawled. "'Cause, like I said, so far it's just a rumor. But this train has been robbed before. One time the scoundrels dynamited a Wells Fargo safe to get a gold shipment. But they miscalculated and blew up thirty-thousand dollars along with it."

"Really?"

"Yep. Pieces of paper flew into the air then drifted down all over the ground like green snow. We haven't had those sort of shenanigans for a time, but just in case, you'll be wanting these."

He reached into a drawer and pulled out a handful of gold colored coins. "When they say to turn over your money, you can give the varmints these fake coins. Those desperados ain't playing with a full deck if you get my drift, so that'll fool 'em."

"Yessir!" Scott looked about ready to burst.

"I'm going to owe you for this," Rachel murmured to Cooper as Scott raced out to the station platform, coins clutched in his fist.

"It's my pleasure. But, if you insist on payback, we

could probably put our heads together and think of a way."

When he put his hand on her back, Rachel felt a surge of heat and knew they were thinking along the same lines.

The train had an old steam engine just like the ones she'd seen Paul Newman and Robert Redford rob in *Butch Cassidy and the Sundance Kid*. After they had boarded, Rachel and Cooper sat together while Scott took the window seat in front of them, bouncing up and down as if he had springs in his jeans.

The train took them along the winding river, through the forest and across meadows. In the distance Modoc Mountain soared high into a blindingly clear autumn blue sky. Accustomed to Iowa's rolling hills and the East's older rounded Adirondack Mountains, Rachel found the jagged, snow-capped Cascades stunning.

"Uh oh," Cooper muttered as a cloud of dust appeared in the distance. A moment later, five men on horseback charged out of the cloud, making a beeline for the train.

"Are those robbers?" Scott pressed his face against the window glass.

"I suspect they may be," Cooper said.

"Are you gonna shoot them?"

"Didn't bring my weapon along. Sunday's are supposed to be peaceful."

The masked riders began shooting and waving their cowboy hats in the air as they got closer to the train.

"Oh, no!" A woman Rachel recognized as the clerk who'd checked her out at the market, leaped up from her seat across the aisle, obviously part of the performance. "Look what just came through the side of the car!" She pointed at a copper bullet slug rolling around on the passenger car floor.

"Wow!" Buying into every boy's good guys/bad guys fantasies, Scott didn't seem the least bit upset. "You need to take that bullet for evidence," he told Cooper.

"Good idea." Winking at Rachel, he scooped it up and put it in his front shirt pocket.

As they watched, one of the outlaws leaped into the engine. Then the train's wheels came screeching to a halt on the iron tracks.

The outlaws boarded the car, guns drawn. "Now all you ladies and gents do what you're told, and no one's going to get hurt," the leader, a short, scrawny man holding a six-shooter in each hand, said.

"You should tell them you're the sheriff," Scott hissed to Cooper.

"I'm not sure this is the time," Cooper murmured. "Besides, the Oregon Rangers will be on their trail."

"I didn't realize Oregon had rangers," Rachel said.

"Sure," Cooper lied deftly. "They may not get as much press as those in Texas, but they've been capturing bad guys for a long time. They're really good at their job."

As if to confirm his words as the outlaws began walking down the aisle, instructing everyone to put money in the bags they were carrying, another cloud of dust appeared.

"It's them danged Rangers!" a second outlaw, who was definitely Cal Potter, shouted. "Time to vamoose!"

They leaped off the train, jumped onto the back of their waiting horses, and raced away.

As the passengers watched, another group of men rode by in hot pursuit.

"Wow! That was the best thing ever." Scott exhaled a long breath. Then his small brow furrowed. "It was make-believe, wasn't it?" he asked Cooper. "Like Pirates of the Caribbean at Disney World."

"It was a re-enactment," Cooper said. "Bad Bill Barkley robbed trains from here down to Tulelake across the state line in California. This gives people a taste of what it would've been like in the old days."

"I wish I'd lived then," Scott said. "It must've been way cool."

"Might have been," Cooper agreed. "But if you had lived back then, I wouldn't have gotten to meet you. Or your mom."

"Yeah," Scott decided after a moment's thought. "And there wouldn't have been any TV or X-Men or anything. So, I guess this is better."

"Much better," Cooper agreed. Then smiled at Rachel in a way that had her heart melting like the spiced butter atop this morning's pancakes.

13

BACK IN HIS early MP days Cooper had awakened each morning juiced and ready to go out and save the world. It hadn't taken him long to realize that a great many places in this world didn't really want to be saved. At least not that he'd been able to tell.

Even in the supposedly laid-back city of Portland, he'd discovered that justice could be deaf and dumb as well as blindfolded. After nearly losing his partner and his own life while serving a warrant for a parole violation to a guy who'd been in and out of the revolving prison door so many times the length of his rap sheet rivaled War and Peace, now all Cooper wanted was an uneventful life where he didn't have to worry about some crazed meth addicts with assault rifles trying to pump him full of bullets.

In Afghanistan, where his brother Sawyer was currently deployed, he'd bounced over rocky roads in an MRAP—Mine-Resistant, Ambush-Protected—vehicle.

After returning Stateside, he'd patrolled Portland's streets in his police cruiser. Although River's Bend town council had sprung for the snazzy new Jeep when he'd accepted the job, he spent a good deal of time walking, passing the time of day with the people who paid his salary. Keeping his ear to the ground let him know which citizens might have had spats, were harboring grudges or, especially in these times, falling into an economic hole that might have them creating trouble.

Like Jake.

Which was why he figured that by getting out of the office and making sure he remained part of the daily ebb and flow, folks would realize that whatever might happen, the sheriff had their backs.

In many ways, River's Bend brought to mind a western town from the late 1800s. Located fifty miles from the interstate in a valley surrounded by mountains, the town boasted three stop lights, which were two more than when Cooper had headed off to San Diego for Marine basic training.

The trees along Front Street were turning a tapestry of red and gold. Mums filled planter boxes below store windows, adding a spicy tang to the fall air.

He passed by Harry's Barber Shop, where Harry and Hank Young were sitting on a wooden bench out in front, taking advantage of the fall sunshine playing checkers as they'd been doing for as long as Cooper could remember.

"Hey," he greeted them. "How's it going?"

"Can't complain," the hardware store owner said as he double jumped, capturing two of his opponent's red pieces and getting crowned king in the process.

"Probably not as good as it's been going for you," Harry drawled. "Heard you've been keeping company with the widow lady."

"If by keeping company, you mean taking her son on the outlaw train, I guess you've caught me."

"Heard you took more than just her son."

"She's been working her butt off. I figured she could use a day off to see the sights."

"Speaking of sights and butts," Hank said, "the lady does fill out a pair of jeans right nice."

"Really?" Cooper adjusted his hat and appeared to be giving the matter some thought. "I guess I hadn't noticed," he lied.

"Better get your eyes checked out," Harry suggested. "Because you're probably the only male in town who hasn't."

"She's a nice woman."

"Did we say she wasn't?" Harry shot back with an arched grizzled brow.

"You could do a lot worse," Hank put in his two cents. "If I weren't old enough to be her daddy, I might make a move on her myself."

"More like her granddaddy," Harry harrumphed. "As if you would've stood a snowball's chance in hell back when you were Coop's age."

The men were second cousins on their mother's side, and to hear Cooper's grandfather tell it, along with the marathon checkers match, they'd been ragging each other for all of their lives. "You'd better make your move, Sheriff," the barber suggested. "Before some other guy stakes a claim on her."

"Well, thanks for the advice," Cooper said. "I'll keep in it mind. Meanwhile, I'd better get back to the office in case a crime wave hits town."

"Town's probably safe enough," Hank said. "So long as your father-in-law stays out on his ranch."

"Not that the dang government's gonna let him live

there that much longer," Harry grumbled, his teasing mood disintegrating.

Despite Jake's recent problems, he'd always been well liked and respected. Cooper guessed not a single person in the county doubted his father-in-law's claim of having made that missing payment.

Correction. Unfortunately, there was one: Mel Skimmer.

Deep in thought, he continued down the street, absently waving back to Jenna Janzen, who was painting autumn leaves on her Chapter One bookstore window.

Jake Buchanan had never been one to shy away from the odds. Ranching had always been a high stakes game, with losing years as likely as not. Unfortunately, right now Skinner was holding all the cards.

Something Cooper was determined to change. Somehow.

He was pondering a new plan of action when a familiar voice called out his name. "Hey, Cooper!"

He turned around and saw Scott running down the sidewalk toward him, a cardinal red book bag banging against the back of his blue jacket.

"Hey, pardner," he said. "How's school going?"

"It's really cool. We're going on a field trip next week."

"You're taking a trip out to a field?"

"Nah." The intended joke flew right over the nine-year-old's curly head. "To the River's Bend historical museum. My teacher said it has a bunch of cool stuff from the olden days."

"It does." Some of that cool stuff included the dented tin pan and wooden rocker his great-great-great-grandfather Malachy had used to pan for gold in the river

along with Mary Murphy's antique porcelain-faced dolls.
"So, I guess you're going to the café?"

"Yeah. Mom came up with this schedule for me to do
my homework in the cafe's dining room before we go
home for dinner." His small face frowned. "But I don't
have that much to do, so mostly I just play video games
on my PSP."

"Nothing wrong with video games. But how would
you like to help me clean out some files?"

Scott's eyes widened with astonishment. "You mean in
the sheriff's office?"

"That's what I'm talking about."

"Wow! You bet I'd like doing that." His mouth turned
down in a frown. "But I promised Mom I'd walk straight
to the café without stopping along the way."

"No problem." Cooper pulled out his phone. "We'll
give her a call, and I'll bet she'll go along with the idea as
long as I promise you'll finish your homework first. Which
you will, right?"

"Sure." The nine-year-old looked skeptical about their
chances. "But she's pretty strict."

"She cares about you." Enough, Cooper figured, that
she'd see the value in her son hanging out with some guys
for a while.

The conversation was short. Cooper figured he'd
guessed right about her liking the idea, or she'd hadn't
wanted to waste time arguing when she could get back up
on the ladder Cal had called her down from.

"It's a go," he told Scott, who'd appeared to be holding his breath as he'd shifted back and forth from foot to
foot during the brief conversation.

Rachel's son pumped a small fist in the air. "Sweet!"

14

SCOTT HAD BEEN to Disney World lots of times. He'd also been to the top of the Empire State Building and a year before his dad had died, his parents had taken him to Italy, where he'd eaten lots of spaghetti and had his picture taken dressed up like a gladiator.

But as neat as all those places had been, none were as cool as Cooper's sheriff's office. It wasn't that fancy. Not at all like his dad's New York office with the thick carpet and all the heavy antique furniture.

The tops of these black metal desks and filing cabinets were piled high with papers. United States and Oregon state flags stood in the corner, and on the long wall, instead of framed posters of ads like in his dad's office, there were framed photos of the President and the Oregon governor. Scott recognized the governor from the photo in the office of the Sacajawea Elementary School.

There was also a white board with people's schedules written on it with a Sharpie and next to it, a corkboard with various notices stuck on it with colored pushpins. Many were layered on top of others, some had official looking raised seals.

But the coolest thing of all was the poster with pictures of the FBI's top ten most wanted criminals. Scott studied them, just in case he ever spotted one of the baddest of bad guys.

A huge yellow dog, nearly as big as the pony Bobby Erickson's parents had rented for his birthday party last year, thumped his tail, then unfolded himself from beneath one of the desks. He ambled across the room, stood on his hind legs, put his baseball mitt sized paws on Scott's shoulders and swiped Scott's face with his big, pink tongue.

"Hummer," Cooper said, sounding strict, like a real sheriff for the first time since Scott had met him at the New Chance. "Attention."

After one more swipe that covered the side of Scott's face from his chin up to his hair, the dog dropped to the floor, sat on his butt, his back straight, big brown eyes looking straight up at Cooper's.

"Good boy." Cooper's approval caused the dog to whine, just a little, but he stayed put. "Scott, meet Hummer. Hummer, this is Scott. You may now shake his hand."

On command, the dog stuck out his paw, which Scott shook. "Hi, Hummer."

The dog's butt wiggled, but Hummer stayed where he was.

"Rest," Cooper instructed.

Hummer immediately plopped down.

"That's really cool," Scott said.

"Sometimes he comes on patrol with me, so it's important he behave when he absolutely has to."

At that, Hummer rolled over and began scratching his

back on the floor. "Does he do tricks?" Scott asked as he rubbed the dog's stomach.

"That would involve expending energy. Hummer is deeply into energy conservation. Aren't you, fella?" When Cooper scratched the dog behind his ear, Hummer moaned with canine pleasure.

"Well, well." A woman with white hair looked at Scott over the top of her glasses. "What do we have here, Sheriff?" She tilted her head. "A new deputy recruit?"

"This is Scott Hathaway," Cooper introduced him. "He's come to help me clean out my files."

"The good Lord knows you need help." Dangling orange pumpkin earrings jiggled as she nodded. "You'd be Rachel Hathaway's son. Your mom's going to give us our restaurant back."

"Yes, ma'am." Scott said, remembering the manners his mom had drilled into him as Hummer wiggled in delight while the big pink tongue lolled. "But the food'll be a lot better."

"I've no doubt of that," she agreed with a smile. "You look like a healthy young man, so she obviously feeds you well."

"Yes, ma'am. She's the best cook ever."

"Aren't you the sweetest thing?" She glanced up at Cooper. "The boy's polite, too. Would you like a cookie?" she asked Scott.

"Yes, ma'am." With one last pat to the dog, Scott stood up.

"Oh, don't fuss with all that ma'am stuff. It makes me feel old," she complained, but not in a grumpy way. "My name's LuluBelle, which I'm well aware sounds like a saloon girl from back in town's wild west days and caused me ever so much grief back when I was your age."

She shook her fluffy white head, which reminded Scott of the cotton balls his mother had taken her makeup off with. Back when she'd worn makeup.

"I had a friend, Jimmy, back in Connecticut, whose mom changed her name," Scott offered helpfully. "She went to this psychic who told her she'd been Cleopatra in a previous life. Since she said she'd never felt like a Brooke, she went to a judge and had her name changed to Cleo."

At the time, Scott had overheard his dad telling his mom that Mrs. Walker was crazy. His mom had said that if it made her happy, then it really didn't hurt anyone.

But that was the way his mom always was. Or had been, before his dad had died and their lives had changed. She was always smiling and laughing and had told him lots of times that one of the reasons she liked cooking for people was it made them happy.

"Well, isn't that interesting," LuluBelle said. "And as it happened, I did consider changing my name to Debbie the summer before I went to high school, but when I brought the idea up to Mama, she cried and wailed like I'd just told her the world was coming to an end since she had, after all, she felt moved to remind me, named me after her own dearly departed mother.

"Mama," she confided, without seeming to take a breath, "was a very sensitive woman and tended to get the vapors at the least little bit of unpleasantness, so I never brought the topic up again.

"She passed a couple years ago, so after all this time, I guess I'll just stick with the name she gave me. Especially since people around here don't take well to change, so I'd just be stuck with them all still calling me LuluBelle. Oatmeal raisin or chocolate chip?"

It took Scott a minute to make the switch back to the lady's original question, and when he took a bit of time trying to make up his mind, she decided for him.

"Why don't we just give you one of both?" She stood up and bustled over to a counter on the far side of the room that had a coffee maker, some cups, and a white box of cookies.

"They're not exactly homemade," the woman said as she plucked two cookies from the box, put them on a paper plate, and handed him a wet wipe to clean his hands. "But they're not store-bought, either. I picked them up this morning at Chapter One. That's a bookstore here in town that serves fresh baked goods. Do you like to read?"

"Yes, ma'am."

"Good for you. I've always said that you're never alone if you've got a book for company. I have books at home that belonged to my children. I've been saving them for my grandchildren, but none of my brood seems inclined to make me a grandmother anytime soon, so I'll bring them down here for the next time you visit."

She handed him the cookies, then took a pint of low fat milk from a little refrigerator next to her desk, stuck a straw in it and held it out to him.

"You can sit over there," she said, nodding to an empty desk. "We've been short one deputy since Frank Thurman up and retired. Which is why I thought maybe you were the new recruit Cooper's been looking to hire."

"I'm only nine."

"Is that so?" A white brow rose above her red-framed glasses. "Well, I would've thought you were older than that. You're very mature for your age."

"Thank you, ma'am," he said.

"It's LuluBelle, honey," she reminded him. "We don't go much for formality around these parts. I guess you'd have some homework in that book bag of yours?"

Since he'd just taken a big swallow of milk, Scott could only nod.

"Well, you'd best get to it right after you finish your snack," she said.

"In case you couldn't tell, LuluBelle is the one who really runs the sheriff's department," Cooper said.

"Well, I'm not out keeping the streets safe," she said as she sat back down, hit a computer key that got rid of the River's Bend photo screensaver and brought up a page of numbers. "But I do keep the trains running as the old saying goes."

"Cooper took me and my mom on the outlaw train," Scott said. He hadn't seen LuluBelle working at the train station when they'd been there.

The pumpkin earrings danced again as she nodded. "So I heard." She winked up at Cooper, who shook his head, then sent his hat sailing across the office. It landed smack on an antler hat rack, just like Jason Kidd shooting a three-pointer.

When he took his gun out of his holster and locked it away in a drawer, Scott remembered how Cooper hadn't taken his pistol on the outlaw train because it was Sunday. Maybe the sheriff didn't have to wear his gun all the time because, like everyone kept saying, River's Bend was a peaceful town.

As he dug his spelling test words out of his backpack, Scott thought maybe that was because Sheriff Cooper Murphy kept everyone safe.

15

FOUR DAYS AFTER the outlaw train ride, with the men gone to pick up more supplies at Young's Hardware, Rachel was alone, sanding peeling paint from the walls, when Cooper walked into the kitchen. Engrossed in her task, she wasn't immediately aware of his presence.

"The view around this place has definitely improved."

At the sound of his deep voice, Rachel froze. A million scattered thoughts flashed through her mind. The first was that she shouldn't be so pleased that he'd finally decided to make an appearance. The second, third, fourth, and millionth were that she looked a mess. Taking a breath in a futile attempt to relax, she glanced back over her shoulder.

"If you've dropped in for lunch, I'm afraid you're a bit premature. We're not quite open."

"So I see." He glanced around the kitchen, which looked as if it had recently been the battleground for World War III. "Looks like you and the guys have been busy."

Rachel laughed. "Goodness, Sheriff, are you always so tactful? Working nearly around the clock, except for that day I took off for the outlaw ride, we've managed to turn an unholy mess into a world-class disaster."

She grinned with undisguised pride as she took in the scene. "Believe it or not, there is an order to this chaos."

"I figured any woman as organized as you would have a plan."

"Oh?" She climbed down from the ladder and met him halfway in the center of the room. "And where did you get that insight?"

"Your son."

"I've been meaning to talk to you about him stopping by your office after school," she said.

Rachel had worked out a detailed schedule that had Scott walking the few short blocks to the New Chance after school, where he'd do his homework while she worked. Since the sheriff's office just happened to be on the way, he'd begun stopping by to visit with the man who'd obviously become his hero.

Because it was already dark at six o'clock this time of year, Cooper would drop him off at the New Chance after which she and Scott would return to the house for dinner and a conversation about his day.

At seven Mrs. Macgregor, who lived across the street, would arrive to stay with Scott while Rachel went back to the café until around midnight, after which she'd return home with bones aching and muscles protesting.

After a too-brief bath to soak out the aches, she'd spend at least another hour poring over her accounts, searching for ways to turn red ink to black. Despite having given up believing in fairy tales, during those lonely dark hours, Rachel found herself wishing for a fairy godmother to sweep in, wave her magic wand and chant some gibberish which would whisk her away to an enchanted tropical island where tanned and buffed-up cabana boys would cater to her every whim.

Or at least tell her a way to cut ten percent off plumbing costs.

When her fairy godmother failed to make an appearance, she'd crash into bed, where it seemed as if she'd no sooner get to sleep when the alarm would go off and it would be time to begin the process all over again.

"Scott assured me that you don't mind him being at your office, but—"

Cooper waved off her concern. "Don't worry about it. I like having him visit. And LuluBelle, my dispatcher, is tickled to pieces."

"Your dispatcher's name is LuluBelle?" An unbidden image of a woman in a red satin dance hall dress and fishnet stockings popped into her head.

"Yep. And I'd advise against mentioning it when you meet her or you'll get treated to the entire story with complete orchestration and five-part harmony. LuluBelle's a warm, friendly sixty-something woman who's still waiting for one of her grown kids to give her a grandchild, so having a little boy around the place brightens her day. And you needn't worry about Scott not being taken good care of if I have to leave on some sheriff business."

"Still, surely you all have more important things to do than babysit my son."

"It's no problem. Scott's a great kid, Rachel. Bright, inquisitive, polite. You should be proud."

He couldn't have said anything that would have pleased her more. "I am."

"Good. Then you won't be upset when I tell you that

he filled me in on all your secrets."

Rachel certainly hoped that wasn't true since her biggest secret was that she'd been all too aware of Cooper Murphy's absence. "Secrets?"

"Secrets," he confirmed. "Such as your vast organizational skills. I'm in the process of trying to clean out the office files and it's driving me insane. Your son assured me that you could straighten both me and my files out in no time." His green eyes narrowed. "He says you make lists."

"I do."

"And you color code the categories."

"Of course."

"Why am I not surprised?"

He'd made it sound like a character flaw. "Creating a well-ordered plan prevents disruption and chaos." Two things she definitely knew a great deal about.

"It also disallows for serendipity."

She folded her arms. "Serendipity?"

"Yeah. The act of experiencing happy or pleasant surprises by accident. Which can more easily be discovered by occasionally going with the flow."

"I know what the word means. But going with the flow doesn't always lead to happy events." Another thing she was more than a little familiar with.

"Yet one could argue that your finding Mitzi's ad for the New Chance was a serendipitous event."

"One could also argue that the jury's still out on whether or not that turned out to be a happy accident."

"Well, we'll just have to make it one, won't we?"

Cooper's answering grin warmed Rachel to the core. She decided that if they could only find some way to harness the power of that smile, she'd save herself a bundle on her electric bill every month.

"I'm not a control freak," she insisted a bit defensively. It wasn't entirely a lie. She'd only become one after her well-ordered life had spun totally out of control.

"Just a perfectionist," he guessed.

Despite the conversation bringing up memories she'd been trying to move beyond, Rachel almost laughed at that. "I'm far from perfect."

"I'm glad to hear that. Since perfect people tend to be intimidating," he said.

"I can't imagine you being intimidated by anyone. Or anything."

"It's the badge. It gives people the wrong image. Actually, if you want to know the truth, beautiful, sexy women have always intimidated me."

"Then you should feel completely comfortable around me."

Damn. From the way that came out sounding, he'd be bound to think she'd been fishing for compliments. Which she wasn't, Rachel assured herself. Not really.

"Funny, you should mention that," he murmured. "As it happens, I've been giving the matter a great deal of thought the past few days."

He rubbed his jaw as he studied her, his leisurely inventory missing nothing, from the top of her head down to her worn running shoes. Rachel had a sudden urge to smooth the wrinkles from her New York Giants sweatshirt. An urge she managed to resist.

"Well?" she asked when she couldn't stand his silent scrutiny another minute.

He didn't immediately answer. Instead, he approached within inches of her suddenly too-tense body. "Like I said,

I've been thinking about you, Rachel Hathaway."

"Oh, really?"

"Really." His thumb skimmed the curve of her jaw, leaving a scattering of sparks on her skin. "A whole lot. Have you thought about me?"

"No." Her voice was calm. She was not.

Cooper laughed softly.

Rachel's heartbeat quickened.

"It's a good thing you're not under oath. I'd have to run you in for perjury."

"Do you always arrest women who resist your advances, Sheriff?"

"I never have before, but now that you bring it up, I'll keep it in mind," he said amiably. "Would you accuse me of police harassment if I kissed you, Rachel?"

She was going to kiss him because she wanted to. Not because the warmth of his gaze was making her knees weak.

"I suppose that would depend on what type of kiss it was."

He smiled, accepting the dare. "Why don't we try it and find out?"

As he lowered his head, Rachel felt a flutter of nerves. And excitement.

His lips, as they moved on hers, were clever, experienced, but that wasn't a surprise. A man as handsome as Cooper Murphy would have had plenty of opportunity to perfect his kissing technique.

What was a surprise was that such an impossibly light touch could kindle such scintillating warmth.

The kiss began soft and slow, a lazy exploration of tastes that only had her wanting more. As it turned deeper, hotter, needs too long untapped rose to the surface.

It was, Rachel thought as her lips parted on a throaty moan, as if she'd spent the past eighteen months crawling across a desert, only to finally come to a sparkling clear, sweet oasis. Linking her fingers together at the back of his head, she molded her mouth to his, pouring herself into the kiss that was bringing all her body parts back to life.

It grew hot. Wild. Reckless. Somehow she'd become trapped between her new stainless steel counter and his rock-hard body and as his hands dove beneath her sweatshirt, his roughened fingers skimming over her torso to cup her breasts, Rachel's skin turned feverish.

Encouraged by her ragged whimper and the way her hands had begun racing up and down his back, he thrust a strong thigh between her legs just as Toby Keith's "Honkytonk U" blasting from Fred's truck signaled that her work crew was back.

"Damn." Cooper blew out a deep, frustrated breath and slowly lifted his head, breaking the heated contact, leaving Rachel's mind clear as glass.

Shaken, struggling to find some connection between her spinning brain and her hand, she bent down to retrieve his Stetson that had fallen to the floor. When she thought that she could meet his eyes with some semblance of calm, she straightened.

"Well . . ." She dragged an unsteady hand through her hair. "That was . . ."

"Along with being a pleasant surprise, definitely something else to think about," he said. He ran the back of his hand down the side of her face. After that shared burst of sexual combustion, the caress felt extraordinarily tender.

"Believe it or not, I'm here on official business." After

putting the hat she'd handed him back on, he reached into his shirt pocket and pulled out a piece of folded paper. "The town council met last night. I was asked to drop this by."

Rachel scanned the lines of text. "It's a contract?"

"With the town, to provide meals for the jail. Johnny's always had a verbal agreement, but we've got a new mayor, George Masterson, owner of Masterson's Mercantile, who's gung ho enough to want everything in writing.

"The price is the same as Johnny's been getting for the past three years, but if it's not enough, feel free to negotiate. As you can probably tell from the way he fell behind on his insurance payments, Johnny was a miserable businessman."

"How many prisoners are we talking about?"

"Not that many," he assured her. "Probably two or three a month, and most of them are ranch hands who've had a bit too much to drink on Saturday night. They're usually gone by Sunday lunchtime, so we're not talking about anything that's going to take much time away from your work here at the café. Or make you much money," he said apologetically.

"Well, the price is fair, so I guess this makes it official." She signed the paper and handed it back to him. "I'm a bona fide resident of River's Bend."

He took the paper, folded it, and put it back into his pocket without looking at it. "You've no idea how happy that makes me."

Reaching out, Cooper gathered her dark hair in his hand, drawing her to him with a gentle tug.

"For someone supposedly on official town business, your behavior isn't exactly businesslike," Rachel said as her pulse spiked.

"We've already gotten the business part of this visit out of the way. And for the record, Rachel, that kiss was entirely personal. You might want to keep that in mind, next time."

The hint of amusement in his tone had her lifting her chin. "What makes you think there's going to be a next time?" But there would be. Until Cooper had kissed her, Rachel had forgotten how glorious kissing could be.

"If I didn't believe there was going to be a next time, I wouldn't be so willing to leave things unfinished this time." He brushed his lips teasingly against hers, creating another flare of heat. "I'll be seeing you."

As he left the kitchen, Rachel sank down onto a stool, closed her eyes and pressed a hand against her still pounding heart. Oh, yes. Despite his laconic, easygoing attitude, Sheriff Cooper Murphy was definitely going to prove a problem.

16

A S THE DAYS GREW shorter, and September sped with lightning speed into mid-October, work on the New Chance continued practically around the clock, during which time Rachel couldn't stop thinking about Cooper. Despite instructions to the contrary, her rebellious mind continued to replay their shared kiss in riveting, sensual detail.

She'd almost forgotten how good it felt to have a man kiss her. Hold her. Touch her. Want her.

Cooper had taken to dropping into the café each day on his foot patrols around town, but they were seldom alone, which, while frustrating, was also a relief because Rachel was so confused.

Part of her wanted to jump his bones whenever he walked in the door. If she'd been alone, living in a more anonymous city, she might seriously consider having a fling.

But she wasn't alone and was all too aware that life wasn't solely about her wants or needs. She was the mother of a young child whom she'd moved to this small town where not only did everyone know your name, gossip provided a major form of entertainment. The last thing Scott needed was to go to school and hear about his mother sleeping with the sheriff.

So, despite the fact that Cooper's visits had become the high point of her work-filled days, she struggled to keep her emotional distance. And, seeming to sense her ambivalence, he'd backed off a bit, keeping the New Chance a seduction-free zone, even as the shared attraction arced between and around them.

Scott was no help at all as he continued to tell her stories of life around the sheriff's office. Then there was the day he showed up with a law-enforcement recruiting poster.

"It's really neat, isn't it, Mom?" he asked that evening for the umpteenth time.

The poster depicted a scrubbed and polished young man and woman clad in starched khaki uniforms standing beside a patrol car looking like the last bastion between the bad guys and the general public.

Bearing the title *Exploring Law Enforcement*, it had immediately been assigned the spot of honor on Scott's bedroom wall.

"Neat," she agreed as she pressed the ground beef into patties. Cheeseburgers might not win her a pedestal on Iron Chef, but they were her son's favorite and didn't take much time or effort to prepare.

"Warren offered me all his Transformer figures for my poster," he divulged. "But I told him I wouldn't trade for anything."

"I hope you thanked Cooper."

"Sure. What kind of kid do you think you raised?" he complained with a grin.

Rachel returned the smile. "A dynamite kid."

"I think you're great, too," Scott said as he went to the refrigerator and took out a carton of milk. He poured it into a glass emblazoned with X-Men's Wolverine they'd bought at a truck stop/gas station/restaurant/souvenir shop in Wyoming on their drive across the country, then climbed up onto the bar stool. "Can we invite Cooper to dinner?"

"I suppose. Sometime," she answered vaguely as she turned on the burner.

"When?"

"I don't know, honey. Cooper is a very busy man."

"But he doesn't work nights unless there's an emergency. He told me."

"Still, he undoubtedly has his own plans."

"No, he doesn't. Most nights he and Hummer just eat frozen dinners."

"I take it you've met Hummer." Rachel sliced cheese from a block of cheddar onto a wooden cutting board.

"Yeah." Scott picked up a piece of cheese and popped it into his mouth. "He mostly hangs around the sheriff's office. He's really neat. Can we get a dog, Mom? There's plenty of room in the backyard."

"I don't know, Scott." Alan had been allergic, so a pet had been out of the question. "A dog might get lonely, with you at school all day and me at work."

"I could take him to play with Hummer."

"I don't believe a law-enforcement office is any place for boys and dogs to be playing."

"But—"

"Let me think about it," Rachel said, interrupting what she knew was going to be a long drawn-out plea.

"Sure." Surprising her with such easy acquiescence, he

took a long drink of milk. "Maybe if you came down to Cooper's office and saw what a neat dog Hummer is—"

Rachel held up her hand as he wiped a milk mustache off his top lip with the back of his sleeve. "I said, let me think about it."

The doorbell rang before Scott could answer.

"I'll get it," he said, sliding off the stool. He was out of the room in a flash, and a moment later Rachel heard the low murmur of voices, one youthful, one deep and compelling.

She instinctively lifted a hand to her hair, remembering the meat on her palm just in time.

"It's Cooper!" Scott shouted as he raced into the room. "And look what he brought me!" Breathless with excitement, he held up a sheet of paper, looking as if he'd just been given the golden ticket to his own private candy factory. "Fingerprints. From a real live stage coach robber!"

At least the man had original taste in gifts. Rachel hadn't seen Scott so excited since . . .

Actually, she wasn't certain she'd ever seen him that excited.

"Hello, Sheriff," she said with measured calm as Cooper strolled into her kitchen carrying a brown paper bag. He wasn't wearing his gun, which she took to mean he was officially off duty. "What can I do for you?"

"I've come for dinner."

"Dinner?" Rachel glanced over at her son, who was busy matching his fingertips to the smudged ink stains.

Picking up on the situation, Cooper turned to Scott. "I thought you said your mother wanted me to come to dinner."

"She does," the boy insisted. "Don't you, Mom?"

"I believe my exact words were 'perhaps sometime.'"

Scott's anxious, coaxing gaze went back and forth between his mother and his new friend. "Well, this is sometime," he pointed out. "I think I'll go next door and show my fingerprints to Warren. He'll be really jealous."

He escaped through the kitchen door before Rachel had a chance to object.

"You have fifteen minutes," she called out to his back. "If you're not home by then, your burger will end up in a doggie bag for Hummer."

"I think that kid might have a great future as a politician," Cooper said.

"If he lives that long," Rachel muttered.

17

DESPITE HAVING WORKED as hard as the guys all day, the woman Cooper had not been able to get out of his mind looked good. Damn good. Rachel Hathaway had been so slender when she'd first arrived in town she'd looked as if a stiff mountain wind could have blown her over. Even working as physically hard as she had been at the New Chance, she'd begun to put on much-needed weight. As he took in the curves beneath her oversized sweater and the way those skinny jeans showcased her long, shapely legs, a bolt of lust shot through him.

Knowing how many changes Rachel had been through since her husband's death, he'd resisted the almost overwhelming urge to touch. To taste. Instead of dragging her off to bed to act out those hot dreams that had had him waking up with major wood every morning, he'd physically backed away so she'd have time to adjust to the idea of a new man in her life.

When Scott had asked him to dinner this afternoon, he'd mistakenly assumed the invitation had come from the mother, not her son.

"You're welcome to stay if you don't mind cheeseburgers and fries," she said.

"Love 'em. Need any help?"

"Thanks, but I have everything under control."

He certainly couldn't argue with that. If she were any more cool, calm, and collected, Cooper would begin to think he'd imagined that kiss they'd shared in the kitchen of the New Chance.

"I brought some wine," he offered, pulling the bottle out of the bag. Not trusting George Masterson's inventory of jug wine, Cooper had driven to a newly opened wine and cheese shop in Klamath Falls. The proprietor of the Cork and Cleaver had assured him that Rachel would approve of the vintage cabernet Sauvignon.

Rachel's brows rose as she studied the label. "Goodness, I feel as if I should dump the hamburgers in the disposal and whip up some fillet of beef Périgourdine."

"Does that mean I did okay?"

"Better than okay. But you needn't have spent so much money."

Cooper shrugged. "It wasn't that much." Okay, he'd admittedly been stunned by the price, but had immediately decided that Rachel was worth every dollar. "Do you have a corkscrew?"

"In the top right-hand drawer, next to the refrigerator. And don't forget, I'm in the business. I know how expensive that vintage is."

"Hey, lady, for your information, this happens to be my favorite adult beverage to drink with burgers."

She studied him curiously for a moment before forming a third hamburger patty. "Well, you certainly needn't have bothered on my account."

"I didn't," he lied blithely as he uncorked the wine.

"Glasses?"

"In the upper cupboard to the left of the sink."

Cooper found the glasses and was prepared to pour the ruby wine into them when something from a Bond flick popped into his mind. "I suppose we ought to let this breathe for a while."

"I suppose so," Rachel agreed. "Not that I'd be able to tell the difference, having never managed to develop a discriminating wine palate. Don't tell anyone, but my teachers used to call me the class Philistine."

"Teachers?" Deciding that the wine had breathed long enough, Cooper poured it into the stemmed glasses.

"At the New York Restaurant School."

"So, that's where you learned to cook?"

"Among other things. We studied everything from boiling eggs to restaurant design. The final thesis was a restaurant proposal including everything from menus and tableware to negotiating your way through New York City's building codes."

"No wonder Mitzi wasn't any match for you."

Rachel shrugged off his compliment. "I picked up a lot about financing, even though I nearly flunked wine."

"That's handy to know. The Mercantile carries a Muscatel that's just one step above antifreeze."

"What year?"

"Last week. And I have it on good authority that it's spent all that time aging in mason jars."

She laughed. "I think even I could spot that. Would you really like to help?"

"I never say anything I don't mean, Rachel." His tone made it clear that he wasn't talking about fixing dinner.

"Well." She met his gaze. Message received. "If you

wouldn't mind, you can peel those potatoes."

"You're in luck." Cooper picked up one of the brown Klamath Russets. "Peeling is one of my few culinary skills. That and taking the plastic wrap off microwave dinners."

"You're certainly fast," she murmured as he covered the bottom of the sink with curling brown potato skins.

"It's not that different from whittling. Fortunately, by the time I joined the Marines, KP duty wasn't part of boot camp, like in Dad's time."

"You were in the Marines?" She filled the deep fryer with cooking oil, then plugged it in.

"My younger brother, Sawyer, and I both followed in Dad's boot steps. Sawyer's currently deployed. I did two tours, then opted out." While his youngest brother was still in harm's way.

Daniel Murphy was typically western rancher stoic, and didn't share his feelings all that much, but just because they didn't discuss Sawyer 24/7, there wasn't a day that went by Cooper didn't think about his brother and worry. He figured it was probably even harder on his dad. And also difficult on his grandparents who'd lost a Marine son of their own, Cooper's Uncle James, whom he'd never met, in Vietnam.

"My other brother, Ryan, who's in the middle, joined the Navy, which put him through med school. After he left the military a few months ago, he went into partnership with a Nurse Practitioner who'd opened her practice after old Doc Willard retired last year. We consider ourselves real lucky to have them. Especially since not that many medical professionals are willing to work for quarters of beef."

"Surely you're kidding."

"Mostly. Though it does happen from time to time. But family practice isn't at the top of the pay scale even in larger markets. By the time you get down to a place the size of River's Bend, you're definitely not in it for the bucks."

"I imagine not. I was relieved to see that the town had a local family physician, though when I met you I had other things on my mind, so the sheriff and the doctor both having the same last name didn't click.

"What did you do?" she asked as the burgers sizzled in a cast-iron pan. "When you were in the Marines?"

"I was an M.P."

"So, you were in law enforcement even then."

"My dad was sheriff of River's Bend, so I guess, growing up with a cop, military police seemed a natural choice."

"Did you become sheriff once you left the Marines?"

"No. I spent a few years working for the Portland Police Bureau." He began slicing the now-peeled potatoes. "Then five years ago Dad had a heart attack which put him out of commission for a while, so I came home to finish up his term as sheriff. By that time, he'd started crossbreeding his Angus with Japanese Wagyu, blending Wagyu's sweet buttery taste with the flavor of grass fed Angus. Which is probably more information than you were asking for."

"I cook for a living," Rachel reminded him. "I love talking food and remember, I tasted your father's beef. It's amazing." She also hadn't been at all surprised that Chef Madeline, who was known for her farm-to-table cooking, was a customer.

"Yeah. It is, and the demand for it is growing exponentially. Which is why he decided he'd rather concentrate on ranching. So, I stayed on, got myself elected to the job, and since it suits me, I figure I'll probably stick around until they vote me out."

"If what I've heard is any indication, you could continue being sheriff for as long as you live," she said, making Cooper wonder if she'd been asking around about him. He liked the idea that she might be as interested in him as he was in her.

"Do you miss the city?" she asked.

"Not at all. Actually, I'd been thinking about coming home for a long time. Dad's situation simply pushed me to make up my mind a little sooner, and although I sure as hell wouldn't have thought it when I was eighteen and looking to get out of River's Bend and see the world, I've found it to be a good fit."

"I'd think being a city policeman would be exciting. Though dangerous."

He shrugged as he dumped the raw potato slices into the stainless steel fryer basket. "Sometimes." They sizzled as he lowered the basket into the hot oil. "Although it's not at all like on TV, where the good guys have exactly sixty minutes, minus commercials to catch the bad guys and put them behind bars.

"Mostly it's boring detail work. Patrolling the streets, filling out reports, stuff like that. And there are days when being sheriff of River County is about as exciting as watching two guys fish."

"Don't tell Scott it's boring. He'd be heartbroken." Rachel turned the burgers. "If it's so boring, why do you do it?"

"Because I love this town. And the people. Also, looking back on the sequence of events that brought me home,

I think it might've been predestined. My great-great grandfather was the first sheriff of River's Bend. He was followed by my great-grandfather, Gramps, then Dad, and now me."

"That's quite a family legacy."

"Yeah. It seems to have become the Murphy business. Probably because no one else is all that eager to take the job."

"So, between all the lawmen and your Navy doctor and Marine brothers, it sounds as if service is woven into the Murphy DNA."

"I guess you could put it that way. Maybe when you come from a small place, where everyone knows everyone else, the world just seems more personal, so you try to do what you can to make it better . . .

"The potatoes are ready. Want me to set the table?"

"If you wouldn't mind. There are paper napkins in that drawer to your right and the plates are there on the shelf. Is that the only reason you're sheriff? Predestination?"

"Not really." Damn. She would have to ask that.

"Well?" her tone invited elaboration.

"It'll sound corny," he warned.

"Corny?"

"Like something from an old John Wayne movie. You know, all that red, white, and blue stuff about honor and integrity."

"I like those old John Wayne movies. And there's certainly a great deal to be said for honor and integrity."

Cooper had Googled Rachel. He'd read her advertising executive husband's obituary, which consisted of pages and pages of achievements and accolades from names even he recognized.

Digging deeper, he'd unearthed the website for her now defunct catering business still lingering out there in cyberspace and checked out the menus, none of which featured cheeseburgers and fries. The glowing reviews from her obviously wealthy clients had pointed out exactly how different a life she'd come from.

Despite what she'd said about having grown up on a farm, she was definitely city now. While he was country to the bone.

He was domestic beer in a long neck bottle.

She was imported French champagne.

Her husband had probably worn a fancy tuxedo to take Rachel to the opera.

He'd worn faded jeans, a blue chambray shirt, and smoke-smudged boots to take her on an outlaw train ride.

Cooper was realist enough to know that while Rachel might be attracted enough to kiss him, hell, maybe even go to bed with him, she'd probably never end up with a small town sheriff like him.

But knowing that didn't stop him from wanting her. Bad.

"Okay, but don't say I didn't warn you. During the years I spent all over the globe, I began to realize that my roots go a lot deeper than I'd thought. So, while I might've come back home because of Dad, I stayed because I'm old-fashioned enough to believe I might actually be able to make a difference in people's lives."

"And you couldn't have made a difference in Portland?"

"I might have, from time to time. But the system was too impersonal for my tastes. How about you?"

"Me?"

"What made you give up the big-city lights of Manhattan for the sleepy ambience of River's Bend, Oregon?"

"Manhattan was where Alan's office was located. We lived in Connecticut."

He knew that, having seen the video the real estate agent had made when she'd listed the Hathaway McMansion for sale. This entire bungalow probably could have fit into the two-story library that had been paneled and furnished like some aristocratic English gentleman's club.

"But you still went to school in New York City. Probably had date nights. Lunches in fancy Michelin star restaurants with friends and potential clients."

"True." Hedging the issue, she pulled the sunshine yellow curtains aside and looked out the kitchen window. "I wonder if I should call Scott. Dinner's nearly ready and he's not home."

"He's still got a couple of minutes," Cooper pointed out. "Conversation getting a little too personal again, Rachel?"

"Not at all," she insisted as she stacked cheese on top of the burgers and slid them into the oven beneath the broiler. "It was merely a question of the most return on my dollar. I couldn't afford to buy anything along the lines of Chez Maxime, but I could afford the New Chance Café."

Cooper topped off their wineglasses and asked the question he'd been wondering about since meeting her. "Surely there were other restaurants between here and New York or Connecticut you could afford to buy. Why this one? And why sight unseen?"

"The cheese is bubbling," she complained, pulling the

broiler pan from the oven as she continued to dodge his questions. "Where is he?"

Scott chose that moment to burst in the door. "Dumb ole Warren doesn't believe these are a real outlaw's fingerprints," he complained, tossing his jacket on the back of a chair, where it slid down onto the floor.

"Pick that up and hang it and your hat on the rack," Rachel instructed. "Then wash your hands and sit down before the burgers get cold."

"But what about Warren?" His face was flushed with frustration and indignation.

"Warren can get his own dinner. I only made three burgers. Wash."

Apparently recognizing her no-nonsense mom tone, Scott scooped up the jacket and hung it on the wooden rack next to his cowboy hat. Then he went over to the sink, where he pumped liquid soap onto his palms and waved them briefly under the water before wiping them on his jeans. Which had Rachel rolling her eyes, but she didn't call him on it.

"They really are an outlaw's prints, huh, Cooper?"

"Sure are. Bad Bill was one of the most infamous stage and train robbers in Oregon. Which is why he always leads the gang on the outlaw ride."

He didn't mention that Bad Bill was usually played by his father-in-law, who also belonged to the Boothill Ghostriders, a western re-enactment group that performed for rodeos throughout Oregon, Nevada, and northern California.

"Is it all right for Scott to have them?" Rachel asked as she brought the cheeseburgers to the table.

"We were cleaning out the files," Cooper assured her.

"You were throwing away official records?"

Her tone was so serious, her expression so sweetly grave that it was all Cooper could do not to bend down and kiss her, right now while her hands were filled with plates and she couldn't push him away. Since her son was right there, he merely smiled.

"Rachel, Bad Bill Barkley escaped from the Oregon State prison in 1925, after which time he was rumored to be hiding out for a while with Butch Cassidy and the Sundance Kid in Utah. I doubt there'll be any immediate need for his fingerprint file."

Scott frowned as he bit into his cheeseburger. "Butch and Sundance died in Argentina," he said when he'd finished chewing. "I've seen the movie lots of times."

"That's what they say," Cooper agreed. "However, Butch's sister, Lula Parker, insisted that the men killed in Argentina were intentionally misidentified to give Butch and Sundance a chance to bury their past and go straight. She said Butch died in Spokane after spending his last years as a trapper and prospector."

"Wow!" His eyes were saucers. "Just think, Mom, my fingerprints belong to a friend of Butch Cassidy and the Sundance Kid!"

"Just what every boy needs," Rachel said dryly. "An outlaw hero. Do you believe that story?" she asked Cooper.

"I don't really know. Gramps swears they escaped, having heard the tale from his dad, who'd heard it from this lady, Pearl Hughes, who used to have a small spread outside town. Apparently some people around here claimed she was actually Etta Place—who may or may not have married Sundance—hiding out under a new name.

Rumors had her buying the farm with money Sundance had given her. There were also reports of Etta living up in Marion, in the northern part of the state."

"Geez." Scott was clearly awestruck. "Now I know what I'm going to write my Oregon history paper on. Can you help me, Cooper?"

"I'd love to, sport, but Gramps would probably be able to give you a lot more facts since most of what I know is just rumor and passed-down family stories."

Scott mulled it over while he chewed on a ketchup soaked French fry. "Okay," he decided. "Mrs. Wilson said the papers have to be non-fiction. That's the truth, not made up," he elaborated for Rachel's benefit. "So I guess facts would be better. But the stories are great, too," he tacked on as if afraid of hurting Cooper's feelings.

Amused, Cooper winked. "Glad you like them. How about after we do the dishes since your mom cooked dinner, you and I go next door to Warren's and I'll verify your fingerprints."

"Geez," Scott, said happily, "this is turning out to be a great night!"

18

"IT'S BEEN A lovely evening," Rachel said a few hours later.

Scott, his reputation and fingerprints vindicated, had gone to bed, leaving her alone with Cooper. A gentle autumn rain sounded a steady tattoo on the roof and contributed to the intimacy of the small living room.

"You sound surprised."

"I suppose I am. And while I'll probably feel guilty in the morning, I have to admit that it's nice to take some time off. Mrs. MacGregor certainly didn't seem surprised when I called to tell her not to bother coming over this evening."

Cooper didn't need to be a mind reader to tell that taking these few hours off made Rachel uncomfortable, but the fact that she wasn't rushing back to the New Chance revealed he was making progress.

"That may have something to do with the River County Sheriff's Department Jeep parked in front of your house," he suggested.

"Probably." She sighed. "By tomorrow it'll be all over town that we had dinner together."

"Does that bother you?"

She shrugged. "I suppose not."

But it did. Cooper could tell. Knowing that it took time to get used to the fishbowl existence that came with life in River's Bend, he sought to put her mind at ease.

"I can tell everyone that I was testing out the cook," he said helpfully. "So they'll know what they're getting when the New Chance reopens."

"Just don't tell them I fed you a cheeseburger."

"Hey, don't knock cheeseburgers. They're considered gourmet fare here in ranching country."

His smile encouraged one in return, and he could feel her relax as she told him of her plans for the café. "I'm covering up the interior log walls with sheetrock that'll be textured like plaster," she said. "While I understand why Johnny stuck with the original logs in the dining room and bar, they're dark and impossible to clean. I suspect decades of nicotine are embedded in them."

"I wouldn't be surprised." They were sitting on the overstuffed couch in front of fireplace. Although it no longer worked, she'd placed half a dozen fat white candles where logs would have gone. Cooper put his arm along the back and played lightly with her hair.

"I'm sticking with that Navajo white Fred was generous enough to donate in the kitchen, and going with a warm gold for the dining room. And although red's considered a death color for restaurants, I decided on a wonderfully rich terracotta brick color for an accent wall. And we're stripping all the horrid layers of paint off those wonderful original wooden moldings."

"Sounds great."

Encouraged when she didn't move away, he allowed his hand to slip down and rest on her shoulder. Just like high school, Cooper thought wryly. Building up to necking with Ellen while parked in his pickup at the old Pelican drive-in theater that had closed during his first deployment.

"And we tore out all those terrible fluorescent lights that make people look like zombies and food look like something the dog would turn down."

"You pretty much just described Johnny's menu."

She laughed as he'd meant her to. "Well, I'm using LED pendant lights and wall sconces. Not only are they energy efficient, they're much more natural. And Hank Young just happened to come up with some wonderful antique embossed copper ceiling tiles. Apparently he bought them a few years ago for song at an auction in Medford, but the woman who'd ordered them changed her mind, so he figured I might want them. He offered to donate them, but I insisted on reimbursing him. Which turned out to be an amazingly low price."

Cooper knew Hank had found the tiles for sale at a restoration wholesaler after Cal told him Rachel had mentioned wishing that she could squeeze a hammered copper ceiling into her budget. But that bit of information, along with what the hardware store owner had actually paid for them, would remain Hank's secret.

"Lucky," he said.

"Isn't it? And you have to see the skylight Cal put in. It makes the entry look so much larger. I'm thinking of getting a tree. Nothing too big. Maybe just a Norfolk Island pine, or Ficus or maybe bamboo, though bamboo's too oriental for the menu. A banana tree would be wonderful, but again, it doesn't really fit into a western theme and it needs so much humidity. Also, Ficus can have a leaf drop problem, so perhaps I ought to stick with the pine."

"I've found it's usually best to go with your first impulse," Cooper said, wondering why he was sitting here talking about trees when he'd rather be tasting her mouth.

"You're right." Rachel nodded decisively. "The pine it is."

"I'm glad we got that settled."

She was so lost in thought that his dry tone went right over her head. "So am I. It's one less thing to worry about. I'm also beginning to interview people who worked for Johnny. Even starting out small, I can't do everything myself.

"Oh, and you'll never guess what we found when we pulled up the linoleum in the dining room today."

"The bodies of everyone who died of ptomaine poisoning after eating Johnny's cooking?"

"Haha. A wood floor. Cal says it's Oregon white oak, which these days can mostly only be found in salvage yards, so it has to be original. The color's so much richer than eastern oak and it's also hand-fitted tongue and groove. Isn't that marvelous?"

"Marvelous," he murmured distractedly. The scent of her lotion was swirling around in his head, making it difficult to concentrate.

"I'm sorry," she said.

"For what?"

"I've been talking nonstop about myself and haven't let you get a word in edgewise."

Actually, she'd been talking about the restaurant, not herself, but he wasn't about to quibble. "That's okay. I'm perfectly content just to sit here and smell your neck."

She suddenly stiffened. "Really, Cooper . . ."

"Really. You always smell like sunlit wildflower meadows after a warm spring rain." When he trailed his fingertips down her neck, she trembled.

"Cooper." It was little more than a whisper, but easily heard in the stillness of the room.

"Is that a complaint?" He pressed a kiss behind her ear. "Or an invitation?"

Cooper sensed her building hunger in the way her body softened beneath his increasingly intimate touch. He felt it in the quickening of her pulse; viewed it in the way her eyes were turning to dark and gleaming pewter as they met his.

But he could feel her vacillation, as well. Her hands were pressed against his chest as if trying to decide whether to clutch at him, or push him away.

Slowly, reluctantly, once again, he solved the problem for her and backed away.

"You really are so damn lovely," he murmured. Still needing to touch, he ran the back of his hand down the side of her face. "I like your mouth. A lot."

Cooper planned to spend a lot more time tasting that luscious mouth. But, it appeared, not tonight.

"Did I thank you for dinner?"

"You did. Several times. Did I thank you for the wine?"

"Three times."

"Well. I guess we've covered everything, then."

"I suppose so. Except for what you're doing for Thanksgiving."

"I'll be working."

"At the café." It was not a question.

"Where else?"

Where else, indeed? Cooper was starting to get a handle on Rachel's workaholic habits. Cal had told him that although all the men tried to get her to take a break from time to time, she steadfastly refused.

He took hold of her hand and turned it over. Her soft skin was marred by angry blisters at the base of each finger. A few of the blisters were hardening to calluses. "Look at what you're doing to yourself."

"Those calluses are merely the sign of hard, honest work," she countered. "Do you have something against work, Sheriff?"

"Of course not. Do you have something against moderation?"

"There'll be time for moderation once the New Chance is open for business."

Cooper wondered about that. From what he'd seen and heard about Rachel, the lady was definitely driven. He could understand ambition. Could even respect it. But he couldn't shake the feeling that Rachel was carrying things too far.

"Look, I understand why you want to get the place open, but you're only human. You can't keep working around the clock indefinitely."

"It's not indefinite. The café will be open before Christmas. I've hired a student at the Oregon Institute of Technology in Klamath Falls to set up a Facebook page and make me a basic website and bought ad space in both the Klamath Falls *Herald and News* and the *River's Bend Register*.

"But Mitzi says people like to ski on Modoc Mountain over the holidays, so I'm considering running a grand opening ad in the Rogue Valley papers, as well. And maybe even go east and try the *Lake County Examiner*. Of course, that would increase the advertising budget, but if I picked up some repeat vacation business the additional cost might be worth it. What do you think?"

"I think you're working too hard."

"Thank you for your concern, Sheriff. But I don't believe that's any of your business."

Her tone had turned city cool and Cooper could practically see the *No Trespassing* signs going up all around her.

"Actually, your son sort of made it my business."

"Scott?" She looked at him disbelievingly. "What does Scott have to do with this?"

"How about the fact that he's forced to talk to a virtual stranger about his father because his mother's too busy to take time to listen?"

Every bit of color fled Rachel's face.

Damn. Cooper immediately regretted his reckless words. "Hell, I'm sorry." His hands cupped her shoulders. "That was a low blow. And totally uncalled for."

"No." Her shadowed eyes glistened. Dear God, please don't let her cry. Cooper would rather face down a dozen gangbangers than deal with a woman's tears.

"It's true," she said on a long sigh. "Scott doesn't talk to me about Alan. I've tried, so many times, but he always changes the subject."

She was tense. Too tense. Feeling lower than a Western diamondback in a rut, Cooper caressed her shoulders with his palms, seeking to soothe the cruelly twisted muscles.

"In case you're worried, I haven't been pumping him for information."

"I know you wouldn't do that. And although my maternal pride is admittedly dented, I'm glad he has someone he feels he can talk with."

"If it helps, the only reason he doesn't discuss his dad with you is because he's afraid of hurting your feelings." The pain in her moist eyes tore at something deep inside Cooper. "It seems he's got the mistaken impression that it's his job to protect you."

"The man of the house." Rachel gave a long, weary sigh. "I wasn't the one who put that idea into his head. Honestly, I wasn't."

He pressed his lips against her temple. "I know." Ambitious Rachel might be. Even driven. But she was not the type of woman to play complex emotional games, especially with a child.

"The first time I heard him make that ridiculous statement was at the funeral, when he assured Father O'Malley that we'd be okay. Seven-years-old and he was suddenly the self-proclaimed man of the house. I couldn't believe my ears. If it weren't so tragic, it'd be funny."

"I think it's genetic," he said. "Woven into a male's DNA, carried over from when men left their caves each morning with their sturdy clubs over their shoulders and returned home at the end of the day with a bunch of brontosaurus steaks."

"It's crazy."

"Probably. But I wouldn't worry too much about Scott, Rachel. He seems to be doing okay. Better than okay. He's fitting in just fine."

"I know. It was the same way he did when I had to move him from the private school he'd known since preschool to a public one."

"Nothing wrong with public," he said. "My brothers and I attended them."

"So did I."

"And see how well you turned out? Besides, although I admittedly don't have any of my own, from what I've seen, kids are resilient."

"It's been a difficult time."

"I can imagine."

"I've tried to give Scott the stability I knew he needed, but there was so much to do." She gave him a weary look. "So much still left to do."

Her hands were twisting agitatedly in her lap. Cooper captured them in his. "You have to give yourself, and Scott, time. Even Rome wasn't built in a day."

And wasn't that just what she needed? A frigging cliché? Could he screw this evening up any more?

"I'm not worried about Rome. I am worried to death about not getting the New Chance renovated in time for the holidays."

"This isn't a marathon. And you're not running against any clock."

"Easy for you to say," she countered with a bit more spark. "I have to have the New Chance open by Christmas," she insisted yet again.

Stubborn. The word didn't begin to describe this woman. Cooper told himself that the smart thing to do would be to get off this couch, walk out the door to the Jeep and drive away, leaving the delectable, but frustratingly intransigent Rachel to her unbridled Eastern ambition.

"So what, exactly would happen if you didn't get the place open by Christmas? Would the world as we know it come to an end? Would thousands of vacationers starve without the chance to sample a piece of Rachel Hathaway's incomparable mincemeat pie? Would the entire economic foundation of our country crumble down around our feet?"

"I'd run out of money, that's what would happen!" Jerking her hands from his, she jumped to her feet.

Cooper watched her cross the room to the window to stare out into the well of darkness. He'd suspected her funds were limited, but hadn't realized she was in danger of completely running out of money.

"I didn't know."

"Well, now you do." She leaned her forehead against the window glass and closed her eyes. "I'm sorry. I never lose my temper. Ever."

"If anyone needs to apologize, it's me. I had no right to push."

"I shouldn't have flown off the handle like that." She turned back toward him and let out an unsteady breath.

"You're entitled. I overstepped my bounds." He crossed the room to take hold of the hand she'd dragged through her hair. "Don't look now, but I think we've just had a milestone moment."

"What milestone would that be?"

"Our first fight."

Her lips hinted at a smile. "Still, I shouldn't have taken my troubles out on you."

"That's what friends are for."

"Is that what we are?" she asked quietly. "Friends?"

In spite of the seriousness of the conversation, Cooper couldn't resist a slight smile of his own. "You're an intelligent woman, Rachel. Surely it hasn't escaped your attention that I'd like to be a great deal more than a friend."

"As in friends with privileges?"

"I'm not saying I haven't been there," he admitted. "But it doesn't feel right with you." He paused, watching the soft color drift into her cheeks in confirmation of his words. "So, if you're not ready for more, I'll settle for friends."

For now.

"We don't even know each other."

"I think we've begun to over the past weeks. Besides, I know Scott, and there's a great deal of you in your son."

"Do you think so?" she asked softly.

"I know so. Undoubtedly there's also a lot of your husband in Scott. From everything he's told me, Alan was a great guy."

There. He'd done it. After hearing about his rival for two weeks, and thinking about him a helluva lot more than he should have, Cooper had finally said the man's name out loud.

"He was."

"Scott worries that you still miss his father." Although he'd promised himself that he wouldn't pry, Cooper couldn't quite keep the question from his voice.

"I do still miss him," she admitted, dragging her hand through her hair again. "Oh, not as much as I used to. But there are times, when something good happens, like finding that floor today, when I instinctively turn around to share it with him."

"I can understand that."

He'd been there himself. After Ellen's death, he'd taken to talking to the framed photo of her in her wedding dress, sharing bits and pieces of his day with his bride.

"Or when I'm afraid," Rachel continued, unaware of the path his thoughts had taken. "Or late at night in bed . . ."

Cooper flashed her his sexiest grin as her cheeks flamed. "I'm well acquainted with that one."

Before he found himself volunteering to help her out on that score, he decided the time had come to turn the conversation back to something less personal.

"I'm afraid the job of sheriff doesn't pay all that much, but I've managed to put some money away, Rachel. You're welcome to as much as you need."

"Thank you," she said. "I appreciate your offer, really I do, but this is something I have to do myself."

Cooper understood pride, having a fair share of it himself. Accepting much-needed help was one thing. Charity was quite another, and there was a razor-thin line between the two.

"I wasn't offering you charity."

"Weren't you?"

"No. I was thinking of making an investment."

He'd caught her unwilling interest with that one. "In the New Chance?"

"No, in the woman running the New Chance. But I suppose, in the long run it works out the same."

"I'll think about it," she said after a long pause.

It wasn't much, Cooper decided, but it was a start. "You do that."

He rose from the couch, reluctantly deciding that he'd made about as much progress as he could hope to this evening. Cooper had always considered himself an easy going guy, but since Rachel's arrival in River's Bend, he'd discovered an impatient streak he'd been unaware of possessing.

"I'd better be going so Mrs. MacGregor can get some sleep."

Rachel smiled as she walked him to the door. "I really did have a lovely evening."

"We'll have to do it again sometime."

"I'd like that," she said, sounding as if she meant it. "Thank you for being so nice to Scott."

"I've already told you, he's a super kid. It's easy to be nice to him. Damn."

She looked up at him. "What's the matter?"

"We got sidetracked, and I nearly forgot that the reason I asked about Thanksgiving is because Dad and Mitzi wanted me to invite you and Scott to have dinner at the ranch."

"I'm sorry, but I really—"

"Have to work."

She didn't hesitate. "Yes."

Cooper studied her, taking in the calm, unwavering determination in her eyes, the taut line of her unpainted lips. He wanted Rachel, more than he'd wanted any woman since Ellen. He also was certain that were it not for that damned New Chance Café, he and the lovely young widow wouldn't be wasting time talking about linoleum, paint color, and indoor trees.

The most important part of law enforcement was not, as TV and movies so often projected, chasing down bad guys, but problem solving. The solution to this problem was readily apparent: if he wanted to make love to Rachel, he'd simply have to help her get the damn place open.

As soon as possible.

"If I promise that the New Chance will be open by

Christmas, will you take Thanksgiving off for some much needed R and R?"

"I already went on that train ride," she reminded him. "I stayed home tonight. And how can you possibly guarantee that?"

"Believe me, Rachel. I never promise anything I can't deliver."

"I don't know," she murmured, obviously tempted.

"Which do you think Scott would enjoy more?" he asked. "Hanging around watching you sand floors or spending a day at the ranch learning to ride a horse?"

"Of course he'd rather learn to ride. But if I take another day off and the New Chance doesn't open for Christmas—"

He held up a hand, cutting her off. "It'll open on time. Trust me."

"Do you always get everything you want?"

Cooper thought of Ellen, of the giddy, love-filled plans they'd made, of the children dreamed about but never born. "No. Not always."

There was another long silence as Rachel studied him, seeming to sense that there was more to his short reply than he was saying. Then, apparently deciding there'd been enough personal revelations for one evening, she thankfully didn't pursue it.

"Just most of the time," she suggested quietly.

"Most of the time," Cooper agreed. He ran a hand down her hair, the sleek dark strands feeling like silk as they flowed through his fingers.

It was a good thing that crime was practically nonexistent in River's Bend because kissing Rachel again had been almost all he'd been able to think about the past few days. And kissing was just for starters.

With free-spirited women accustomed to following their feelings and living for the moment, desire would be enough. With Rachel, things would always be more serious.

More complicated.

It was just as well, Cooper decided. Experience had taught him that most things that came too easily were often not worth having.

"I'm a reasonably patient man, Rachel. I'm willing to wait."

"You'll have a very long wait." Her eyes, wide gray pools of need, belied her words.

"Perhaps." He ran a slow, teasing fingertip over her lips. "And then again, perhaps not." Unable to resist, he ducked his head, dragged her up onto her toes, and took her mouth.

The kiss was quick, hot, and potent.

And not nearly enough.

Patience, Cooper warned himself as he opened the door, letting in a gust of brisk autumn air. Some things, some women, were worth waiting for.

"We may have less crime than in the city," he said. "But make sure you lock up."

That said, he walked away into the rainy night.

Patience.

19

SCOTT CREPT OUT of bed, avoiding the floorboard he'd discovered squeaked, padded over to the window and watched the Jeep drive away. He hadn't wanted to go to bed. What he'd wanted was to hang out and have Cooper tell him more outlaw stories, but Warren had told him that guys didn't like kids hanging around when they were dating their moms.

Not that Cooper and his mom had gone on a real date. But Scott didn't want to screw things up if the sheriff did decide to ask her out. Cooper didn't seem to mind Scott hanging around, but Warren's mom had been married three times and Mrs. MacGregor was always saying how she babysat a lot at Warren's because his mother, who was between husbands, liked to go dancing and changed men as often as she changed hair color, so Scott figured Warren should know what he was talking about.

What he hadn't shared with Warren, or anyone, especially his mom, was his wish that Cooper would become his new dad. Scott really, really wished his dad hadn't died, but sometimes Cooper felt more like a dad than his own had.

His dad had worked even more than his mom did

these days. He'd leave the house for New York City in the dark and usually didn't come home until after dinner. Sometimes even after bedtime. Lots of nights he stayed at the apartment he kept in the city, which overlooked the Macy's Parade, but Scott would've given up the parade to have his dad home more.

It wasn't any different on the weekends when his dad would break his promise to come to one of his basketball or baseball games. Sometimes he did show up, but even if he didn't get called away by some advertising emergency, he was always on his phone, talking, answering emails, and texting.

When Scott had been a little kid, their family had seemed normal. Most of the parents in his private school were the same way. Their dads worked while their moms volunteered at Junior League stuff, played tennis, and in the summer, hung out at the country club pool while their kids took swimming lessons and played Marco Polo.

But when his mom moved him to public school six weeks after his dad's funeral, he'd noticed that a lot more dads came to root for their kids and even played video games at home with them. Like Cooper had done this afternoon after Scott had finished his homework. It'd be easier to imagine his dad morphing into Iron Man and battling evil enemies than playing *Iron Man* or *Rango* with him.

Back in Connecticut, whenever he wished out loud that his dad would be around more, his mother would look upset and remind him that his father had a very important job.

Scott felt queasy in his stomach, like the time he'd gone on the Tilt-a-Whirl at the Oyster Festival, for even thinking that a sheriff's job was probably more important than advertising.

Just the other day, Cooper had rescued a guy who swerved his pickup and plowed into a tree after a deer ran in front of him. Cooper and the firemen had to cut the driver out of the truck's cab with the Jaws of Life. Thanks to them, the man only ended up with a broken wrist and some burns from the airbag.

Scott had seen the video—taken by a fisherman who'd been driving by and stopped to help—on the news. But when Scott told Cooper how awesome it had been, the sheriff just shrugged and said he was doing his job.

Which was just what Sheriff Andy Taylor would've said.

Jimmy had a boxed set of *The Andy Griffith Show* he'd gotten one Christmas from his grandmother, who lived in Mount Airy, North Carolina, where Andy Griffith had grown up.

Sometimes, when they'd watched the show on the TV in Jimmy's bedroom back in Connecticut, Scott had wondered if any kid really had a dad like Opie's. A dad who'd take you fishing and ask how school had gone, and help out when you screwed up. Which in Opie's case seemed like almost every week.

Scott bet that if Mayberry had had an outlaw train, Sheriff Taylor would've left Barney Fife in charge of the office while he took Opie and Aunt Bea for a ride.

The Jeep's red taillights disappeared around a corner. Scott sighed, crept back into bed and lay in the dark and tried not to feel guilty for being barely able to remember what his dad looked like.

And for wishing that he could have a dad like Opie Taylor's.

Or at least a dog.

20

THE FOLLOWING MORNING, after a restless sleep, Rachel was back at the New Chance where things were beginning to take shape. The warm white enamel that had replaced the peeling olive-drab paint made the cleaned and polished copper hood appear to gleam even more brightly.

Pouring herself a cup of coffee from the new machine—one glance at Johnny's oil-encrusted vat had been more than enough to make her throw it away—Rachel leaned back against the counter to savor her feeling of satisfaction.

For the first time since she'd begun the Herculean task of renovating the New Chance Café, she could actually envision the restaurant opening on time.

"Looking good," a familiar deep voice broke into her reveries.

Her fingers tightened on her mug as she slowly turned around. Cooper was standing in the doorway, looking better than any man had a right to look.

"It is, isn't it? The paint Fred donated turned out perfectly. It's bright, but has a warm undertone that complements the copper, don't you think?"

Instead of looking at the wall, he took in her faded red sweatshirt, the silk-screened fat striped cat advertising the wonders of the Metropolitan Museum of Art and her worn jeans, which had splotches of white on one knee from when she'd knelt in dripped paint.

"It's great," he said. "But I was referring to the painter."

She shook her head, even as her lips curved into an answering smile. "Don't you ever give up?"

"Not when it's something I want badly enough. And I believe we've already determined that I want you, Rachel."

"Really, Cooper . . ."

"I see you finally got rid of the steer," he said, changing the subject before she could continue her complaint.

"The steer? Oh, yes, that horrid thing. Cal took it down for me this morning."

"That old steer's been a fixture on the New Chance since before I was born," Cooper said. "It'll seem kind of strange to have it gone."

"It isn't exactly gone."

"Really?" He picked up a cardboard cup from the stack on the counter and filled it with coffee from her new brewer. "What did you do with it?"

"Promise not to tell Scott?"

He held up his right hand. "Scout's honor. What's the matter, are you afraid he'll ride his bike out to the dump, retrieve it, and bring it back?"

"It's not at the dump."

"You put in out in your garden to use as a gigantic scarecrow," he guessed.

"Close. I had Cal put the cow—"

"Steer."

Rachel shot him a frustrated look. "Cow, steer, what's the difference?"

"Let's just say that a steer's a bull who's lost his motivation for getting up in the morning. Actually, if you want to get technical, thanks to a little snip job, the poor guy can't get it up at all."

As his eyes danced with humor, Rachel felt a familiar zing race through her.

"Thank you for that image," she said dryly. "Well, anyway, I scrubbed it with hot soapy water and disinfectant then had Cal put it in our backyard for a surprise."

"That's great. Scott's wild about that steer. He was really feeling bad when he thought you were going to get rid of it."

"I know. That's why I decided to keep it, although it's got to be the world's largest garden ornament and even worse than a pink plastic flamingo. I also needed to try to come up with something that could compete with those bank robber's fingerprints you gave him."

"I hadn't realized we were in competition."

"Aren't we?"

"Believe me, Rachel, we both have your son's best interests at heart."

Things were becoming too complicated too quickly.

Desire was one thing. Rachel could deal with that. Well, perhaps not exactly deal with it, considering those dreams that had kept her tossing and turning all night. But Cooper was, after all, a very sexy man. She'd probably have reason to worry if she weren't attracted to him.

However, as well intentioned as the man might be, encouraging him to grow closer to her son would be entering into something far more serious than a sexual encounter. Scott had already been wounded by the loss of his father. Rachel wasn't about to risk his happiness for some fleeting physical pleasure.

"You haven't told me what you're doing here, Sheriff."

Although he lifted a brow at her brisk tone, he didn't immediately answer. Instead, he looked down into the mug he'd poured himself with surprise. "This is good. What did you do with Johnny's battery-acid maker?"

"I threw it out. And if your sole purpose in dropping by was for a cup of coffee, now that you've had it, have a good day protecting and serving the citizens of River's Bend while I get back to work."

She turned away, picked up her brush and began slapping paint on another wall.

"I understand you're working on a tight deadline," he said. "Which is why I'm here."

She glanced suspiciously over her shoulder. Instead of his usual jeans and blue chambray shirt he was wearing an unfamiliar starched khaki uniform with his badge pinned to his chest. The fawn Stetson was on his head and his boots were polished to a gleaming sheen. He certainly didn't look like a man prepared to do manual labor.

"You're here to paint walls?"

"Sorry."

"I didn't think so."

"Hey, you're lucky I'm not volunteering. I'm the world's worst painter. Just ask Dad, who put me to work painting the barn after he caught me sneaking back into the house after a summer kegger down at the river the week before my senior year. Believe me, it wasn't pretty. I brought you a restaurant-warming gift."

"An automatic paint sprayer?" Not that she'd know

how to use it. She'd considered renting one, but had decided she'd probably end up spraying paint all over everything she'd already replaced or repaired.

"Better."

She put down her brush and crossed her arms. "Are you going to let me in on exactly what this gift is? Or is it a secret?"

His grin broadened. "A fireplace."

Rachel could only stare at him. "A what?"

"A fireplace. Didn't you tell me after dinner last night that you wanted a beehive fireplace in the dining room?"

"I hadn't realized you were listening to anything I said."

Cooper's smile didn't fade in wattage, but a gentle censure appeared in his eyes. "Just because I find you a very appealing distraction doesn't mean I wasn't listening, Rachel. I heard everything you said."

The intimate affection in his gaze tugged at something elemental deep inside her. Struggling against its appeal, she said, "Then you should recall I'd decided I couldn't afford to put one in."

"Now that you mention it, that does ring a bell."

"I also told you that I don't want to borrow any of your money."

"I remember. Although you did promise to consider taking on an investor."

"I only promised to think about it," she stressed. "And after giving it more consideration—"

He held up his hand, forestalling her planned refusal. "The fireplace isn't going to cost a cent, Rachel. Hank Young volunteered to donate supplies and I've got one of the best stonemasons in the county sitting out in my

Jeep."

"Mr. Young has already donated the roofing material and been kind enough to give me a contractor's discount on the paint, copper ceiling, and other supplies. Why would he want to give me anything else?"

"Simple. He's getting hungry and figures that anything he can do to get the New Chance reopened in a hurry will be worth the price."

"I don't understand."

"Hank's a bachelor. He's getting sick and tired of eating out of cans and boxes. Besides, it just so happens that his brother-in-law, Willard, ordered too many bricks from the supplier three months ago and it's getting expensive to keep carrying them on the books."

"Why do I have this feeling he didn't come to this generous decision all on his own?" she asked suspiciously.

"Beats me. So, how about it? Do I bring the stuff in or not?"

"Even if you're telling the truth, I'm not certain I can accept."

"Why not?"

"Because building a fireplace has to be a time-consuming, difficult job and anyone who actually knows how to do it is a skilled craftsman who deserves to be paid for his labor. And I really can't afford to do that."

"Don't worry. It's all taken care of."

"I'm almost afraid to ask."

"It's simple. Building your fireplace is a condition of Jake's parole."

"Parole?" Rachel was beginning to get a headache. She rubbed her fingertips against her throbbing temple. "Your bricklayer is a criminal?"

"Not really. It's sort of complicated to explain."

The pounding in her head increased. "Why don't you try?"

He took his time answering, instead drawing circles in the sawdust on the counter, which drew her gaze to his large, dark hands, which in turn reminded her how they felt on her body. Which caused a glimmer of heat to race up her spine.

It wasn't wise being alone with a man who could make her feel this way.

Not wise at all.

"Jake's had a run of bad luck lately." As he switched to squares, the brim of his hat shielded his face from her view. "Drought two years in a row cost him most of his cash hay crop, then we got a period of heavy rain up in the mountains where his cattle were grazing for the summer. Some flooding released anthrax spores into the soil. Unfortunately, the disease can kill in days."

"He lost his cattle?"

When he lifted his head to meet her gaze, Rachel could read the terrible sadness in his eyes. "Most of the herd. And the rest were put in isolation quarantine, since people can contact anthrax by eating contaminated meat."

"That's terrible." Didn't she know all too well about loss? "Isn't there any way to prevent it?"

"There are vaccinations and Jake had all his cattle inoculated, but for some reason the stuff didn't take. The state health department's looking into that particular batch of vaccine, but even if they find it's defective, it isn't going to get Jake his herd back."

"Can't he at least sue the manufacturer?"

"I suppose so, if it turns out to have been defective.

The problem with that scenario is that we're talking about a drug company with thousands of lawyers and Jake would be lucky to be able to afford one. And his odds of finding one who'd work on contingency are slim to none. Meanwhile, he's flat out of money and about to be run off his land."

"Oh, no." Personal economic disaster was something Rachel could definitely identify and empathize with.

"As rotten as Jake's luck has been, I think he could live with that. After all, it's part of the gamble of living off the land. His granddaddy knew that ranching was a gamble, his daddy knew it, and Jake knows it. The problem that got him into trouble with the law is that he's convinced the government's taking his land illegally."

"Do you believe that?"

He rubbed his chin thoughtfully. "I don't think anyone would do such a thing intentionally. But Jake insists he made all his payments on time and I've never known him to lie."

He flashed her a quick grin at odds with the seriousness of the topic. "Unless it's about the size of the fish that got away or the ten-point buck he almost shot the opening day of hunting season. Or that redheaded waitress down in Tulelake who has supposedly been lusting after his body for the past ten years."

"It sounds as if you know this Jake well."

His fleeting hesitation suggested he was choosing his words carefully. "His land borders the Bar M and we've always been close."

"And now you were forced to arrest him."

"Yeah." He blew out a breath. Broad shoulders lifted and fell in a weary shrug. "He's not really that bad, Rachel.

The poor guy just gets frustrated, has too much to drink, then gets rowdy. I'm driving up to the government offices in Salem today to see if I can track down someone willing to search for the payment he swears he's made, and the truth is, I'm asking you to baby-sit him while I'm gone. If he's busy building your fireplace, he won't be able to get into trouble."

"Surely taking on a maze of governmental red tape isn't part of your job."

"Jake's all caught up in that tape. Someone's got to help him."

Rachel wasn't as surprised by that simple declaration as she would have been when she'd first arrived in River's Bend.

"I wouldn't bring him here if I believed he presented any danger to you or Scott," he said. "Whatever doubts you might have about me personally, Rachel, you have to believe this."

She had not a single doubt he was telling the truth. "You're a very good friend," she said quietly.

Amusement. Desire. Affection. All were present in his once again smiling eyes. "I believe that's what I've been trying to tell you."

He crossed the space between them to stand directly in front of her. Then ran his knuckles down her cheek in a way that was as gentle as it was sensual.

"You've got paint on your face."

"That's no big surprise. I may be a fast painter, but I can't claim to be neat."

"Good thing . . . You also have a white nose." He skimmed a finger down the slope of that nose.

Tilting her head, Rachel frowned up at him. "Are you

going to spend all morning criticizing my painting skills, or are you going to introduce me to my fireplace builder?"

"In a minute." He picked up a rag from the counter and rubbed at the white spot on her cheek. "That's better." Cooper rubbed his chin as he studied her thoughtfully. "Perhaps we should leave your nose as it is. It's kind of cute. Makes you look more accessible."

Tossing the rag back onto the counter, he curved his fingers around the back of her neck. "Do you know what I did after I left your house last night?"

"What?"

"I went home and spent several long and frustrating hours fantasizing about making love with you."

As hard as she'd tried not to think about Sheriff Cooper Murphy, especially not in that way, hadn't she done the same thing?

"Really Cooper . . ."

The slight tightening of his fingers on her nape was the only sign he'd heard her. "I imagined pulling you down onto that rug in front of the fireplace and undressing you. Taking off your clothes piece by piece, your skin gleaming in the glow of the firelight."

The evocative vision was definitely too close to some of the fantasies she'd been having lately. "Please," she said softly. "You shouldn't . . ."

He was only touching her neck, but his gaze had the physical impact of a caress as it moved down her body.

"And then," his deep, hypnotizing voice continued as she fought against an urge to fling her arms around him and drag him down to the sawdust covered floor, "after I'd caressed every bit of your creamy flesh, I'd enter you slowly, giving you time to adjust to my incredible—"

"Incredible?" Despite the fact that he was driving her crazy, Rachel couldn't resist a ragged laugh. "No one could ever accuse you of having a less than robust ego, Sheriff."

"Just wait," he promised easily, bending his head to brush his lips briefly, without pressure or force, against hers. "Besides, as I was saying, that's how I imagined making love to you last night. Seeing you in the bright light of a new day, with paint on your nose, has altered things."

"Changed your mind?"

Why, oh why, did Rachel find that idea vastly disappointing? She had no intention of becoming involved with Cooper. None at all.

Hell. Whom was she trying to fool? Anyone who'd believe that she wasn't interested in River's Bend's sheriff would be a prime candidate for beachfront property on Front Street.

"Oh, not about the act," he assured her. "Just the location." His smile was quick, sexy, and oh, so dangerous. "I don't know if it's the paint, or how sexy your butt looks in those jeans, but I'm struck with this urge to tumble you in a hayloft."

He nibbled on her neck. "How about it, Rachel, my sweet," he murmured enticingly. "Have you ever made love in a warm bed of hay?"

Even as she sought to ignore the havoc his teeth were creating, Rachel's rebellious mind conjured up the pungent scent of hay warmed by a slanting buttery sunbeam. Cooper's skin, where the sun touched it, would be dark, contrasting vividly with the hay and his body, as it pressed against hers, would be hot and hard and . . .

No. It was happening all over again!

Ducking out of his light embrace, Rachel grabbed up the wet rag and began scrubbing furiously at her nose.

"We can't do this."

"Don't look now. But we have been. And from my point of view, it's been going pretty well. Though I sure wouldn't mind kissing you again. All over."

"You have to stop talking to me like that," she insisted, pressing her fingers against a temple where a new headache threatened. "Someone might hear you."

He shrugged. "Cal and Fred are outside working on the roof, Dad drove out to the ranch to get some linseed oil, and Jake's still sitting in the truck, waiting to come in. You don't have to worry, Rachel. We're all alone."

That knowledge did nothing to instill calm. Nor make her feel any safer. Needing to change the subject, Rachel glanced pointedly at her watch. The face was spattered with pinpoint drops of white paint, but she could still read the Roman numerals.

"If you're planning to get any work done in Salem, I'd suggest you'd better leave now. Government employees have a habit of closing up shop and going home earlier than the rest of us."

"Going up there sure as hell isn't my first choice." He plucked the rag from her hands and disposed of the remainder of the white paint on her face with a few deft strokes.

Then he lowered his head and laid his mouth on hers, drawing forth a sigh as his lips cruised over hers, as soft as snowflakes on a silent, moonlit night. Oh, he was good she thought, as the floor started turning beneath her.

His lips took a slow, almost languid journey up her

face, warming her temples, causing her lids to close as they skimmed over them, down her cheek and around her jaw. By the time he'd returned to her lips, she was clinging to the front of his shirt to keep from slipping off the suddenly, spinning, tilting floor.

He cradled her face. "Feel free to kiss me back," he murmured as he nipped at her bottom lip. "If you feel inclined."

As if she could stop herself if she tried. Which she didn't.

Just as she had the first time, here in this very kitchen, Rachel didn't think five steps ahead. She didn't plan or weigh all her options. Responding only to Cooper and the moment, she dove into the kiss, her mouth avid. Greedy. Tangling her tongue with his, she arched against him as he drove the heated kiss deeper. Darker.

Her mind was swamped with sensation, which was why it took her a moment to recognize the buzzing against her hip. A moment later, she heard it.

"Damn." Cooper dragged his mouth away and apparently as battered as she'd been by the kiss, rested his brow against hers. "Hold that thought," he said roughly. He dug his phone from the front pocket of his jeans, the gesture pulling the denim tight against his groin in a way that did nothing to calm Rachel's racing heart.

"This had better involve flashing lights and sirens," he answered. Then rolled his eyes. "Okay. I'll be right there." He ended the call and shoved the phone back into his pocket. "I've got to go."

"What's wrong?"

"Two rustlers were caught trying to coax a cow into an old Suburban. Turns out she wasn't going along with the program. Nor was her owner, who'd noticed her missing and was riding the fence line looking for how she might've escaped."

"Rustlers?" For a fleeting moment, Rachel wondered if he'd somehow managed to take her back in time with that mind-blinding kiss. "I had no idea they still existed."

"As long as there are cattle, there will be rustlers."

"But isn't that why there are brands?"

"In theory, but there are ways to get around brands. One popular old trick is to steal a cow, get her pregnant, though it's even better if someone else's bull has already done that for you. It's not that hard to keep her hidden during the winter, then set her free on the range after the calf is born come spring. Cows have a strong homing sense, so chances are she'll eventually end up back on her own ranch."

"But meanwhile, the rustlers have an unbranded calf."

"Got it. A calf they can add to their herd without all that much risk of being caught."

"You would've caught them."

His deep, low chuckle had her feeling the ground begin to shift beneath her feet again. "Now you sound like your son."

"I may not be ready to go to bed with you. Not that I'm saying it's ever going to happen," she tacked on when she saw the look of satisfaction flash in his smiling eyes. "But I can recognize dedication and intelligence when I see it."

"You're damn good for a man's ego, Rachel." He skimmed a roughened finger down the slope of her nose. "I'll go get Jake."

After Cooper had left the kitchen, Rachel squared her

shoulders and took three deep breaths. "The thing to do," she reminded herself. "Is keep your eye on the goal of getting this place open without becoming sidetracked by a sheriff who's too sexy for his badge."

Which, as Cooper returned with her bricklayer, looking lean, hard, and unreasonably hot, was proving easier said than done.

·

21

JAKE BUCHANAN, WHOM Rachel immediately recognized as Bad Bill Barkley from the outlaw train ride, didn't look like a criminal. He was neatly dressed in a red plaid shirt and jeans. His scuffed brown boots had wedge heels that, along with his leathery dark skin, revealed a lifetime spent in the saddle.

To her vast relief, neither did he behave like a criminal, but greeted her politely when Cooper introduced them, exchanged greetings with the other men and went straight to work. Rachel returned to her painting.

By lunchtime she had three of the four walls finished and was ready for a break. Taking a brown paper bag out of the refrigerator, she entered the dining room to find Jake still hard at work.

"Where are the others?" she asked, glancing around. Cal, Fred, and Dan were nowhere to be seen.

"They went to pick up some supplies in K. Falls. Said they'd get lunch there," he replied without turning around.

"Oh. What about you?"

"What about me?"

"Wouldn't you like some lunch?"

"I'd just as soon keep working if it's all the same to

you, ma'am."

"Surely you're hungry," Rachel coaxed.

Jake's only response, as he cut a brick in half, was a nonchalant shrug.

Well, at least she didn't have to worry about the man talking her to death. Rachel decided to try again. "I got a little carried away this morning," she said with a smile. "I'll never be able to eat all this by myself."

Although she was loath to admit it, she'd packed the extra food in hopes that Cooper happened to drop by for lunch.

Nothing.

Jake continued measuring and cutting.

"It's meatloaf," she offered.

The older man slowly put the saw down and turned around. "With ketchup?"

"Tons."

"And onions?"

"Ever hear of a meat loaf without onions?" Rachel countered.

"I like mustard in it, too," he said, testing her further.

"Got it covered."

"The yellow kind or that fancy European stuff they advertise on television?"

Strike one. "I'm afraid it's brown," she admitted.

"Figures," Jake harrumphed. "I'm partial to the yellow kind, myself."

"I see." So was Scott, but Rachel didn't think it prudent to accuse the man of having the palate of a nine-year-old.

"No offense meant to your cooking, ma'am, but the yellow kind is spicier," Jake said.

"No offense taken, Mr. Buchanan," Rachel assured him. "However, this mustard has horseradish mixed into it."

He arched a wiry brow. "Horseradish?"

"That's right."

She waited while Jake thought the matter over. "I reckon horseradish might give it the right amount of kick," he allowed finally.

Rachel repressed her smile. "I've always thought so."

He rubbed his unshaven chin as his eyes drifted to the brown paper bag she was still holding. "I suppose I could give it a try. Seein' as how Cooper didn't see fit to feed me a proper breakfast. Never have figured out how a grown man can eat all that sugarcoated cereal first thing in the morning," he complained. "Not to mention how the stuff turns the milk different colors." He fixed her with a direct look. "You ever try eating blue milk with a hangover?"

"No, that's something I've never experienced."

"You haven't missed much, that's for sure. Those Murphys have always been crazy. And Cooper's the worst of the lot, 'cepting old Malachy."

"Malachy?"

"Cooper's great-great-great-granddaddy. He founded River's Bend."

"So you spent the night with Cooper?" she asked conversationally as she took out a foil-wrapped sandwich.

"Thanks," he said as she handed it to him. "Didn't Coop tell you? I spent last night in jail."

"Oh." Rachel was momentarily nonplussed. "I didn't know. I mean I did know that you've had a few unfortunate brushes with the law, but I hadn't realized that—"

"Cooper arrested me for being drunk and disorderly

outside Mel Skinner's house around one o'clock this morning," Jake said matter-of-factly. "And disturbing the peace."

"Were you?" Rachel couldn't resist asking. "Disturbing the peace?"

"Sure. But I didn't have any choice. If the bastard would've let me in, I'd have been drunk and disorderly inside his house. That way I wouldn't have woke up the entire neighborhood." He unwrapped the sandwich, wadded the foil into a ball and tossed it into a nearby cardboard box.

"Just Mr. Skinner's sleep."

"Hell—sorry about the language, ma'am—but Mel Skinner is nothin' but a double-faced, two-tongue lying polecat. He deserves a helluva lot more than having his sleep disrupted. The fiend stole my money. Now he's tryin' to steal my land. Land that's been in the Buchanan family for five generations."

He took a forceful bite of the thick sandwich. "Well, I'm not about to let that happen," he mumbled around the spiced meatloaf.

It was more than an idle threat made by a man with a hangover. Viewing the icy determination in Jake Buchanan's brown eyes, Rachel found herself hoping that Cooper would be able to solve his problem with the government while in Salem this afternoon. Because, if not, he might just find himself having to arrest his friend for something a great deal more serious than drunk and disorderly.

"This is real tasty," Jake said, breaking the silence.

Now that she'd witnessed the simmering anger inside the man, Rachel no longer felt as comfortable around him as she had earlier. "You sound surprised."

"I kinda figured you'd be one of those fancy Eastern cooks who whips up things with fou fou names nobody can ever pronounce. Stuff made outta eel gizzards or brains, or some such thing."

"Eel gizzards?"

He nodded as he chewed. "Yeah. You know, all that highbrow stuff. Like sushi."

"Sushi." She handed him a small plastic bowl of potato salad.

"Yeah. Never have understood the appeal of that stuff," he said around a mouthful of salad. "I used to have this lady friend. Taught English at Klamath Community College. She was from California and plumb crazy about the stuff. Acted kinda like a horse on locoweed, if you know what I mean."

"I believe I get the picture," Rachel murmured. "And although I do happen to like sushi myself, I've no plans to put it on the New Chance's menu."

"Good idea," he agreed, looking over the food she'd spread out onto a two-by-four. "Wouldn't think you'd have too many customers if you did. Are you gonna eat that pie?"

"It's yours," Rachel offered, handing over the piece of apple pie she'd never had any intention of eating.

"This is damned good." Jake looked at her admiringly. "You're gonna do real good in River's Bend, Miz Hathaway."

"I fervently hope so, Mr. Buchanan."

He took another bite and rolled his eyes. "Real good," he repeated. "Folks around these parts like good, basic food. Not that raw fish stuff." His eyes danced with the first humor she'd witnessed. "Course, we've had sushi around here for a real long time," he revealed. "Probably as far back as the time River's Bend was founded."

"Really?"

"Sure . . . But we've always called it bait."

When Rachel laughed, as she was supposed to, Jake grinned.

The uncomfortable moment had passed.

22

EVERY HALLOWEEN OF Scott's life, his parents had taken him to the country club for a party. He'd rather have gone running from door to door, yelling trick or treat and having people put candy in his bag. But whenever he brought up that idea, his father would point out that the houses in their neighborhood were too far apart. Then his mother would bring up the possibility of bad people putting razors into candy bars. Which had never made any sense because he'd been pretty sure they hadn't had any bad people living in their neighborhood.

Instead, they'd go the club, where the kids would have to stand in lines to play stupid games like tossing beanbags into plastic pumpkins and throwing orange tennis balls into the mouths of more pumpkins painted onto a wooden board. The only halfway good part was when they were blindfolded and put their hands into bowls of weird food that was supposed to be creepy stuff like guts, brains, zombie eyeballs, and maggots. The boys all thought it was cool, mostly because the girls would squeal and scream about how icky everything was.

Finally, they'd put on a costume parade for parents

who had their own grownup party in the club dining room. All the moms and dads would clap and cheer. Then every kid left with a costume prize. Which pretty much took any specialness away from winning.

Here in River's Bend, because so many of the kids lived out of town on ranches, where it would be even harder to trick or treat than back in Connecticut, all the stores on Front Street had gotten together to offer treats.

Instead of candy, the bookstore lady handed out cupcakes with tiny books made of sugary stuff on top of the frosting. The two ladies at the scrapbook shop handed out sheets of stickers and though Scott had been warned that the market gave out the dreaded boxes of raisins, he left with a blue glow stick.

Some of the stores still gave out candy, but the very best stop of all was the sheriff's office where Cooper, Cal, the new deputy Travis Yates, and LuluBelle had sheriff's badges for everyone. Not real ones, like Cooper wore, but as he pinned it onto his blue cowboy shirt Scott didn't care.

"So," his mom asked after they'd returned to the house and he was sorting through his loot, "did you have a good time?"

"It was the best Halloween ever," Scott said truthfully.

"I'm glad. That girl with the pretty blond hair you were talking with at the sheriff's office seemed nice. The one wearing the tiara."

"It was a crown," Scott said. "That's Ariel."

"I recognized the cameo on the tiara. Crown," Rachel corrected. "What's her name?"

"I told you. It's Ariel."

"Oh. I thought you were talking about her character."

"Her mom named her after the movie."

"Well, it's a pretty name for a pretty girl."

"It is pretty. She's pretty." Scott bit into a coconut covered doughnut hole decorated to look like a bloody eyeball he'd picked up at the hardware store. "I love her."

"Do you?" Rachel felt her heart twinge, just a bit, at the thought of this child she'd not that long ago brought home from the hospital in a soft blue blanket and knit booties growing up.

"Yep." Coconut fell onto the front of his new shirt that was sporting the metal badge he'd gotten at the sheriff's office. Rachel suspected the badge would be showing up on his pajamas tonight. "We're going to get married."

"Not right away, I hope."

"I'm nine-years-old," he reminded her unnecessarily. "That's too young to get married. But when we're grown up we're going to live on a ranch and have lots of dogs and cats and horses. And five children."

"Well, it sounds as if you have it all planned. What does Ariel say about all this?"

"She's all for it. The cats were her idea. She says we need them to catch mice in the barn, and since she lives on a ranch, she should know. She decided to have five kids because she has two brothers and two sisters and says it's the perfect size family."

Rachel tamped down a twinge of guilt that her son didn't have any brothers or sisters. An only child herself, there had been times when she'd wished for siblings. As she realized that quite a bit of discussion had gone into this plan she was only now hearing about, she felt her metaphorical mom apron strings begin to untie.

"Well, as your mother, I'm happy to hear you plan to stay in River's Bend."

"I knew we belonged here as soon as I saw the cow," Scott said. "It was the same way I felt when I saw Ariel the first day of school. She says sometimes you just know."

Although Rachel was certainly in no hurry for her only son to leave home, that fact that he'd given his nine-year-old heart to his first girlfriend indicated that he'd turned the page to an optimistic new chapter in his young life.

And wasn't that what this move had all been about?

A new beginning for them both?

∾

"ARE ME AND you gonna have Thanksgiving dinner alone again this year?" Scott asked the next night as he set the table.

He'd dragged the fiberglass cow—steer, Rachel reminded herself—into the kitchen, unwilling to let it out of his sight. She knew it was silly, but she found herself hating the way it seemed to be staring at her through its dark brown glass eyes.

"Are you and I," she corrected.

"Are you and I gonna have Thanksgiving dinner alone again this year?"

She stopped in the middle of mixing waffle batter. For a restaurant owner, since moving to River's Bend she certainly wasn't very innovative with her home cooking. Fortunately, Scott, like all nine-year-olds, much preferred chili to calamari, tuna fish sandwiches to truffles, and waffles to wasabi.

"Don't you like the company?"

"It's not that." He began twisting the paper napkin to shreds. "It's just that it's kind of nice to do something different."

"Such as having Thanksgiving dinner with Cooper at his father's ranch?"

He lifted slender shoulders in an exaggerated shrug. "I guess we could do that. If you wanted to."

"How about you? What do you want to do?"

He turned to her, his expression as earnest as Rachel had seen it since she'd told him his father had died. "Cooper said I could ride one of his dad's horses. A real cowboy horse, Mom," he stressed. "Not like that stupid pony Bobby Erickson had for his birthday party last year."

Rachel poured the batter onto the preheated waffle iron and closed the lid. "Goodness," she said. "Imagine that. A real horse."

"Well?"

The pieces of napkin scattered over the floor looked like Hansel and Gretel's trail out of the forest. Rachel handed him another. "I don't know, honey," she said truthfully. She'd been vacillating since Cooper had first mentioned it. "It's not as simple as it sounds."

Scott took a deep breath. Then blurted out, "Is it because you don't like Cooper?"

She would have had to be deaf and blind not to hear the distress in her son's voice, or see the anxiety written in bold script across his freckled young face. "I like Cooper," she hedged.

"He sure likes you," Scott revealed, placing the napkins and the stainless steel cutlery that had replaced her wedding silver beside the plates.

"Oh?"

"Yeah. Whenever I complain about having to study my spelling words or eat my vegetables, Cooper tells me that I'm real lucky to have you as a mom. But I already knew that. Could we, Mom? Please? I'll go to bed an hour early for a month."

"You don't have to do that."

"How about I promise never to call Mrs. MacGregor a snoopy old walrus again?"

"Surely you don't ever call her that to her face," she said, truly aghast.

"Nah. Just when I'm joking around with the guys." He took the milk carton from the refrigerator and filled his glass. "Want some?"

"Thank you, I would. And from now on, I don't want you insulting Mrs. MacGregor ever again. Even to the guys."

"She does have a big old mustache, just like a walrus," Scott pointed out.

"Mrs. MacGregor's mustache is nothing like a walrus. Nor is it any of your concern, young man."

"But she does always snoop on everybody. Every night she asks about how things were back in Connecticut and did you have any boyfriends after Dad died, and how often Cooper visits us."

"She does?"

"Yeah. It gets so bad I have to go into my room and do extra credit homework to escape, instead of watching TV."

Rachel wasn't surprised. Irritated, perhaps. But not surprised. "Well, a little extra studying certainly won't kill you," she said. "But I'll have a talk with Mrs. MacGregor and ask her not to discuss our personal life."

"Okay, but I bet that won't do any good. I think she's really, really nosy, mom."

Rachel smiled at that. Reaching out, she ruffled his hair. "I suspect you're probably right, kiddo."

"So," Scott said, after they'd finished their light supper, "can we go to the ranch for Thanksgiving?"

The thought of preparing an elaborate Thanksgiving dinner while she was working so hard at the New Chance was less than appealing. But Scott had experienced so many changes in his young life Rachel didn't want to give up the traditional meal. She tried telling herself that the only reason she was tempted to take Cooper up on his invitation was to get out of all that cooking.

Liar.

"I'll think about it."

"Thanks, Mom!" Scott threw his arms around her waist. "I knew you'd say yes!"

"I said I'll think about it," Rachel pointed out.

"I know. But that's always what you say when you're going to give in."

"It is?"

"Yep."

"Every time?"

He nodded. "Every time."

"Hmmm," Rachel mused. "Perhaps, to keep from being too predictable, I should just say no this time."

"Mom!"

She grinned. "I'll think about it."

Scott's young face relaxed into a broad grin of his own. "Sweet! You rock, Mom!"

23

RACHEL WAS SURPRISED when Cooper changed tactics. At the end of his shift the second evening after Halloween, he showed up at the New Chance, declaring his intention to work. Behaving as if the sensual moments and heated kisses they'd shared had never occurred, he began treating her as a merely a friend. Rather than a potential lover.

Even as Rachel told herself that she should be relieved and grateful that he'd seemingly abandoned his seduction campaign, she found herself missing the way he had, for a brief time, made her feel, not like the exhausted, widowed single mother restaurant owner she was, but like a desirable woman. There were times, during those nights when they were all alone, staining woodwork or sanding chairs for refinishing, she found herself wanting to drag him into the new cooler and jump him.

Over the next week, he proved to be a willing, albeit less than skilled manual laborer, throwing himself into his work with an enthusiasm that reminded her of Scott tackling a new project. He hadn't lied about his painting skills. They were, if anything, even weaker than her own.

She set him to countersinking the nails on the shelves,

but when he hit his thumb twice and scarred the dark wood with the head of the hammer, Rachel sought to find something else to keep him occupied.

When she suggested he help his father install the stained-glass in the front door, Dan immediately threatened to quit if his son got anywhere near his pet project.

Unfortunately, as bad as Cooper's painting and carpentry skills were, he proved to be a terrible bricklayer. Ten minutes after he'd begun working as Jake's apprentice, the older man had threatened to quit if Rachel couldn't find something else for, in Jake's vernacular, "that ten-thumbed jackass" to do.

"The new sink's been leaking in the men's room," she said thoughtfully as Cooper stood cheerfully by, waiting for new orders. "How are you with plumbing?"

"I'll never know until I try."

His offhand answer didn't exactly instill a great deal of confidence, but Rachel reminded herself that it was, after all, only a small leak. More like an occasional drip. Probably all that was needed was a washer. And it would keep him in another part of the restaurant, safe from the usually good-natured Cal, who'd threaten to go after Cooper with his nail gun if he put another ding in the shelving.

"Just change the washer," she instructed. "Don't try anything fancy."

"What's the matter, Rachel, don't you trust me to do the job right?" There was a glint of laughter in his eyes.

"Of course I do," she said, not quite truthfully. While she'd already discovered that Cooper Murphy had many talents, especially when it came to his people skills, he'd proven to be a remarkably inept handyman.

Cooper grinned at her blatant lie. "I'll call if I get in over my head."

Rachel found herself smiling as she watched him saunter away. Then, dragging her gaze from his Wrangler butt, she set to work on the miles of pantry shelves that still needed a final sanding.

She'd lost track of how long she'd been working. The men had left. Outside, a harvest moon was rising, bathing Modoc Mountain in a blood-red glow that was almost otherworldly. Immersed in her work, Rachel had actually forgotten about Cooper.

Until she heard him call her name from the restroom.

"Uh, Rachel?"

"Cooper?" She set down her sanding block. "Are you still here?"

"Yeah. I think I've just about got it."

"Great." She glanced at her watch. Sixty minutes. Not bad for a simple washer change. Not when it was Cooper doing the plumbing.

"If you could just hold the pipes steady while I turn the wrench, that should do it."

"Pipes?" A tingle of trepidation skimmed up Rachel's spine as she headed down the short hallway. "Cooper, all I asked you to do was . . ."

She broke off as she stood in the doorway, staring down at the long booted legs. Cooper was lying on his back, his head and shoulders inside the new vanity Cal had installed yesterday.

"What on earth?"

"I replaced the washer, like you suggested," he explained. "But then it started dripping even worse. So, I decided that the problem is in this joint right here, but the damn thing's stuck."

He hit the handle of the pipe wrench with the palm of his hand.

Once.

Twice.

Then a third time.

"Damn!"

Without warning, a flood of water burst out of the pipe like a miniature Niagara Falls, drenching him. Sitting up too quickly, he slammed his head against the bottom of the cast-iron sink. The water kept coming. While he shouted a string of curses, Rachel raced outside and turned off the water at the source.

He was struggling to his feet when she returned to the restroom. "Who the hell turned the water back on?" he asked, accepting the towel she handed him without a word of thanks.

His hair was plastered down, water trailed down his scowling face, and his clothes clung wetly to his body.

"I'm afraid that was me," she admitted.

"You?" Cooper stared at her unbelievingly. "You knew I was working in here, Rachel."

"Yes. Well, you see, I thought everyone had gone, and I wanted to make a pot of decaf, so I had to turn the water back on, and—"

"Wait." Cooper up his hand. "You forgot I was here?"

"Not exactly. I mean, if I'd thought about it, I would've realized that I hadn't said goodnight to you when the others left. But I got busy, and well, you just sort of slipped my mind."

Cooper stared at her. "I slipped your mind?"

From the stunned expression on his handsome face,

Rachel had the feeling that were she to glance down at the floor, she'd see Cooper's male ego lying in water-soaked tatters.

"That's not what I meant to say," she hastened to assure him. Walking handyman disaster or not, he'd given up his evenings to help her. Surely that deserved some special handling. "What I intended to say was, that after the others left, I got lost in work, and—"

"Forgot all about me," he put in glumly.

Rachel was feeling more and more like the Wicked Witch of the West. "Not exactly," she mumbled, twisting her fingers together in front of her.

Cooper's wet chest rose and fell as he exhaled a long, suffering sigh. "No. That's exactly what you meant, Rachel. You forgot all about me."

"Oh, Cooper." She took the towel from his hands and looped it around his neck. "You couldn't be any more wrong."

Looking slightly appeased, Cooper put his hands on her hips. "You did forget me."

"If that's the case, and I'm not saying it is," she said, "it's partly your fault."

"My fault?" He arched a brow and drew her closer. Rachel could feel a low ache spreading through her body.

"You've seemed distant."

"Distant."

"Like perhaps you changed your mind about wanting me."

"I can't freaking believe this." He lifted his gaze to the new ceiling awaiting a fresh coat of paint. "Are you telling me that after I've spent all these damn evenings trying to prove to you that I'm interested in more than getting you into bed, you're pissed off because I haven't been trying to drag you down onto the sawdust covered floor every chance I get?"

"I'm not pissed off."

"Hurt."

"No. Not hurt, either." Not really. At least that's what she'd been trying to tell herself.

"How about disappointed?"

"Perhaps." She pressed a hand to his chest. "Just a bit."

It was all the encouragement Cooper needed. He pulled her tight against him, letting her feel the heat of his erection through his wet jeans. When he began rubbing his hips in a slow, primitive rhythm, Rachel wouldn't have been surprised to find them surrounded by clouds of steam.

"I have wanted you," he insisted against her mouth.

Rachel thrust her fingers through his hair, pressing even closer against his rock hard body. "Really?"

"Really. You've had me feeling like I was back in high school, forced to hold my books in front of a perpetual boner. Do you have any idea how many times I've fantasized ravishing you on top of that pile of Sheetrock?"

The thought of Cooper ravishing her anywhere was vastly appealing. "Sheetrock is awfully hard."

His tongue flicked into her ear, then retreated. "I have a difficult time believing we'd even notice."

He was probably right. "Still," Rachel said, even as her knees weakened, "if we're going to make love, Cooper, I think a bed would be preferable."

His hands had been cupping her butt; his lips had been playing at the all-too sensitive skin behind her ear. At her words, Cooper suddenly went very still.

"Are you saying what I think you're saying?"

Rachel felt as if she were teetering on a very high cliff over a rushing river. Taking a deep breath that should have calmed, but didn't, she dove into the storm tossed waters below.

"Mrs. MacGregor isn't expecting me home for another hour."

"Well then," he said, punctuating his words with kisses, "why are we wasting time standing around here?"

24

THE NIGHT WAS clear and chilly, tinged with a promise of the winter soon to come. By the time Rachel walked up to the front door of Cooper's log home, situated on the river, the crisp air had cleared her head, forcing her to view her behavior free of the sensual cloud that had been fogging her mind.

Oh, she wanted him. There'd been too many late nights over the past weeks that she'd tossed and turned in her lonely bed, fantasizing making love to him.

She was a normal, healthy woman, approaching her sexual peak. And Cooper was an impossibly sexy man. These feelings she'd been having toward him were entirely natural. In fact, she'd probably have something to worry about if she didn't want him.

But want was an uncomplicated emotion, easily felt and just as easily satiated. What worried Rachel was that her feelings were more complicated than mere lust. Try as she might, she couldn't quite shake the misgiving that when she did go to bed with him, she'd risk too much.

What she had no way of knowing was that it was coming as a shock to Cooper how, in such a brief time, Rachel had managed to infiltrate every corner of his mind. She was never out of his thoughts: he envisioned making love to her in front of a crackling fire, under a canopy of stars, in the hand-milled bed where three generations of Murphy brides had spent their wedding nights.

He wanted her with a need that bordered on obsession. But having been in love before, he realized that something else besides lust might be happening between Rachel and him. Something they'd both have to explore further.

Later.

When they entered the living room, Hummer lifted his head, eyed Rachel with interest, and thumped his tail once on the wooden floor.

"This must be Hummer," she guessed.

"It is. He'd get up and greet you properly, but he's never been one to move when he doesn't have to. I think your son wore him out playing fetch the police baton this afternoon."

"Poor Hummer." Rachel bent down to pat the enormous head. The dog rolled over and groaned in canine ecstasy as she obligingly rubbed his stomach. "I hope Scott isn't proving too much of a nuisance," she said, looking up at Cooper.

"Not at all. In fact, I should probably pay you for having him exercise Hummer every day."

"That's not necessary. If you want to get technical, I should be paying you for baby-sitting services."

They'd been over this before. Each time Rachel had brought it up, Cooper had steadfastly refused. "Why don't we just call it even," he suggested easily. "For now."

Rachel nodded as she straightened. "For now."

A slightly uncomfortable silence settled between them. That she was nervous was all too obvious. She was twisting her hands together as her eyes darted around the room like nervous birds, never lighting anywhere.

"Would you like to sit down?" he asked, scooping some newspapers off the leather sofa and tossing them onto a nearby chair.

"Thank you." She perched on the edge of the cushion as if on the verge of running away at any moment. Not an encouraging sign.

"How about a drink while I go change?" Seducing a woman while you were soaking wet might work in some cases, especially if she was, too, but it wasn't how Cooper wanted to start out.

Her smile was forced. "I don't think so. But thank you."

"Okay, then. I'll be right back."

Well, this was going well. As he changed in the bedroom where he'd hoped to end up, Cooper was coming to the conclusion that he should have just gone ahead and made love to Rachel on that Sheetrock. Because the mood was rapidly slipping away.

"So, since I can't get you a drink, how about we just talk for a while," he said as he returned to the living room where she looked, if possible, even more tense than when he'd left.

She looked up at him with surprise. "Talk?"

"Yeah. You know, as in having a conversation. That's where you say something, then I respond, then the ball's back in your court. I'm told some people manage to go on like that for several minutes. Sometimes even hours."

She appeared not to have even considered that idea. What, had she expected him to rip off her clothes the minute they walked in, then take her standing up against the wall? Not that the idea wasn't one of the scenarios he'd imagined. It just wasn't the way he wanted their first time to play out.

"What would we talk about?" she asked.

"Anything you'd like," he said as he sat down beside her. "The New Chance—"

"Just for one hour, I'd like to forget that place even exists," she muttered.

"Done. We could talk about the weather."

She latched onto that one. "Hal Potter says that according to his Farmer's Almanac, we're in for a long, cold winter."

The thought of making love to Rachel in front of his fireplace while snow fell outside flashed yet again through his mind. "Hal's an electrician. Not a farmer. I'm not sure he qualifies as an expert on the weather."

"Ah, but how does that explain the caterpillar?"

"What caterpillar?"

"The one Fred gave Scott."

"Fred Wiley gave Scott a caterpillar?"

"A fat, furry, orange and black one. According to Fred, something about the stripes—I forget exactly what—forecast a long winter."

"Well, that settles it," Cooper said. "You just can't argue with a caterpillar. Sure you don't want something to drink?"

For a moment, Rachel appeared to have begun to relax and enjoy herself. At the mention of the drink, she seemed to remember her reason for being here.

"I'd better not. After the day I've put in, I'd probably be out like a light."

This time her attempt at a smile faltered badly. When she dragged her left hand nervously through her hair, Cooper noted the unmistakable glint of gold and wondered exactly how emotionally ready Rachel was to move on. Eighteen months was a long time. Yet, he knew firsthand that there was no universal time period for mourning.

"I really am attracted to you," she said.

He caught her hand in his. "That's encouraging. It might become a little awkward if this were totally one sided." He brushed his fingers over her knuckles. When he began toying with her slim gold wedding band, he could feel her tremor.

Dragging her eyes from his gaze, she stared down at the wooden floor. Hummer, who apparently thought she was looking at him, thumped his tail encouragingly. She didn't appear to notice.

"I thought I was ready." A small, regretful sigh escaped before she could prevent it. A sigh that told him more than words ever could. "But I don't think I'm in a place yet where I can enter into a new relationship."

"I'm getting that."

It took a herculean effort, but Cooper kept his tone from revealing exactly how much he wanted to fling Rachel over his shoulder, caveman style, and carry her into his bedroom, where he'd toss her onto his Grandmother Murphy's wedding-ring quilt, strip off her clothes and spend the rest of the night making mad, passionate love to her, with her, until they were both too exhausted to move.

Cooper hadn't been living the life of a saint. There'd been a time when his body, dormant for months after Ellen's death, eventually had begun to stir to life. Rather than expose himself to River's Bend's spotlight, he'd driven across the mountains to various Rogue River Valley towns where he'd indulged in short-lived relationships with women who weren't looking to get emotionally involved any more than he'd been.

Okay. They hadn't even been relationships. Or even affairs. What they'd been were hookups, pure and simple. A solution that had worked for both parties in the beginning. But after a few months, sex without an emotional connection became depressing, so he'd locked his once lusty libido away.

Until Rachel Hathaway had arrived in town and blown the lockbox to smithereens.

"I know how much you loved your husband," he said.

Apparently not having expected him to bring up the late Alan Hathaway during a conversation that had begun as a prelude to sex, Rachel visibly tensed.

Not wanting to let her get away until he'd gotten this off his chest, Cooper cupped her shoulders comfortingly with his palms. "I'd never ask you to deny what you and Alan had together, Rachel. Because it's obvious that your marriage was special."

"Really, Cooper," she protested. "I don't think this is the time or the place—"

"That's where you're wrong. If we don't talk about him now, he'll always be there between us."

"Alan isn't standing between us," she insisted.

Cooper had been a cop long enough to know when someone was being less than truthful. "Isn't he?"

Before she could deny his softly spoken accusation, his next words came as a complete surprise to Rachel.

"You've never asked about my marriage."

"I didn't think it was any of my business." But oh, how she'd wondered.

"I think it is," he quietly corrected her. "Ellen and I grew up together. She lived on the neighboring ranch."

"The neighboring ranch? But that would make her—"

"Jake Buchanan's daughter," he confirmed.

No wonder Jake and Cooper were so close. "How did she . . ." Rachel couldn't make herself say the word. "What happened?"

"We'd been back here six months and talking about

starting a family when she flew to Denver to visit a friend from college who'd just had a baby. On the way home a freak spring snowstorm blew in. The plane went off course and flew into Modoc Mountain." He scrubbed his hand over his face, as if to expunge the bitter memory. "I headed up the search party that found the wreckage. There weren't any survivors."

"I'm so sorry." She couldn't begin to imagine how painful that must have been.

"So was I. After having been friends all our lives, once I was old enough to decide that girls were a lot more fun than fishing, she and I became the quintessential high school sweethearts and I always figured we'd be spending the rest of our lives together. In fact, her being homesick while we'd been living in Portland was the main reason I decided to stay here in River's Bend after Dad's heart attack."

He sucked in a deep breath. "I didn't tell you this so you'd feel sorry for me, Rachel. I told you about Ellen so you'd understand that I know, firsthand, what you're going through. I loved my wife. And although we weren't married nearly as long as you and Alan, I'll always value those years we had together.

"I also want you know that your love for your husband only makes you more special to me."

"How?"

He took both her hands in his. "Because all those years with Alan have contributed to the woman you are today." Despite the topic, he smiled down at her. "And believe me, sweetheart, you are one extraordinary woman."

Over the past weeks Rachel had come to realize that Cooper was more than a sexy, desirable male. He was a genuinely kind and generous man. She could only hope that he was also a patient and forgiving one.

She pulled her hands free. "You're going to hate me."

"Never."

"I'm so sorry." There were words for women who'd lead a man on, only to pull away when he was primed for sex. None of them pretty.

Taking hold of his arms, feeling their strength, she knew she'd be safe in them. Protected. It was that, more than anything else about the man that worried her.

Cooper Murphy was a man accustomed to being in charge. She'd already determined that River's Bend, as charming and friendly a town as it was, tended to be more traditional than Connecticut or New York. Would he truly be happy with the independent woman she'd become?

She'd never be able to return to the passive, protected woman she'd been during her marriage. She'd come too far to allow herself to retreat to the security of a man's protection just because things had gotten a little rough.

Okay. A lot rough. But every day, as work on the New Chance progressed Rachel could begin to see the light at the end of the tunnel, shining like a beacon, leading her steadily forward.

"I want to be with you." That was the absolute truth. She thought about him too much during the day. Dreamed about him every night. "And I'm honestly not playing coy. It's just that I need more time."

Until the New Chance opened. Then, as soon as she was standing fully on her own two feet, she'd be able to handle an affair with Cooper without getting into this relationship over her head.

"Then you'll have it."

Without taking his eyes from hers, Cooper lifted her hand to his lips and pressed a kiss against her palm, which she'd never realized was an erogenous zone until he caressed her skin with the tip of his tongue, causing a jolt of hot need to arc between her thighs.

Apparently satisfied with the vivid response she knew he'd seen in her startled gaze, he lowered her hand.

"How would you like some hot spiced cider?" he asked with a surprising amount of calm. Surely she wasn't the only one who'd felt that spark?

Rachel's body was screaming at her to give into temptation and make love to Cooper now, if only to cool the flames raging inside her.

As a battle raged between her mind and her body, she struggled to listen to reason.

"I really should leave. Mrs. MacGregor will be anxious to get home."

"You said she wasn't expecting you for another hour," he reminded her. "Come on, Rachel, what could it hurt? We'll share some Antelope Valley Orchards cider, talk a little, then I'll take you home."

The idea was more than a little appealing. Especially since they'd had so few chances to be alone together. "I'd like that."

"Terrific. I'll be right back." He bent, brushed a quick, unthreatening kiss against her lips, then left the room.

"I'll probably regret this," she said to Hummer. "But your master is proving difficult to resist."

Appearing happy to be included in the conversation, Hummer rose from the rug and ambled over to her, tail wagging. As she patted the dog's enormous head, Rachel decided that describing Cooper as difficult to resist was an understatement.

He was impossible to resist. And the more time Rachel spent in his company, the more she wondered why any woman would even want to try.

25

THE CIDER WAS hot, fragrantly spiced and, coming after a long day's work, definitely appreciated. As she sipped it slowly in front of the crackling fire, Rachel gradually relaxed.

"Who carved the menagerie?" she asked, picking up an intricately detailed wooden antelope from the coffee table.

"That would be me."

"You?"

"Surprised?"

She ran a finger over the smooth wood. The antelope was remarkably lifelike, as were all the other animals scattered around the room. "Let's just say that you've kept your woodworking skills well hidden."

"You've forgotten about my potato peeling."

"That's right," she recalled. "You said something about pretending you were whittling." But at the time she'd imagined a stick and pocketknife.

"I may be a klutz with a hammer or wrench, but my grandfather's a world-class carver who won a lot of awards in his day. I grew up spending summer evenings sitting on the front porch, watching him bring a piece of wood to life. I suppose it only figures I'd pick up some of his tricks."

"They're wonderful." She replaced the antelope on the table.

"Thanks."

"And I really like your home."

Two of the room's walls were made of logs, the others distressed wooden planks she guessed to be barn siding. Perhaps from the family ranch? The fireplace had a river rock surround with a rustic wood mantle holding books and some of the carved animal figures. A framed print of a Native American in full headdress hung above the mantle and a tall case Grandfather clock she recognized as dating back to the early 1900s stood in the corner.

The furniture was leather and a lustrous antiqued pine that had been hand-rubbed and distressed for a rich and mellow look. Or, she considered, thinking of his family history here in River's Bend, maybe the distressing had been done the old fashioned way, by generations of Murphys living with it.

It was a room designed for comfort and relaxation.

"I like it, too," he said. "I built it a couple years ago, but Mitzi's responsible for the rug and the pillow. Apparently the decorating police show up at your house if at least one chair in any given room doesn't have a pillow on it."

While Rachel was a fan of decorative pillows, Alan had been less enthusiastic. "She's right."

"It figures you women would stick together," he said. "At least Hummer enjoys it when he sleeps on that chair. The paneling's from Dad's old barn," he confirmed what she'd been thinking.

"I thought that might be the case." She sipped on the

cider. "That's a lovely way of keeping in touch with your past."

Most of her parents' belongings had been sold at an estate sale after their deaths. As Alan had pointed out, the New York apartment they'd been living in at the time, the one he'd kept for those nights he'd stay in the city, couldn't handle a houseful of sturdy farmhouse furniture. She had kept her grandmother's Depression-era calico star quilt.

"My great-great grandfather built that barn, with the help of his neighbors, the weekend before he got married," Cooper revealed. "They spent the first six months camping out and sleeping in the hayloft because they didn't have enough money to build both a house and a barn."

Rachel shot him a suspicious glance. "Is that true?"

"My hand to God." He raised his right hand. "Fortunately, they managed to get a one-room cabin built before winter set in." He flashed her one of those quick grins she was finding more and more difficult to resist. "While we Murphy men are renown for our lovemaking prowess, I'm not sure even he could've kept his bride warm once the temperatures dropped down into single digits."

"Is the cabin still standing?"

"Sure is. Except now it's the master bedroom in my dad's house. Each generation added more rooms as they needed them. Once Ryan, Sawyer, and I got older, the main house got too crowded, not to mention rowdy with three boys under roof, so we built that log house Gram and Gramps are living in next door."

"You were lucky, growing up surrounded by so much tradition." It sounded as if she and Cooper had much the same childhoods, although he'd come back home. While, with no family left in Iowa, there'd been no reason for Rachel to return.

He shrugged. "I never gave it much thought. A lot of folks around here are descended from one of the original settlers, so yeah, there's a fair amount of shared history. Although we do get more and more people like Mitzi, who visit, fall in love with the place, and decide to stay."

"I suspect her reason for choosing to live here has more to do with her falling in love with your father."

"That's undoubtedly true. But small town life isn't for everyone. Mitzi's a savvy woman. If she weren't sure she'd settle in, she wouldn't risking making them both unhappy by trying to live here."

"I'm sure you're right." The real estate agent definitely seemed to be a woman who knew her own mind. And heart. "Cal mentioned that your great-great-great grandfather founded the town."

"He did. Malachy Murphy was the third son of a Boston lawyer and politician, who eschewed the political life that was the family tradition and became a librarian."

"A librarian?"

"Yep. He was well-educated, highly respected, and supposedly the least adventurous of the Murphy brothers. Which was why everyone was so surprised when he suddenly packed everything he and my great-great-great-grandmother Mary owned into a wagon and headed off to California, where he promptly came down with a serious case of gold fever."

"I think I'm beginning to suspect where the idea of all the Murphy men being crazy started."

He grinned good-naturedly. "Heard that one, have

you?"

"Jake mentioned it." Rachel opted against telling him that not only had Cal and Fred offered a similar appraisal, Mitzi had mentioned it, as well. "Tell me more about Malachy."

"Well, according to the stories, the first two claims he bought from speculators turned out to be salted. That was an old trick pulled by the precursors of modern land developers and junk bond traders. They'd sprinkle a little gold dust on the bottom of the creek so they could sell the claim for an exaggerated value to unsuspecting green-horns. As intelligent as he was, poor Malachy was a trusting soul. It took him a while to catch on."

"And when he did?"

"After getting a stake from a guy he met in a poker game, in what's now a ghost town on the Sacramento River, he went out on his own. Six months later, he struck it rich."

Rachel smiled. After such a run of bad luck as she'd personally experienced, she was pleased to hear of Malachy Murphy's good fortune. "I'm glad."

Cooper had slid his arm around her shoulder and his fingers were playing idly with the ends of her hair. "The only problem was, the word of his strike made it back to town before he did. When he arrived at the recording office, he discovered the guy who'd staked him had already filed a claim."

"I don't believe it. He was cheated again?"

"According to family lore, that's pretty much the same thing Mary, who was not happy, said. She convinced him that he was too naïve and too trusting to make it in the California gold fields. All the rascals and scoundrels could see him coming a mile away."

"Sounds as if Mary Murphy was a clever woman."

"Supposedly a firecracker," Cooper said. "So, she and Malachy packed what was left of their belongings back onto that wagon and headed north to where he'd heard of a big strike up in Washington State."

"A stubborn man was Malachy," she murmured, thinking that tenacity must run in the Murphy men's genes.

"True." He polished off the cider and put his mug on the coffee table in front of them. "But he never made it to Washington, because one memorable afternoon, when he and Mary were camping out along this river, right where Dad's ranch is today, he spotted some small gold nuggets gleaming in the water. He staked a claim, which immediately brought in others, swelling the population of River's Bend to over fifteen thousand."

"That's nearly five times more than today."

"Sure was. When no more gold was ever found around these parts, for a time the settlement became known as Murphy's Folly as miners moved on to greener—or golder, as the case may be—pastures, leaving behind others who'd come to enjoy the new, freer way of life they'd found here."

"That's why I came," she admitted.

Cooper's only response was an arched brow.

"It had been a horrible day," she explained. "I'd spent the morning with the IRS trying to arrange payment for the back taxes Alan owed on his business, and that afternoon I'd met with the broker who was going to list the house, and the auctioneer I'd hired to sell off all my furniture. I returned home, overwhelmed by desperation, when I opened that magazine and saw Mitzi's ad."

"Advertising the New Chance."

She smiled at the memory. "I don't even remember what the ad said. All I saw was the name. It was like fate."

Grinning, Cooper tugged on her hair. "What if you'd known fate came with a life-size steer on the roof?"

"I still would've come."

"And now?"

"Now?" He was suddenly so close their thighs were pressing together. Had he moved? Or had she?

"Are you glad you've come?"

Their eyes met and held for what seemed like an eternity. Rachel knew that they were no longer talking about the New Chance, but something far more important.

"Very," she whispered finally.

He brushed his smiling lips against hers. "I'm glad, too."

His breath was warm, spiced, reminding her of autumn in New England. Rachel heard her empty mug fall to the floor as she framed his face with her hands, continuing the kiss, deepening it, stroking his tongue with hers until she felt the greedy, answering heat of his mouth all the way down to her toes, which were curling in her sneakers.

And still she needed more. When she dug her fingers deep into his biceps, leaning backwards on the couch, urging him down so she could feel the rock wall of his chest against hers, a rough groan rumbled deep in his throat.

He slipped his hand between them, beneath her sweater, his clever, calloused fingers gliding over her skin, leaving sparks wherever they touched.

She could feel his erection straining against her and if

her hands weren't already busy grabbing his very fine Wrangler butt to pull him even closer, she would have been yanking down his zipper.

She was hearing bells.

No, not bells, Rachel realized. It was the Grandfather clock in the corner announcing the hour on a peal of Westminster chimes.

It was Cooper who finally broke away. "I'd better be getting you home," he said, his rough voice revealing that it wasn't his first choice.

Rachel's head was spinning; her body throbbed; her lips tingled. "Yes," she agreed, understanding how Cinderella must have felt when her magic had run out at the stroke of midnight.

Rising unsteadily to her feet and pulling down her sweater, which was bunched up over her white cotton bra, she considered that if Cooper Murphy could create such weakness from a mere kiss, she was afraid to think what would happen were she to give into impulse and make love to him.

Unfolding his long length from the leather sofa, Cooper stood in front of her, not attempting to conceal the bold outline of his erection pressing against the placket of his jeans.

"Poor Rachel," Cooper murmured, reading the undisguised desire in her eyes. "This isn't turning out to be as easy as it should be, is it?"

"It is difficult," she admitted. "It seems as if we're hardly ever alone, and then, even when we are—"

"You're racing the clock. Literally, tonight," he said with a frustrated look toward the clock. "Along with the calendar."

She nodded and looked inclined to say something when his phone buzzed.

Damn. Cooper had discovered that unlike when he'd been a city cop, one problem with being sheriff of a town the size of River's Bend was that it tended to be an around-the-clock job. People who'd never bother their banker or doctor outside of office hours felt perfectly free to track him down with their personal grievances.

Having appointed Cal chief deputy six months ago had made little difference. People in River's Bend were used to having Cooper Murphy solve their problems. The same way his father and grandfather had done.

The news wasn't good. But not as bad as it might have been.

"Jake got drunk and showed up at Mel Skinner's house again," he told Rachel after ending the call. "Cal's got him in a cell to sleep it off."

"Oh, dear." Her eyes filled with a very real concern. "He's been doing so well."

"The government set the date for the auction. I suppose that's what set him off."

"No doubt. I know all too well how upsetting it can be to lose everything. When is it?"

"December twenty-third."

"That's terrible timing. You'd think they could have waited until after Christmas."

"You'd think so, wouldn't you? I keep hoping some proof of the payment he swears he made will turn up. If only we had more time."

They exchanged a bleak look. "Perhaps I could talk with him," Rachel suggested. "Sometimes it helps to know that someone understand what you're going through. And

I definitely know how it feels to lose my home."

Cooper shrugged. "It sure couldn't hurt. Jake likes you. A lot."

"I like him, too."

"He keeps telling me that I'm not good enough for you."

Despite the seriousness of the topic, Rachel smiled up at him. "Why don't we let me be the judge of that?"

"Good idea. I don't suppose you'd be open to a little personal lobbying for my case?"

"Feel free to give it your best shot, Sheriff."

"I've never been one to turn down a challenge."

Cooper forced himself to linger over the kiss, even as he felt the now familiar flare of heat rising. They couldn't keep it banked for long, he knew as he tasted her lips from one silky corner to the other, feeling her tremble in his arms. Not from nerves, but the same emotions that were burning through him.

As he finally backed away, he considered that when they finally did make love, the challenge would be to keep the flames from consuming them both.

26

D R. RYAN MURPHY had set up shop in a historical building two blocks north of Front Street on Eureka Way. Quarried from Rogue River Valley sandstone, it had originally been built as an inn and restaurant by Wong Kee, a Chinese miner who had deposited over a million dollars in gold dust in various Oregon banks.

When restrictive anti-Chinese legislation forced Wong to return to China with his fortune, it had become a bordello that transformed into a speakeasy during Prohibition. After liquor became legal again, the building spent three decades as a boarding house before finally falling into disrepair.

While Cooper and his brothers had been growing up, like probably every other kid in River's Bend, they'd sneak into the boarded up Victorian, scaring themselves spitless with ghostly tales of twin prostitutes who'd supposedly been murdered in one of the second floor bedrooms.

Then damned if Ryan hadn't returned to town, cash in hand, and surprised everyone, Cooper included, by restoring the building with the colorful, not always legitimate past. His medical offices were on the first floor with living quarters on the second. The jury was still out about whether the ghosts had stuck around during all the construction.

After dropping Scott off at the New Chance, as he did every weekday, Cooper drove to his brother's office/home. As soon as he turned off Front Street, Hummer, who'd been sprawled lazily in the back seat, leaped up and began to bark.

"Yeah, yeah," Cooper muttered. "We're going to visit Layla."

Layla Longstreet—Ryan's partner, Nurse Practitioner, office manager, ill child soother, and keeper of dog biscuits—stood up from behind the antique counter as Hummer came dashing into the office, his nails clattering on the wood plank floor.

"Well, look who's here," she said, bending down to pat him. "The handsomest male in all of River's Bend." She scratched the dog behind his ear.

"Damn mutt broke my eardrum about a block away," Cooper said. "He may be the laziest animal God ever put on this green earth, but there's no denying that he has excellent taste in women."

"Flatterer," she laughed as she reached into a ceramic jar and pulled out a MilkBone the size of a small tree limb. She tossed it up, clapping in approval as Hummer snatched it out of the air.

"It's not flattery if it's true."

And it was. Tall, with a wild mass of auburn hair laced with lighter gold, and a face that could have earned her a fortune had she decided to try her luck in Hollywood, she'd been Ellen's best friend since first grade.

In a rare act of rebellion for a "good" girl who always

made honor roll, her senior year she'd started going out with motorcycle riding, black-leather-jacket-wearing Keifer Foster, who, on the rare occasion he worked, was a planer at the sawmill outside of town.

Instead of going off to Oregon State to major in pre-med as planned, Layla was two months pregnant when she married her bad boy the day after high school graduation.

Cooper had been on his second tour in Iraq when his dad arrested Foster for domestic violence. Which had him suspecting that Layla's husband could have been responsible for that miscarriage she'd suffered a few weeks after their quickie wedding.

Whatever, apparently finally realizing that some people couldn't be redeemed, Layla divorced the loser, took back her maiden name and returned to school. After receiving a B.S. and MNP, she set up a nurse practitioner office in a small retail space next to the bookstore and had been doing a brisk business when Ryan had returned home and offered her a partnership.

They made a good team and somehow Layla managed to do the work of three people without breaking a sweat or losing that dazzling Julia Roberts smile.

"So," she said, "I hear you've been busy."

"No more than usual," he said. "Though Cal did catch Tyler Parker papering the maple in the Young's front yard last night."

"I thought Tyler had a thing for Heather Young."

"He does. According to the report Cal wrote up, Madison Parker told her brother that Heather would never go for him because she was team Edward. Which, I have to admit, makes no sense to me."

"Hello." She waved a hand in front of his face. "What

planet have you been living on? It's a mega book and movie series centered around an innocent, virginal girl who has to choose between a beautiful, sparkly bad boy vampire or a kind and caring werewolf."

"Edward's the vampire," Cooper guessed.

"Got it in one. Jacob's the werewolf. My guess would be that after Madison told Tyler that he was playing for the wrong team, the kid decided he needed to do something dramatically bad to get her attention."

"Like get arrested for papering her house?" Despite having been one himself, Cooper had long ago tried to figure out the workings of any teenage boy's mind. He also hoped Heather had switched to team Jacob.

"Well, you can't deny he got her attention," Layla said with a laugh and a shake of her head. "And girls do tend to be attracted to bad boys." She sighed, suggesting she was thinking back on her own bad boy. "I wouldn't want to relive my high school days for anything."

"Me neither. But there were some good times," he said, remembering parking with Ellen on a bluff overlooking the river one warm summer's night. The wide sky had been filled with stars and a full moon had cast a silver streak on dark water as Clay Walker sang about a woman who could hypnotize the moon on his pickup's radio. That was the night he'd first made love to the girl who'd become his wife.

"You and Ellen had a lot of good times," Layla agreed. "That was so unfair, what happened to her."

"Won't get any argument from me."

A reflective silence stretched between them.

"I'm really glad you're back," Cooper said.

"I'm glad I'm back, too. I'm also glad to hear your love

life is finally picking up."

"Small towns," he murmured, thinking about all the interwoven circles and connections.

"Nothing stays secret for long," she agreed.

Their stroll down memory lane ended as Mrs. Johnson, who'd been Cooper's father's English teacher, entered the reception area/front parlor from the door leading to the examination rooms.

"Well, Mrs. Johnson," Layla said as she ran the Medicare card, "I hope Dr. Murphy took good care of you."

"Boy's a fine doctor," the elderly woman said. "Always takes time to talk and hear a person out. Not like some who are always on the run and talk so fast without a break that you forget what you were going to say. Which is why I always write my complaints down," she said, lifting up a small yellow sheet of paper, "though some don't pay any mind to that, either. They're just out to make a quick buck by treating folks like cattle."

"Well, we definitely don't believe our patients are livestock." Layla printed out the patient instructions that Ryan had sent to her computer. "Now, you'll want to get this prescription for lotion filled at Parker's Drugs. And follow these instructions. If you have any questions, don't hesitate to call. Any time.

"He's done for the day," Layla said as Mrs. Johnson shuffled out the door Cooper held open for her. "You can go on back."

Cooper found his brother in his office, which had once been a formal parlor where scantily dressed women had served drinks to men who'd come to pay for pleasure.

"You actually look like a doctor in that white coat," he said.

"I am a doctor, and I wear it to help counter the rumor that all us Murphys are crazy."

"Mrs. Johnson certainly sings your praises."

Ryan shrugged as he took off the coat and hung it on a rack next to a wall of framed diplomas with embossed gold seals. "She's lonely. I listen to her, which, along with a prescription lotion for dry skin is all she needs. Woman's in her nineties and healthy as a horse."

"She calls the station two, three times a week," Cooper said. "The latest was a complaint about people ringing her doorbell, but whenever she'd look through the peephole, they'd be gone."

"What was it? Kids doing a ring and run?"

"No. Being the brilliant cop in the family, I solved the crime before I even rang the bell. Turns out the UPS guy had been leaving packages on her front porch, which she couldn't see through the peephole. Apparently she'd ordered a bunch of stuff online, then forget about it."

"Actually, that's important for me to know." Ryan opened a file on his computer and typed in a note. "I'll have Layla call her back in for a dementia test."

That bit of physician business done with, he turned back to Cooper. "So, you do know you're overdue for your flu shot?"

"Yeah, yeah. I'll get to that. Meanwhile, I wanted to give you a head's up on something."

Ryan leaned back in his chair. "This sounds personal."

"It is. I may be bringing someone to Thanksgiving dinner."

"The widow and her son. Whom you took on that train ride."

"That would be them."

"I've been away and may have missed it, but except for Ellen, I don't recall you ever taking a woman to the ranch."

"Rachel's different. I'm halfway in love with her."

"The fact that you even came by to tell me about her suggests you've crossed the line over halfway. And that she's not just another quick lay like those out-of-town women you were sneaking off to visit."

"How the hell did you know about them?"

"Word gets around."

All the way to freaking Afghanistan?

"It wasn't as bad as it sounds." Cooper threw his body into the chair on the visitor's side of the desk. "But yeah, she's the one."

"Well, it's about time. The family's been worried that you were planning to keep Ellen up on that pedestal forever."

"It wasn't so much that I'd put her on a pedestal. More that I was choosy. What she and her husband had was the real thing. I wasn't willing to settle for anything less."

"So this should be good news. Why am I hearing a but in your announcement?"

"She's not quite ready to move on."

"The woman moved all the way across the country, took on a job that would've sent most people running for the hills, and from what I hear, she's doing a bang-up job of not only refurbishing the New Chance, but turning it into an actual restaurant. To me that suggests she's come a long way."

"She has. But the damn place is taking all her attention. Well, almost." She certainly didn't seem to be thinking about the café whenever she was kissing him. "The thing is, she's not the kind of woman to go for a no-strings affair and with Scott being involved in the equation, I'm willing to give her more time to realize that we're perfect together."

"Well, good luck with that."

"Hey, being a Navy squid, you may not be acquainted with the Marine Corps concept about failure not being an option."

Ryan laughed, not taking offense at the derogatory nickname Marines had given the Navy. "And, as a jarhead," he returned the insult with good humor, "you may not realize that squids just happen to be giant sea creatures who swim around the ocean crapping on lower marine life.

"Seriously though," he said, "we're all rooting for you, bro. If you bring her to Thanksgiving dinner, we can plead your case."

"That's all I need. You, Dad, Mitzi, Gramps and Gram putting on a full-court press. I'm already working on getting her there. So if she does show up, could you be casual about it?"

"You've got it. I'll talk to the others."

"Thanks." Cooper blew out a breath. "I thought it would be weird," he admitted. "Falling in love again. Especially since Ellen and I had grown up together, so getting married to her was inevitable and comfortable. And totally drama free.

"But the minute I saw Rachel, I just knew. It was as if I'd been waiting just for her these past years. Then suddenly, there she was, at the New Chance, of all places."

"Okay." It was Ryan's turn to exhale. "Sounds like you've really got it bad."

"Yeah. I do."

And the weirdest thing was Cooper didn't mind. At all.

27

AFTER WHAT HAD seemed like nonstop wheedling from Scott, Rachel accepted Mitzi's and Dan's Thanksgiving invitation. After conferring with Betty, she contributed a bowl of Cabernet Sauvignon orange cranberry sauce. The roasting turkey and bubbling pots filled the house with a fragrance more appealing than the most expensive perfume, the scents reminding her of holidays in Iowa.

Extra tables, set up to accommodate all the people without family the couple had invited, groaned with a variety of dishes. Jake was there, as was Jenna Janzen, the pretty blond owner of the local bookstore who'd thoughtfully brought Scott the latest in his favorite Wimpy Kid series, and Layla Longstreet, a stunningly beautiful redhead whom Cooper introduced as his doctor brother's Nurse Practitioner partner.

Austin Merrill, the owner of a smaller neighboring ranch, whose cowboy husband was away riding bucking broncos in an Australian rodeo, had arrived bearing a lattice-topped cranberry apple pie that looked and smelled delicious. Despite Austin's smile when she and Rachel were introduced, her eyes were shadowed with a sadness that appeared to be more than loneliness. From the way the other women hovered around her like protective mother hens, Rachel had the impression that she'd come into the middle of a personal story that wasn't going to be shared. At least not today.

"You're undoubtedly horribly busy right now," Jenna said to Rachel as they stood at the kitchen counter, drinking wine.

"That would be an understatement," Rachel agreed.

"It's good you were able to escape for the day," Austin said as she reached for the bottle of chardonnay and topped off her glass.

"Every time I looked at my to-do list, I resisted. But Scott and Cooper double-teamed me."

"Well, we're glad you're here," Jenna said. "I dropped by when you arrived in town, but Cal told me you'd left to get a permit from Hester. Which, because it was lunchtime, probably took a while. Since I had to get back to the bookstore, I couldn't wait."

"I take it you've been through Hester's permit process."

Jenna nodded. "I wanted to expand my bookstore into the space that opened up when Layla went into practice with Ryan Murphy. The plan was to include a coffee bar, which probably would've been easy with anyone other than Hester. But I finally got it opened, and we even serve desserts, thanks to Austin."

Rachel glanced over at Austin. "I thought you were a rancher."

"I am. But money's been tight, and since I'm a pretty good baker, I've managed to pick up a bit here and there selling cookies, brownies, tarts and such. Nothing fancy, like you're probably used to. Just basic desserts."

"They're hardly basic," Jenna argued. "They're delicious. And since Johnny didn't serve desserts, they've turned out to be a super draw for the bookstore when people want coffee or tea and something sweet."

"Johnny didn't serve dessert?" Rachel asked.

"Well, not that anyone would want to eat," Jenna said.

"Or would dare to," Layla said. "When I first came back to town and went into practice, I used to wonder why people didn't show up at my office with food poisoning. I finally decided that no one could eat enough of his meals to get sick."

"Austin even offered him her cranberry apple pie, which you'll discover is to die for," Jenna said. "He turned her down flat. Same as he did her amazing, almost better than sex chocolate marble cheesecake. Which was lucky for me." She smiled at Austin as she took a sip of wine. "You should hire her."

"Now, Jenna," Austin protested. "You don't have to push."

"I'm not pushing," Jenna said. "Merely making a suggestion. It can't be that easy for Rachel to do all the cooking and baking while managing the New Chance."

"I don't have much choice at this point," Rachel said. "Though I did manage to hire Johnny's prep cook, dishwasher, and a few of his servers."

"They're good people," Jenna said after Rachel had named them. "They're probably thrilled to have a chance to work for someone who knows what she's doing."

"There are a lot of days I wonder if I know anything."

The bookseller laughed. "Join the club. I always say the problem with having your own business is that if you hate your boss, you have only yourself to blame. But unless you're seriously passionate about baking, why not get your desserts from the best baker in Southern Oregon? Probably the entire state?"

It wasn't a bad idea. Granted, Rachel wasn't swimming in financial resources. But neither was Austin, apparently. And if the rancher/baker's pie tasted half as good as it looked and smelled, her desserts could draw in even more business.

Also, not only would it be one less thing Rachel would have to worry about, going with the "time is money" maxim, it would give her more time to focus on other things. Perhaps she'd even have more of a life away from work.

"I wouldn't want to take away from your business," she told Jenna.

"Oh, don't worry about that," the bookstore owner said. "I close at five, so I'm not serving the dinner crowd. And as I said, we're talking small item desserts, so we wouldn't be in any competition."

"Maybe we can talk later," Rachel said to Austin. "After dinner."

Sky blue eyes echoed the first real smile Rachel had seen since she'd arrived. "I'd like that."

When Cooper suggested a horseback ride before dinner, Scott, unsurprisingly, jumped at the offer, which is why, after being assured her presence wasn't needed in the kitchen, Rachel was walking with Cooper and Scott toward the barn when a forest green SUV pulled into the circular stone driveway already filled with cars.

"It's about time you showed up," Cooper called out as the newcomer climbed out of the driver's seat and headed toward them.

"Lori Prescott called me at home because her toddler wouldn't stop crying. Since she's already got two kids, knows the teething drill and isn't one to exaggerate, I couldn't ignore her suspicion that the little girl had an ear infection. Which turned out to be the case when I stopped by their ranch on the way here."

"You make house calls?" Rachel asked, remembering the day Scott had come down with a fever and blazing red throat. Unable to fit her son in, the pediatrician had referred them to the Walk-In Care office where they'd had to wait three hours to get antibiotics for a strep throat.

"Occasionally," he said. "Lori's stuck hosting the family dinner this year, and one thing she didn't need was a screaming toddler on her hands."

"Especially given that Dorothy Prescott is one of those mother-in-laws who doesn't believe any woman's ever good enough for her son. Which totally ignores the fact that John and Lori have been happily married for twelve years," Cooper said.

"That would be true on both counts," the man who had to be Cooper's brother said. Although he was taller and lankier than Cooper, there was no mistaking the family resemblance.

"You must be Rachel Hathaway," he said. "The woman who's come to save us all from starving."

"That might be an overstatement, but I'm Rachel. This is my son, Scott." She put her hand atop the crown of his Stetson. "And you'd be Dr. Ryan Murphy."

"That's me. But you can skip the doctor part. Hey, Scott, great to meet you." He held out his hand. "I like the hat."

"Cooper got it for me," her son said, practically bursting with pride.

"I figured that might be the case." Ryan Cooper flashed a grin every bit as devastating as his brother's, making Rachel think the Murphy men should come with a warning label. "If I didn't know you were new to River's Bend, I'd have bet you'd grown up on one of the local ranches."

Scott beamed. "We're going to go horseback riding."

"It's a great day for it," Ryan said.

"I've been meaning to call your office," Rachel said.

"Are you okay?" Cooper asked, shooting her a sharp look.

"I'm fine," she assured him. "It's just that everything was so hectic when we were getting ready to leave Connecticut, then after we arrived here, we haven't gotten around to getting flu shots."

Just getting flu would be bad enough. Coming down with it, or having Scott sick, while she was trying to re-open the New Chance would be even worse.

"No problem," Ryan said easily. "Just call and tell Layla to get you in whenever it fits into your schedule."

"Thank you."

"No problem." He shrugged in a way she recognized all too well. "It's my job."

Oh, yes, Rachel thought. River's Bend's doctor was definitely Cooper Murphy's brother.

"Have a nice ride," he said before continuing toward the ranch house.

The day had dawned a perfect one with a crisp autumn tang in the air. Flaming red willows along the water provided a bright contrast to white-trunked aspen and in the distance the tree-covered Cascades were already wearing their winter coats. Rising above them all, the volcanic peak of Modoc Mountain gleamed like an ice palace.

When everyone else had come up with pitifully flimsy reasons to remain behind, it had been all too obvious that she and Cooper were targets of a matchmaking conspiracy. But on this perfect day Rachel couldn't be upset by the other's heavy handed maneuvering. She was, after all, an intelligent, grown woman, capable of making her own decisions. If she did decide to have an affair with Cooper, it didn't mean that she'd immediately begin planning a wedding menu.

Eighteen months ago she might have been more vulnerable to manipulation. But she'd successfully faced down lawyers, accountants, bankers, and a slug of a therapist with the morals of an alley cat.

"Something funny?" Cooper asked as they rode along the river trail, Scott out in front of them.

"Excuse me?"

"You laughed."

"I did?"

"You did. And you really should do it more often." He was wearing aviator shades against the brilliant fall sun, but Rachel knew, from the warmth of his voice, that his eyes were smiling.

"I was thinking back over the past eighteen months."

"That's good you've gotten so you can laugh about it. It shows progress."

"It does," she agreed. "I'm not where I want to be quite yet. But I'm getting there." She smiled at him. "I'm also having a wonderful day. I'm glad I came."

"I'm glad, too." He tilted his hat back with his thumb, a sign, she'd noticed, he tended to do when he was thinking. But before he could share whatever thoughts with her, Scott called out.

"Cooper! Are those eagles?"

Rachel lifted her gaze to the magnificent bald eagles circling overhead in a wide blue western sky.

"Sure are," Cooper answered. "They're riding the air currents. We're on the Pacific flyway, so you'll see lots of migrating birds this time of year. But these are probably part of our resident population."

"They're really cool." Scott's gaze tracked the white-headed birds while his horse, obviously familiar with the trail, walked along, mindless of the fact that his rider had let the reins go slack.

"They are that. And I, for one, am glad Ben Franklin didn't get his way when he lobbied for the turkey to be named the national bird."

"Is that true?" Scott turned around in the saddle. Rachel held her breath, waiting for him to slide off as they came around the bend just ahead, but his horse, sensing a now total lack of control, simply stopped and waited for the situation to change.

"Sure is. Though he was talking about wild turkeys, which aren't anything like the one roasting away in the oven back at the house. But they're still not as cool as eagles."

"That's for sure. I'd also feel real bad about eating an eagle."

"Me, too, sport," Cooper agreed. "Now, why don't you pick those reins up again, settle yourself in the saddle and we'd better get back before Gram grounds me for keeping you and your mom past dinner time."

"You couldn't get grounded," Scott scoffed. "You're a grownup. And the sheriff."

Cooper's rich, baritone laugh caused an all-too-familiar jittering in Rachel's stomach.

"Wait until you get to know my grandmother better," he said. "You'll discover she's a powerful force to be reckoned with."

"She likes me," Scott said. "She let me lick the spoon after she mixed up a spice cake."

"Of course she likes you. She may be a formidable woman, but she's also smart enough to recognize what a great kid you are."

Scott beamed as if Christmas had arrived a month early, and Santa had been generous. It was obvious that to his nine-year-old mind, Cooper could do no wrong. Just as it was readily apparent that he soaked up compliments from the sheriff like a too-dry sponge.

Which could become a problem. But as they rode back toward the ranch, the sound of the icy river tumbling over rocks nearly drowned out by the loud honking of long-necked geese flying overhead, Rachel decided to put that possible complication aside for now and enjoy the first perfect day she could remember in a very long time.

Even with whatever was bothering Austin and Jake's ongoing government problem, conversation flowed easily both during and after dinner, and by the time they drove home with the leftovers Betty had boxed up and Scott dozing in the back seat, Rachel knew that an entire week at Disney's Magic Kingdom would have paled in comparison to this single day at the Murphy's Bar M ranch.

28

AFTER SCOTT CRASHED into bed, Rachel had just put the leftovers away in the fridge when Cooper put his hands on her hips, drawing her close.

"I have a proposition for you."

Every female part of her body was shouting out *Yes!*

"Oh?"

"What would you say to going away together?"

"Where? When?"

"There's an Oregon Law Enforcement banquet and dance next Friday night. Although I usually try to avoid any event that has me putting on a tie, I have to attend this one and was thinking you might like a night off from the New Chance."

Maybe it was how much she'd enjoyed spending the day with his family and friends. Or how Cooper being in her kitchen felt so right. Maybe it was the way the smoldering sensuality in his gaze warmed her body, but a night away from all her responsibilities sounded like nirvana.

A night off with Cooper Murphy sounded deliciously decadent. Like the molten red velvet lava cake Austin had proposed adding to the New Chance's dessert menu. But better.

Remembering back to the horse ride, when Cooper had seemed about to say something, she wondered if he'd been wanting to ask her then. Putting that together with a few words she'd caught between Dan and Ryan while she'd been refilling the chip bowl during the football game, Rachel had her answer. "You're getting an award."

"Yeah. I guess I am."

"What for?"

"I don't recall the exact wording," he hedged. "Something about valor in the field."

Rachel knew if she'd been receiving the award, she would have memorized every word. "Congratulations. You must be very proud."

He shrugged, appearing uncomfortable. "I was just—"

"If you dare try to tell me that valor is merely part of your job, I'll hit you over the head with my heaviest sauté pan, Cooper Murphy." It was an idle threat, and they both knew it.

"Yes ma'am." he said, not entirely repressing a grin.

"That's better. And I'd be honored to watch you receive your award."

Now that Cooper had cleared the first hurdle, it was time for what he feared could be a deal breaker. "The banquet's being held at an inn on the coast. What would you say to driving up there Friday, then coming home Sunday evening?"

"So we'd be spending the entire weekend together?"

Yes, that was precisely what he wanted. It was what he'd wanted since that first day when she walked into the New Chance Café, smelling like wildflowers in the midst of all that lingering smoke.

"We'd have separate rooms." Which wasn't his preferred choice. But he'd promised to give her the time and distance she needed. "Say yes, Rachel."

Unable to resist touching her, he brushed the back of his hand down the side of her face and decided to play his trump card. "Did I mention the menu's being catered by Chef Madeline Chaffee?"

"Seriously?"

"What's what it says on the program I was emailed."

"I suppose I could ask Mrs. MacGregor to stay with Scott for the weekend."

She sounded less than enthusiastic about that idea. "I was thinking he could stay at the ranch," he said. "He seemed to enjoy himself today."

"He had a wonderful time. I'll be hearing about that horse ride for days. Probably months."

"Rusty's a patient old thing," Cooper repeated what he'd assured her at the time. "Which is why some of the dude ranches around here hire him when they need additional stock for trail rides. You needn't worry about Scott getting hurt if he stays there."

"I wasn't worried about that."

"Then what's the problem?"

"Surely your father has better things to do than babysit a nine-year-old boy."

"Dad came up with the idea of Scott staying with him. He wouldn't have made the offer if he hadn't honestly enjoyed having Scott there."

"You discussed this with your father before asking me?"

"I had a feeling you wouldn't be comfortable with Mrs. MacGregor." Lifting her hands, he put them around his neck. "So, how about boosting my ego by allowing me to escort the prettiest woman in Oregon to the Policeman's Ball?"

"With a line like that," she said, "how could any girl resist? And for the record, I'm going because I want to be alone with you. Chef Madeline's only the cherry atop the cupcake."

Smiling, Rachel lifted her lips to his.

29

THE MONDAY AFTER the Thanksgiving weekend, Cooper was finishing up his daily stroll of downtown when his phone buzzed. The caller I.D. read *Murphy, Ryan, Dr.*

"Hey," he answered. "Thanks for getting Rachel and Scott in for their shots."

"No problem. Are you doing anything right now?"

"I was going to turn the office over to Cal and go to Rachel's for dinner. She's making mac and cheese. With three different kinds of cheese. Who knew?"

"Sounds great. Do you have a few minutes to talk about her visit?"

Cooper's blood went cold. "Is she all right?"

"She seemed fine. I suggested a physical, but she said—"

"She didn't have the time right now." And where had he heard that before?

"Yeah. But she promised to come in as soon as the New Chance has opened."

Cooper hoped to hell that would be true. "Let me call her and let her know I'll be late, and I'll meet you at The Shady Lady in five."

The Shady Lady was one of two bars in River's Bend. It had previously been known as the No Name after a winter storm blew the sign away while Cooper had been in elementary school.

As further proof that the rest of the world hadn't stopped spinning during Cooper's deployment to Afghanistan, a movie company had hung up a weathered wooden sign declaring it The Shady Lady Saloon.

Typically after filming crews would return the storefronts to an even better condition than they'd found them, which had proven a good deal for local merchants over the years. This time the owners opted to keep the name. And the sign.

The interior had been created to match the theme and appeal to tourists with velvet couches, bordello red walls hung with framed paintings of dance hall girls and faded sepia photographs of more girls along with cowboys, outlaws, and miners. A player piano, lassos, antique spurs and six-shooters added to the western theme. As did a mechanical bull that might admittedly be an anachronism, but pulled in a lot of revenue. Especially on Friday and Saturday nights.

His brother had already taken a table in the far corner of the room when Cooper walked in. While waiting for their beers to arrive, by unspoken mutual agreement, they talked about easy things—the weather, which had finally turned autumn crisp, necessitating additional insulation in Ryan's attic and how work on the New Chance was coming along.

"It'll be good to have it open," Ryan said as the waitress, dressed in jeans, a ruffled-front rodeo queen blouse and tasseled red boots delivered chilled mugs of Crater

Lake Amber Ale. "At least you're eating like a king while the rest of us are forced to subsist on microwave dinners, canned soup and sandwiches."

"I'll bring you a doggy bag."

"That would be appreciated. You can get your flu shot when you do. While I've nothing against Cal Potter personally, I'd just as soon have you in charge of law and order, which you can't do if you're barfing your guts out because you couldn't cowboy up enough to handle a needle prick."

"That's not it."

"Yeah, I know." His brother sighed, plucked a peanut from the bowl in the middle of the table and cracked it open. "Guys around here think flu shots are for old ladies, kids, and wusses."

"I can't argue that." Cooper took a long drink of Klamath Basin's flagship ale. "But you're right. If nothing else, getting flu will keep me from helping Rachel with the café and hanging out with Scott in the afternoons."

"He's a cute kid. And I like his mother. A lot."

"She's damn likable," Cooper agreed. "And as a friendly fraternal reminder, you can't have her because I've already called dibs."

Seemingly distracted, Ryan didn't rise to the challenge. "So, did she happen to mention anything about her appointment?"

"Just that she was grateful you got her and Scott in and that you give good shots." Cooper put down his beer and scooped up a handful of peanuts. "Why?"

"If she'd noticed anything off kilter, would she have told you?"

"I'm not sure. Possibly." A blast of ice hit his bloodstream. "You're not going to tell me that you're self-medicating, are you?" He knew vets who'd come back with problems. Even he had the occasional flashback.

"Hell, no." Fire flashed in whiskey brown eyes inherited from their mother. "What kind of doctor are you accusing me of being?"

"I'm not accusing you of anything. It was merely a question. What, exactly, do you mean, by 'off kilter?' "

Ryan sighed heavily as he traced the condensation trailing down the side of the mug with a fingertip. "I was giving her son—"

"Scott."

"Yeah. Scott. Who idolizes you, by the way."

"I like him too. A bunch. Getting back to your reason for calling me . . ."

His brother rubbed the back of his neck, obviously uncomfortable with the topic. "I think you need some backstory. While I was in Kandahar, there was this kid about Scott's age. His hand had been blown off by a detonated mine and they'd operated on him at the local civilian hospital, but whoever did it must've learned surgery from an *Amputation for Dummies* book because after it had been hacked off, the wound wasn't properly closed."

"So it got infected."

Ryan winced and took a longer drink of the beer. "Dealing with an infection might have been workable. It had gone way beyond that to freaking rotting off. I don't think I need to describe it."

"No." Cooper shook his head. "I'd just as soon you didn't."

"I'd never seen a totally black arm before. The flesh

had mummified and there wasn't a pulse. So, obviously, it had to come off."

"It's always hardest with kids," Cooper said, having seen his share of horror. War, unfortunately, wasn't neat and tidy. It killed anything and anyone who happened to get in the way. Even innocent children.

"You don't forget a thing like that," Ryan said quietly.

"No." But there was more. Cooper could see it in his brother's haunted eyes. So, he waited.

"His father must've had him late in life because he looked older than you'd expect for a child that young. Then again, those people live such a damn hard existence, they look older than their years. He'd driven miles over the goat paths laughingly call roads in those mountains, risking IEDs, drone strikes, even getting caught in the middle of a battle, just to bring his son to us. So we'd save him."

Ryan answered the question Cooper had been afraid to ask. "And we did. At least, when he left a few days later, with instructions for aftercare, he was doing a hell of a lot better than I'd initially expected."

"But?"

"It was his dad who got to me." Ryan shook his head and downed the rest of his beer in one long, thirsty gulp. "As we were getting ready to operate, he grabbed my arm, pointed toward his own and, through the interpreter, begged me to amputate it and transplant it to his son."

"Jesus." The chill skittered over Cooper again and caused his gut to churn. "And that's what you flashed back to when you were giving Scott his shot."

"Yeah."

"Okay, that's about as bad as it gets." Now that the

picture was in Cooper's mind, joining his own imbedded images of too many bodies, he was afraid he'd dream of it himself. "Maybe you ought to talk it out with someone."

"I just did."

"I mean a professional. Or a group. There's one over in K. Falls—"

"Yeah, that'll give my patients a lot of confidence in me. Knowing that I'm being treated for PTSD."

He skimmed a hand over hair he still wore in a military cut. Which now that he looked at his brother more closely, Cooper realized that the short hair revealed cheeks that were more hollowed than they'd been the last time Ryan had been home on leave. And while he'd always been rangy, he was definitely leaner.

"Maybe the VA hospital in Roseburg."

"I'm okay," this brother insisted. "It was just a flash-back. And it only lasted a second."

"Which seemed longer," Cooper guessed.

"Yeah. But they don't come that often."

"Jesus." Cooper shook his head. "If you don't get treatment, I'll tell dad."

"Snitch," Ryan complained without heat.

"Sticks and stones." Faking a relaxation he was a long way from feeling, Cooper tilted the wooden chair on its back legs and sipped his beer. "I'd rather be called names than show up here some day and find that you've eaten your gun."

Ryan rose to the bait. "Coming home and setting up an office is what kept me going during all those damn deployments." His face was set, and his eyes were practically shooting sparks. If they'd been kids again, they'd be about two seconds from rolling around on the floor, throwing punches. "No way would I ever do anything like that after finally achieving my goal of coming back here as a family physician."

Ryan hadn't always wanted to be a doctor. When he'd been a kid, he'd spend hours building miniature rockets and setting them off. At seven, he announced his plan to be the first astronaut from Oregon. When their mom's cancer bombshell hit their family, he'd turned on a dime and changed direction to medicine. Accustomed to looking below the surface, and having spent so many years sharing a room with this man, Cooper knew how seriously Ryan took medicine. It was more than a career; it was a calling.

"Damn right you wouldn't," Cooper said, unfazed by fire burning in his brother's eyes. "But if you need to talk about anything, you know I'm always here for you."

Ryan's lips quirked. "That's because you got stuck with the big brother role."

"No," Cooper countered, though it was partly true. His innate need to take charge of things and fix problems was probably another reason he'd become a cop, then a sheriff.

Ryan, on the other hand, was a people pleaser and peacemaker, undoubtedly good traits for a family physician and why all his patients loved him. "Because though I'm about to embarrass us both, I love you, man."

"Ditto," Ryan said. "And now that we've had our beer and brotherly conversation, why don't you drop by Blossoms and pick up one of those mixed bouquets in the window?"

"I was going to do that," Cooper lied, wishing he'd thought of it.

Ryan laughed. A robust sound from deep inside that sounded like the old Ryan and eased Cooper's concern somewhat. "Sure you were."

As he left The Shady Lady, headed toward the flower shop, Cooper was unsurprised his brother knew he'd begun spending dinners with Rachel. At first she'd resisted him buying the ingredients, but he'd been able to win the argument by pointing out that she was saving him from eating Cocoa Puffs and Pop Tarts for dinner.

He also claimed that he was trying out recipes as part of his investment. By the third night, after tasting her short ribs, although he wasn't fool enough to suggest it, Cooper realized that she was wasting her talents in a town as small as River's Bend.

Would she come to realize that herself?

And more importantly, when she did, would she stay?

30

"I DON'T HAVE ANYTHING to wear."

Women said that all the time. Rachel certainly had on more than one occasion, even when her oversized, professionally designed walk-in closet was filled with designer clothes. In this case, it was true.

Not having planned to leap into a social life in River's Bend, and suspecting that there would be no place to wear Valentino or Versace, along with needing the money, she'd sold most of her dressier clothing to consignment stores.

Which was what had brought her to Back to the Rack, a consignment thrift shop she'd noticed down the street.

She was browsing through the scant selection when Mitzi suddenly appeared. "Attending a prom, are we?" she asked as Rachel dismissed a strapless candy pink chiffon dress studded with sequins and moved on to a beaded red and black skin-tight gown with a side slit cut nearly to the waist.

"Surely girls don't wear dresses like this to proms," she said. "It looks more like a *Dancing With The Stars* tango costume."

"Believe me, if this were spring, those would've been snapped up by now. Coincidentally, I was on my way to the café to suggest we drive up to Eugene or Portland to shop for something for you to wear to the banquet."

"I've already agreed to go to the coast with Cooper. I can't take an entire day to go shopping."

"Well, you're lucky I saw you come in here," she said as Rachel held up a strapless scarlet dress with a short bell skirt. Even if she could keep it up, she'd freeze to death before they got to the main course. "Because you're definitely in need of a fairy godmother."

"I've stopped believing in fairy tales."

"Too bad because fairy tales demonstrate compassion, intelligence, courage, coping skills, and determination. All of which you have in spades," Mitzi countered. "As for the charge that they encourage girls to believe in the power of love, I'll be damned if I can figure out what's wrong with that since I suspect it's what most people really want. Deep down.

"However, getting back to the issue at hand, you need a new dress."

She stepped back and gave Rachel a long, considering head to toe look. "Unfortunately, you're too tall to fit into anything in my closet." She pulled an emerald silk sheath off the rack and checked the price tag. "This is a steal."

"Green makes me look sallow."

"I sincerely doubt you'd look bad in anything, but if you don't feel pretty in a special occasion dress, there's no point in getting a bargain."

"This entire idea was a mistake," Rachel said, feeling defeated as she passed on a trio of taffeta gowns in day-Glo colors that could only have been bridesmaid dresses and came to a wedding dress at the end of the rack. The tag on the dress read "Never Worn."

"Don't be ridiculous," Mitzi scoffed. "Call me an unabashed romantic, but I know the night's going to be special. For both you and Cooper."

"Still—"

"Look." Mitzi cut her off again by holding up a manicured hand. "Given your life before moving here, I can't believe there isn't something in your closet that will be perfect."

She managed to frown without furrowing her brow as she skimmed a disapproving glance over Rachel's paint-stained sweatshirt. "Surely you didn't get rid of everything decent you owned?"

"I have clothes," Rachel defended herself as Mitzi made her sound like some pitiful urchin from a Dickens tale. "Just nothing fancy."

"Some of the women at the banquet will go for glitz and glam because they don't have all that many opportunities to get dressed up," Mitzi said. "Or they're like me and just enjoy a bit of sparkle. But you're a lily, Rachel. Classic and beautiful on your own. You don't need gilding. How about a little black dress?"

"I brought one with me, but—"

"Please tell me it's not the one you wore to your husband's funeral."

"No. I gave that away." The same day she'd packed up all Alan's clothing and taken the box to Goodwill. "This is one I was planning to wear to an after-party during Fashion Week."

"Bingo. Let's go look at it," Mitzi said.

Ten minutes later, Rachel was almost unable to recognize the woman looking back at her from the bathroom mirror. All the hard, physical work she'd been doing had resulted in her appetite returning and during the past weeks in River's Bend, she'd begun to gain back the weight she'd lost. While no one would ever call her voluptuous, the dress hugged what curves she had like a second skin.

"Well?" Mitzi called in to her.

"I don't know." She loved the dress as much as when she'd first seen it on Saks Fifth Avenue's pricey third floor on a splurge day with Janet that had included afternoon tea in the SFA café. "I think it might be a little edgy for Oregon."

"In case you haven't noticed, women in cowboy country no longer live in gingham and calico," Mitzi shot back.

When Rachel returned to the bedroom, Mitzi drew in a deep breath. "Be still my fluttering heart," she said. "That's a Herve Leger." She twirled a finger. "Turn around." She breathed out a huge sigh as she took in Rachel's bared back. "I'd kill to be able to wear that. If anyone dared to remake *Breakfast at Tiffany's*, this is the dress Holly Golightly would wear."

"Are you sure it's not overkill?"

"Are you kidding?" Mitzi tilted her head, studying the tight, mid-thigh length dress with an off the shoulder neckline and three-quarter length sleeves. "There's not a man on the planet who wouldn't want to show you off. I'll bet the minute Cooper sees you, he'll forget all about that award."

She studied Rachel. "I know I said there's no point in gilding the lily, but you need jewelry. I have some diamonds—"

"I have some pieces that'll work." Rachel opened the top drawer of the chest and pulled out a lined box. The pearl earrings had been a first anniversary present. Later, Alan had draped the strand of matching pearls around her neck the day she'd returned home from the hospital with their son.

"Now that's class," Mitzi said approvingly. "You're a natural."

Rachel laughed as she thought back on the small town farm girl who'd shown up in the big city with two new suitcases and so many dreams. "I had good teachers." Not only had Alan's taste had been impeccable, he'd handed her over to personal shoppers who'd ensured that she fit the image of a powerful man's wife. It had been like playing dress-up.

"Well, I'd argue that, but we've got one last problem." Mitzi looked down at Rachel's feet still clad in the red wool socks she'd worn to the café this morning. "I don't suppose you happen to have a pair of shoes to go with that outfit?"

Rachel went digging into the back of the closet. "I know it was weak of me, but I couldn't give these away because I bought them to go with the dress." Tugging off the socks, she balanced one hand on the top of the chest and pulled on the strappy black high heels.

"Jimmy Choo." Mitzi nodded approvingly. "You're going to make a dynamite wedding attendant."

"Wedding?" Rachel almost fell off her shoes in surprise. "Are you saying what I think you are?"

"Dan proposed last night," Mitzi revealed. Rachel knew that the gleam in the woman's eyes had nothing to do with her tinted contacts. "We're getting married and I'd love for you to be my matron of honor."

"Oh, I'd love that, too. I'm so happy for you!" Rachel

hugged the woman who was responsible for bringing her to River's Bend. The woman who, in so many ways, was that fairy godmother she'd been wishing for.

"I'm happy, too. And I have you to thank."

"Me?"

"For years after Dan's wife died, he seemed perfectly content to live alone out there on that ranch. Then I came to town, shook up his life a bit, and made him feel like a young stud again. But, try as I might, I couldn't get him focused on the idea that what we had together might grow into something permanent.

"But then you came to town and watching his son fall so fast and so hard for you made him take a deeper look at his own feelings. And Scott has him thinking how much he'd like to be a grandfather while he's still young enough to enjoy the role.

"So, while he was pondering on all that, it finally dawned on the man that he isn't too ancient to take one more ride on the marriage-go-round. Maybe we might just end up making it a double wedding."

"I'm certainly not planning to get married."

Mitzi switched gears with the deftness of a natural born saleswoman. "Well, that is probably too soon," she agreed without missing a bit. "What with your restaurant opening, and all. But the chemistry between the two of you could light up the entire town."

"Chemistry is one thing. Love quite another."

"True. But are you saying that you're not in love with Cooper? Just a little bit?" She held up the crimson tips of her thumb and index finger a smidgen of an inch apart.

"It would be easy to fall in love with Cooper," Rachel allowed, not ready to admit that she feared she might already be half way there. "He's warm and kind, and wonderful with Scott."

"And hot and handsome as sin," Mitzi tacked on.

"That too."

"So, what's the problem?"

As she considered her response, Rachel realized that she'd missed having a woman friend to talk with. Phone calls with Janet weren't the same as talking in person, when you felt you could open up.

How could she share her confused, conflicted feelings about a man her former best friend hadn't even met? How could she describe how Cooper's smile could warm her from the inside out or the way his touch could make her feel as if she were on the verge of melting into a hot little puddle of need? And how to explain that his absolute belief in her boosted Rachel's confidence on days she'd secretly worried that she may have taken on more than she could handle?

"I didn't come here looking to fall in love." It wasn't part of the plan she'd been focused on for months.

Mitzi laughed at that. "Join the club. When I arrived in town looking for a vacation ranch property for a wealthy client, if anyone would have suggested I'd end up staying, I would've accused them of being certifiable.

"But then I dropped into the New Chance for a cup of coffee and there was Dan, risking ptomaine by eating one of Johnny's ghastly burgers. And my heart started doing cartwheels right on the spot." She patted her breast as if just talking about her fiancé could cause the same reaction. "I swear it was love at first sight."

Having seen them together, Rachel wasn't about to challenge Mitzi's statement. While it might have more likely been lust at first glance, the couple's love was obvious.

"That was your heart," she said, working out her own feelings aloud. "What about your head?"

"What about it?"

"Weren't you worried that you'd lose your independence?"

"Not for a minute. Dan knows I love my work. He'd never ask me to stay home all day and cook for ranch hands." Mitzi laughed. "Which would prove dangerous, since, as we've already determined, I can't boil water. And there's also the fact that if I even tried to enter her kitchen, Betty would probably go after me with a cleaver."

"There is that," Rachel murmured.

"Look, honey, I don't know anything about your relationship with your husband, but—"

"It was wonderful. I adored Alan. And he loved me. He also encouraged my catering."

With the caveat that her career plans wouldn't interfere with her continuing to handle everything at home, including being a proper hostess.

The social part of her marriage had been the most difficult because although she'd learned to dress, talk, and act as if she belonged in the rarified circles in which she and Alan had moved, despite having left the farm behind, inside, a very strong part of Rachel had remained a small town girl.

When she shared her sudden revelation that she'd chosen River's Bend, not just because it was affordable, but because it was so far removed from her life in Connecticut, Mitzi wasn't the least bit surprised.

"I see that all the time in my business," she said. "A

move represents change and women, especially, are always re-inventing themselves as they go through life stages. And while we can run, we can't always hide from our inner child.

"I grew up in a coastal logging town not much bigger than River's Bend. Escaping to the big, glittery city was my dream. I loved living in Portland, where I first landed after leaving home, then Eugene after my divorce. I was perfectly content with my life.

"Then I fell in love with Dan and found that returning to my small town roots was as easy as sliding into a warm bath."

Yet Mitzi hadn't abandoned her past entirely. Rachel realized that instead, she'd melded different aspects of her previous lives into one that fit the woman she was now.

"I was swept away by Alan," Rachel murmured. "It was like a fairy tale. Unfortunately, instead of ending happily ever after, it turned out to be more Grimm's than Disney. Lets say, hypothetically, that Cooper was to get serious about me—"

"I suspect that bull has already left the chute, to use the local cowboy vernacular," Mitzi broke in dryly.

"If things got serious," Rachel forged on, "I'm not sure I'm capable of juggling a new restaurant, mother-hood, and marriage."

"I suspect you're capable of doing whatever you set your mind to," the older woman argued. "I've watched all you've accomplished since contacting me about the New Chance. And, sticking with the hypothetical, you wouldn't be doing it alone. Cooper's wonderful with Scott. It would be a partnership of equals."

What Mitzi was saying made sense. But . . .

"I'm getting ahead of myself," Rachel said.

"Perhaps a bit," Mitzi agreed, not sounding convinced. "But meanwhile that is one dynamite dress. Poor Cooper's toast."

"You make it sound so easy." As she smoothed non-existent wrinkles from the tight, short skirt, Rachel's attention was drawn to her wedding ring. Not for the first time, she felt her courage faltering. "I really did love my husband, Mitzi."

"Of course you did," the older woman said soothingly. "But as tragic as his death was, Alan's gone, Rachel. Don't you think it's time to start living for yourself for a change?"

Rachel's grave gray eyes met Mitzi's sympathetic blue ones in the mirror. "What do you think this weekend's all about?"

Mitzi nodded approvingly. "Do you have any wine?"

"In the fridge."

"Good. You change out of that," the older woman said with renewed briskness. "I'm going downstairs to pour two glasses, and we'll toast your romantic weekend and my nuptials before you return to the salt mine."

Before changing back into her working clothes, Rachel took another long look at the sexy stranger in the mirror. Then she smiled.

Take that, Cooper Murphy.

31

AFTER MITZI LEFT, Rachel returned to work, her mind caught in an endless loop between her previous life and the one she was creating for herself in River's Bend.

"Everything okay?" Cooper asked as he did the dishes after having declared her mac and cheese the best he'd ever tasted.

"Fine," she said, hedging a bit.

"You've been quiet this evening."

"Have I?" She'd discovered that not much got past the man. "I guess I'm just tired."

"No surprise there. I'm starting to feel guilty about you cooking for me every night."

"Don't. You've no idea how much it helps to have someone to test my new menu. River's Bend isn't exactly Connecticut—"

"There's a newsflash." After hanging the dishtowel on the oven handle, he began massaging the boulders in her shoulders.

"You know the people. What they like." She tilted her head, giving his talented hands better access to her neck muscles. "And despite hearing what a terrible cook Johnny was, I'm not aiming to be merely better. I want to serve home cooking that local diners will not only enjoy, but could hold its own anywhere in the country."

"I may be a hick from the boonies, Sweetheart. But I've eaten at some fine dining establishments in Portland. And you've got them all beat."

"That's nice of you to say."

"It's the truth." He bent his head and brushed a light kiss against her neck. "All you need is a decent night's sleep for a change. Why don't you cancel Mrs. MacGregor and make it an early night?"

"I think I will," Rachel said.

But not for the reason Cooper was thinking.

After he'd kissed her goodnight, and Scott had gone to bed, Rachel retrieved a DVD she'd hidden away in her dresser. Then, snuggled into her grandmother's quilt, she settled down on the sofa with a cup of cocoa and a box of Kleenex.

By the time she'd watched her wedding DVD three times, the forgotten cocoa was cold and the box of tissues nearly empty.

Alan had looked so worldly, so sophisticated in white tie. Taking in the bold, confident man standing at the altar, Rachel could foresee the advertising titan he would become.

In contrast, as she'd floated down the white satin runner (the third time in slow motion), she'd looked so young. So naive. Like Cinderella crossing the ballroom toward Prince Charming. Her hand trembled when Alan slipped the ring on her finger.

How could she have forgotten that?

"If you'd only known how things would turn out,

would you have run away?" she asked her twenty-one year
old self.

No. Absolutely not.

Dashing at tears with her fingertips, Rachel knew that
if that fairy godmother she'd tried so hard not to believe in
had suddenly appeared at the altar, opening a magic
window into the future, she wouldn't have hesitated for a
moment about going through with her wedding.

She'd been blessed with a good life. A wonderful life.

She'd adored a generous, loving man who'd loved her
back. And yes, Alan had been flawed. But wasn't everyone? Hadn't she been using the same excuse for her
workaholic behavior these past weeks that Alan had used
whenever she'd question his seeming obsession with his
career? He'd always insisted he was only trying to do the
best for his family. As she was attempting to do for Scott.

But, Rachel belatedly realized, by focusing solely on
work as she'd been doing, she'd ignored so many other
aspects of a full life.

Cooper had tried to convince her to take more time to
relax once in a while. His brother, after taking her blood
pressure, had prescribed some R&R. Even Mitzi had
advised her to start living for herself.

Rachel froze the TV screen on Alan's face, drinking in
the unqualified love she viewed in his dark eyes the
moment before he'd kissed her after they'd been declared
husband and wife. And she knew, that were it possible for
him to be able to see her now, he'd tell her the same thing
that the others had.

"Nobody loves a damn martyr," she sniffled as she
blew her nose.

After ejecting the DVD, she put it back in the dresser,

beneath her underwear, then picked up a frame photo of Alan and her on the beach from the bedside table. With all their income going into building his agency, rather than an expensive destination honeymoon, they'd opted for a weekend beach getaway in New Jersey's Cape May. The hosts of the Victorian B&B, who'd gone out of their way to ensure a memorable time, had taken the photo.

Rachel felt a tug in her heart as she looked down at their happy, glowing faces. The honeymoon may have been short, but what they'd lacked in time, they'd made up for in pleasure.

After touching her fingertips to her lips, she pressed them against her husband's glass-covered face before putting the photo away in the top drawer of the table. Then she slipped off the gold band that hadn't left her hand since her wedding day and set it into the blue Tiffany box next to the photo.

As she blew out a deep, shuddering breath, Rachel felt a weight she hadn't even realized she'd been carrying all these months lift off her shoulders.

32

AVING GUESSED THAT Cooper would be strictly a country music fan, Rachel was surprised when he tuned the Jeep's radio to a smooth jazz station that allowed for conversation during their drive across the snow-capped Cascades to lush valleys where vineyards were a blaze of gold and red leaves.

"Thank you," she said as her eyes drank in the brilliant hues.

"You're welcome," he responded as, coincidentally, Al Jarreau began crooning about berries on the vine getting sweeter all the time. "What did I do?"

"The day my furniture was sold off, I stood on the back terrace thinking how much I was going to miss the fall colors. But this is beautiful."

"It is," he agreed. "We'll have to come back next summer for a tasting tour."

"That sounds lovely." And wonderfully romantic.

Rachel was falling for Cooper. She wasn't going to try to deny it, to herself or to him. Which was why she was in his Jeep, headed toward the coast for a weekend she knew would take their relationship to the next level.

The sensible thing would have been to have sex at his

house. That way, afterwards, she could go home. Give them both space.

The problem was that the man had done something to her mind. She didn't feel the least bit sensible. Or cautious.

Rachel had been the "good girl" her entire life. The good daughter. The good wife. She'd never complained or made waves and could probably count on one hand the number of times she'd raised her voice. Even at her husband's funeral, keeping in mind her father's words that big girls don't cry, she had used every bit of inner strength she'd possessed to channel Jackie Kennedy, refusing to shed a single public tear.

Her father, like all farmers, had been a gambler at heart. As had Alan. While Rachel had always possessed a need for peace and security.

And look where that got you a judgmental voice in the back of her mind piped up.

It had gotten her to River's Bend. And into Cooper Murphy's arms.

Which was why, for this one stolen weekend, Rachel intended to throw caution to the wind and take a walk on the wild side.

Then once they returned to River's Bend, desire satisfied, heads cleared, life could return to normal.

❧

SHELTER BAY, WITH its charming Cape Cod style shops and galleries, reminded Rachel of Cape May. Despite the chilly rain falling from a quilted pewter sky, sailboats, white sails billowing in the stiff sea breeze, skimmed along the blue-gray water while Gortex-clad tourists stood at the sea wall, looking through binoculars in hopes of spotting the pod of resident whales. Fishing boats chugged into the harbor while sea lions lounged on wooden docks, barking at one another.

Drops of silvery rain spattered the Jeep's windshield as they drove up a hill, passing a park where a bronze statue of a young woman looked out to sea, eternally awaiting her fisherman husband's return from the sea.

The Whale Song Inn was a turreted, gingerbread-encrusted Victorian with a wide, wraparound front porch that spoke of the opulence and optimism of a bygone era. In contrast to the exterior, the lobby's floor was a simple whitewashed pine and the blue and beige hues of the walls and furniture brought sea, sand, and sky indoors.

"This is lovely," Rachel said as they rode up to the fourth floor in an old-fashioned cage elevator.

"We used to come to Shelter Bay for summer vacations when I was a kid," Cooper said. "We didn't stay here because it was beyond our budget, but since the trip was all about hanging out at the beach, a rental cottage made more sense."

"And was probably more fun." As casual and comfortable as the lobby was, Rachel couldn't imagine bringing a wet and sandy boy through it.

"We had some great times," he agreed as he opened the door to a room painted in sea glass blues and greens. A pair of French doors led onto a balcony that offered a dazzling view of the bay, sea, and a lighthouse.

"Oh." She drew in an appreciative breath as she opened the French doors and despite the drizzle, which had lessened to a mist, stepped out onto the balcony. "It's stunning."

"I realize you had beaches back east," Cooper said, coming out to stand beside her. "But there's something special about the Oregon coast."

"From what I've seen so far, I'd have to agree."

"We'll play tourist tomorrow," he promised.

Her knee-jerk response, which she wisely didn't share, was to remember that Hal would be putting the wall sconces in tomorrow without her there to ensure they ended up in precisely the locations they'd agreed upon.

Then, determined to take her own —and everyone else's—advice, she turned her focus to smelling the roses. Or, in this case, the scents of salt and fir trees on the sea air.

"I can actually feel myself unwinding," she murmured. And it felt wonderful.

He put his arm around her. "That's the idea."

The sun was lowering in the sky, gilding the pewter clouds and turning the white caps to a gleaming gold.

They'd arrived later than originally planned because, on a whim, Cooper had turned down a winding road to a winery, where they'd had a lovely lunch in a glassed-in room overlooking the vineyard. The spontaneity had made both the wood-fired Pacific rockfish tacos and sunshine bright Chardonnay taste even more delicious.

"I suppose I should leave and let you get unpacked," he said just before lowering his head to skim his lips teasingly over hers. In the heartbeat that his mouth was on Rachel's, his hands moving down her sides, she couldn't have responded if her life had depended on it.

Too soon, he drew back. A slow smile curved those dangerous lips. "I'm glad you came, Rachel."

"Me, too," she said as she left the balcony and walked

across the room with him.

He paused at the door. "I know the guy in charge of security here. He used to be Secret Service, assigned to protecting foreign diplomats, so this place should be nearly as safe as the White House. Especially since it's filled with cops tonight. But things can happen, so don't forget to fasten the security latch."

Rachel shut the door and turned the lock. But as she fastened the chain as instructed, she knew that it was too late to protect her heart.

33

RACHEL LAY IN the Jacuzzi tub, luxuriating in the warmth of the scented water and as she imaged the fragrant bubbling foam to be Cooper's caressing hands, her bones turned as soft and pliant as the water.

Her rebellious mind, once stimulated, seemed unable to stop painting erotic pictures as she continued to get ready for the evening. Checking her reflection for the umpteenth time, Rachel wasn't at all surprised that the image gazing back at her was of a woman who wanted to be made love to.

By the time Cooper knocked on door between them, Rachel was feeling as sexually frustrated as Maggie the Cat in *Cat on a Hot Tin Roof*.

"You're late," she said as she opened the door.

Seemingly struck speechless by the vision in front of him, Cooper stared at her. He was wearing a dark charcoal suit, white shirt, and burgundy tie. As handsome as he was, she found herself preferring him in those chambray shirts and jeans.

"Cooper?"

He shook his head as if to clear it. "Sorry. What did

you say?"

"I said you were late."

He glanced down at his leather-banded watch. "Actually, I think I'm early. But I was getting lonely." His slow gaze took her in, from the top of her head down to her stiletto heels, then back up again. "You are the most stunningly beautiful woman I've ever seen."

Except for Alan on their wedding day, no one had ever called Rachel stunning. Usually, pretty tended to be her highest accolade.

Rachel glanced down at the dark green bottle he held in his right hand. His left was holding two long stemmed tulip glasses. "Is that for us?"

Cooper stared blankly at the champagne as if he'd forgotten its existence. "Oh. Yeah. There's an open bar at the pre-banquet reception, but I thought it might be nice to have a drink in private before we go downstairs."

"That's a wonderful idea. I'd love it."

"I'm glad."

When he still didn't budge, Rachel felt a heady surge of feminine power.

"Would you prefer to drink it in my room or yours?" Her lips curved in a slow, seductress smile as uncharacteristic as her sexy, skin-tight dress.

Who knew the Widow Hathaway's legs went on forever? And how the hell had she gotten into that dress? More to the point, Cooper wondered, how would he ever get her out of it?

He glanced past her at the bed, which seemed to have grown even larger, taking up most of the room.

"If I come in right now, Rachel, I might not be able to leave."

"What about your award?"

"What award?"

She'd fastened her hair up into some sort of complicated twist that, along with those pearls gleaming at her ears and between her breasts made her look New York sophisticated and totally out of his league. But that didn't stop all Cooper's blood from flowing south when he imagined plucking the pins from her hair, allowing it to rain over her bare shoulders and breasts as he peeled her out of the black dress.

Hell. In another minute, he was going to need oxygen.

"Poor Cooper." Her husky Kathleen Turner laugh wasn't helping his runaway libido. "Come inside and we'll see if we can restore your memory in time for the banquet."

Intent on showing her that while he might be country, he wasn't a total hick, he peeled the shiny gold foil off the top of the bottle, removed the wire covering the cork, and deftly opened the champagne. The cork came out with a whisper of vapor.

"You weren't late," she admitted what they both already knew as he poured the champagne into one of the flutes and handed it to her. "I was just getting impatient. And lonely for you."

She gave him another of those come-and-take-me-big-boy smiles that hit directly in his solar plexus. Then shot a direct path to below the belt. "In fact, I was tempted to try to bribe the bellman for a key to that door between us."

"It wouldn't have done you any good."

"Oh?" Rachel arched a dark brow. "You think not?"

Call him perverse, but he loved it when she pulled out that Eastern seaboard society tone. Partly because he'd already figured out that it was like one of those silk blouses she'd worn when she'd first arrived in town. Something she could put on and take off at will.

"I know not. Because I beat you to it." Cooper grinned as he pulled the key from his jacket pocket.

"Gracious." Her eyes widened with feigned shock. "What would all those law and order people downstairs say if they knew their medal recipient had committed bribery?"

"One look at you in that dress, and they'd totally understand. Hell, any guy in the place would've done the same thing."

"While I shudder at the thought of compromising the integrity of Oregon's law enforcement community, I believe I'll take that as a compliment."

"Good. Because that's precisely how I meant it." When she would have lifted her glass to her lips, he caught her wrist. "I think a toast is in order."

"That's a lovely idea. What did you have in mind?"

What did he have in mind? How about her naked, rolling around that king sized bed that was taking up half the room? Or in the shower, surrounded by steam, with warm water streaming over that perfumed porcelain flesh.

Against the wall.

On the floor.

And that was just for starters.

He blew out a long breath. "To us. And this weekend together."

"To us," she agreed, lifting her glass. There was a faint chime as the rims of the flutes touched. Looking into her lovely eyes, he could see visions of his own sexual fantasies reflected back at him. "And the weekend together."

"And finally alone," Cooper said. "With the exception of the crowd downstairs in the banquet room."

As they stood there, neither moving toward the door, a burst of fiery hormones zinged back and forth between them.

"Speaking of all those people waiting for the guest of honor, I suppose we'd better get going," she said, that unfamiliar siren's voice suggesting that she was no more eager than he was to leave this room.

She took a sip. When the sight of the crescent imprint on the rim of her glass had him imagining those siren red lips on the aching hard-on he needed to get under control before they got downstairs, Cooper tossed back his own champagne and decided that if they didn't leave now, they probably never would.

34

THE NEXT TWO hours flew by in a blur. Rachel was vaguely aware of meeting a number of individuals, including the governor and a state senator, all of whom had nothing but praise for Cooper. The inn's banquet room was lovely and the autumnal bouquets on the tables were as beautifully arranged as any she'd seen back home.

No. River's Bend was her home. Its people becoming as close, some even closer, than those she'd left behind.

In the past, whenever she'd attend a catered event, she paid close attention to every detail. But tonight, although the meal catered by Chef Madeline Chaffee's Lavender Hill Farm restaurant was excellent, Rachel could have been eating cold franks and burned beans for all she noticed.

All her attention kept drifting toward Cooper. On the way the lines fanned out from his green eyes and the appealing creases that deepened in his cheeks when he smiled at her. And on the gold dusting of hair on his tanned wrists beneath the starched white cuffs of his shirt as he tasted the decadently rich salted caramel sauce that had been spooned over the apple tart served for desert.

Rachel was thinking how much she'd like to scoop him up with a spoon when a familiar, dark-haired woman wearing a tall white hat appeared at their table.

"Well, if it isn't everyone's favorite superhero." When Cooper stood up, Chef Madeline Chaffee greeted him with a hug.

"I'm neither super nor a hero," he insisted.

She patted his cheek. "You can keep saying that, but no one who knows you will ever believe it. Especially all these people who've shown up to watch you receive your award."

She backed away, just a bit, and shared a warm smile with Rachel's dinner companions. "I hope you all enjoyed your dinner."

As everyone around her was quick to assure the celebrity chef that it was the best meal they'd ever had, Rachel was momentarily tongue-tied. Not only had the chef been the star of two popular Cooking Network food shows, Rachel had bought all her cookbooks and made every dish in them. The chef branded cookware was one of the few things she'd brought to Oregon with her from her former life. The woman was, to Rachel, what Julia Child had been to previous generations of eager cooks.

"So," Chef Madeline said, turning toward Rachel. "You're the new owner of the New Chance. I heard about the fire. What a terrible thing to have happen."

"Actually, it turned out to be an advantage," Rachel shared what she'd already decided. "The café was definitely in need of remodeling; this just allowed me to get it right."

"Dan tells me it's looking great. I visit River's Bend two or three times a year. I'll have to drop in next time."

"I'd love to have you visit." Though the idea of cooking for this culinary icon was more than a little intimidating.

"Terrific. Maybe we could cook together. If you don't mind sharing your kitchen with another chef."

"Having had a catering business back east hardly qualifies me as a chef."

"Never knock catering," Chef Madeline said easily. "It was a chance meeting with a Today show producer at a baby shower luncheon I catered that led to my having my first show."

"I know. I attended that luncheon."

"Seriously?"

"Seriously. Not only were the flavors of your lobster salad amazingly layered, it was exquisitely presented. I hope you don't mind, but I've served it myself with a couple small tweaks."

"Talk about your small worlds, and of course you should make it your own." The chef's smile was quick, warm, and genuine. "I've set up a cooking school at my grandmother's herb farm. Perhaps, once the New Chance gets up and running, you'd be willing to come up to the coast again and give a demonstration."

"I'd love to." Rachel's mind flashed into warp speed as she considered what she could possibly create to live up to her idol.

"Terrific. I'll give you a call after the first of the year, and we'll set up a time." Chef Madeline swept another warm smile over everyone before moving on to the other tables.

Later, after the awards ceremony, feeling as if she were back in high school, dancing with the prom king, Rachel swayed with Cooper to a slow, sexy ballad.

"I'm having a wonderful time," she murmured, linking her fingers together behind his neck.

"I'm glad. I hope you weren't too bored by the speeches."

"Of course not." Feeling as if they were in their own private bubble, Rachel brushed the back of his neck with her fingertips. "In fact, I'm flattered."

"Flattered?" Cooper nuzzled that erogenous zone he'd discovered behind her ear.

"To be in the company of Oregon's Lawman of the Year."

"It's no big deal."

She tilted her head back to look up at him. "Only you would consider being a hero no big deal."

"Heroes come and go. And it's a term people throw around too loosely."

"You saved a mother and two small children. They probably wouldn't be alive if it weren't for you."

He shrugged, clearly uncomfortable. "It was a lucky accident. I didn't even realize they were being held hostage by that guy until I stopped the SUV for speeding."

"But when you realized what was going on, you rescued them."

"Any officer in this room tonight would've done the same thing, Rachel. It's part—"

"Don't you dare say it." She pressed her fingers against his lips. "Not tonight." She rested her head on his shoulder, sighing happily as she pressed her body closer against his. "Now I know how Lois Lane would've felt out on a date with Superman."

She felt his muffled laugh. "Just don't get your hopes

up too high. Because I can't leap tall buildings in a single bound."

"There aren't any tall buildings in River's Bend. And even if there were, I certainly wouldn't expect you to."

"And I'm not stronger than a locomotive." His broad, long-fingered hands were on her hips, warming the silk and her skin beneath. Rachel ached to feel them on her body. Everywhere.

"Who is?" They fit together like two perfect pieces of a puzzle. The image of them fitting together equally well in bed caused her blood to spike.

"And I'm definitely not faster than a speeding bullet." His deep, husky voice promised slow, hot sex and had her afraid any response she might make would come out sounding as if she'd been inhaling helium.

"Believe me, Cooper." Okay, maybe not helium, but her voice was definitely more breathless than those times when they were discussing Sheetrock and plumbing. "You've no idea how pleased I am to hear that."

He pressed her against an impressive erection that felt pretty super to her. "What would you say to moving this party upstairs?"

Rachel went up on her toes and pressed a kiss against his lips. "Sheriff, I thought you'd never ask."

35

THE ELEVATOR WAS filled with a contingent of police chiefs and their wives, but Cooper and Rachel were aware of only one another. When he stroked the soft skin at the inside of her wrist, her pulse hummed. When he smiled down at her, a hot wicked grin rife with sexual intent, her blood warmed.

As soon as they exited onto their floor, he swept her up in his arms and carried her down the carpeted hall.

"Cooper," she hissed, looking around, concerned they might not be alone. "Put me down."

"In a minute," he said easily. "There's no one else here. Besides, you wouldn't deny me a Superman fantasy moment, would you? On the night I was named Oregon's Lawman of the Year?"

"I thought that didn't matter to you."

"It doesn't." He managed to balance her while opening the door to her room. "But since it seems to matter to you, I figured I might as well throw it out there."

Despite feeling like an entire New Years' Eve fireworks display about to go off, Rachel laughed.

"You don't need it," she said as he carried her across the room then stood her up next to the bed, which housekeeping had already turned down. The radio had been tuned to an easy listening station and the drapes were drawn.

"We do have one slight problem," he said after throwing his suit jacket onto a nearby chair. While Enya crooned about trains and winter rains, he began taking the pins out of her hair.

"Oh?"

"How the hell do I get that dress off you?"

Her soft laugh came out on a purr. "There's a hidden zipper in the back."

"Thank God. I spent half the evening wondering if I was going to have to peel it off you." Cooper nibbled lightly on her earlobe and put his hands on her hips as she slowly turned around.

Her exposed back gleamed like alabaster. No, alabaster was too cold. Too hard. "I've been going crazy wanting to do this all night," he said.

He felt her breath hitch as his mouth brushed over the nape of her neck, then glided down the delicate bones of her spine to where the warm satin of her flesh gave way to black silk. And back up again.

Although his body was urging him to drag her down onto that inviting white bed and ravish her like a wild man, Cooper was determined to take his time. To do this right.

As he continued to seduce her with his mouth alone, he tried to ignore the fact that his damn knees were shaking the same way they had the day he'd almost passed out while locking them too hard at his Marine Corps graduation.

"You stagger me, Rachel Hathaway."

His tongue gathered into the perfumed warmth of her

skin. When he found the hidden zipper and lowered it. When he pressed a trail of kisses down to the bared small of her back, then lower still, soft, ragged sounds of pleasure escaped her parted lips.

This was how Cooper wanted Rachel. Warm, pliant, holding nothing back. If only for tonight.

Once they'd returned to River's Bend, she could return to the brisk, efficient restaurateur, rebuilding her life the way she was renovating a century-old building.

But for now, for this single night, he wanted to know that he could make her as crazy as she'd made him. Maintaining a rigid self-restraint that had been drilled into him in the Corps, and had served him well in law enforcement, he took his time.

When he lifted her hair and lightly nipped her neck, she trembled from the thrill.

"Cooper." God, he loved hearing her say his name. Especially now, with her voice all breathy, brimming with need. "Please . . . I need you."

"There's no schedule tonight." Turning her in his arms, he looked down to see his own unbridled passion mirrored in her eyes, which were gleaming like sun shining through rain. "No clock. No need to hurry."

Buying his hands deep in that flowing black hair, he cradled her head as he pulled her tighter against him and took her mouth, lingering over the kiss even as his body turned hot. Hard.

Patience.

Finally, without a word, he slipped the dress off her body, where it pooled at her feet, leaving her standing there in those come-and-take-me-big-boy stilettos, a black lace bra that plunged to her waist in back, matching panties, and those gleaming pearls. None of which she could have possibly bought in River's Bend. But Cooper wasn't going to think about the world of difference between them right now. What he was going to concentrate on was what they had in common.

He wanted her.

She wanted him.

And for tonight, that would be enough.

As he watched the color rise on her skin behind his stroking touch, a thought popped into his head. "My grandmother grows roses."

"Oh?" He suspected she was wondering what kind of man would bring up his grandmother at a time like this. Wondering the same damn thing himself, he nevertheless forged on.

"There's this one . . ."

He unhooked the bra, letting it drop to the carpeting as he cupped her breasts with his hands. And fought for control as hunger spiked.

"I don't remember the name, but the outer petals are a soft cream color." She drew in a sharp breath when he flicked a thumb across her nipple and nearly swallowed his tongue as he watched it darken and pebble. "In the very center, there's a soft blush of pink. Which is what your breasts reminds me of."

The pretty flush deepened as he insinuated his knee between her legs, brushing against that other center in a way that sent a tremor through her and had her holding onto his shoulder for balance.

"My head's spinning," she said breathlessly.

Don't feel like the Lone Ranger. Cooper was on the verge of premature blast off. Houston, we have a problem.

"Maybe you'd better lie down," he suggested in a rough, gravely voice.

"Maybe I should," she agreed. "But first, you're wearing too many clothes."

Since it was his numbnuts idea to take this first time slow, though Cooper's choice would've been to rip the damn shirt off himself, he forced himself to stand there as she unfastened the buttons. One by one. Which seemed to take an eternity.

"I knew it," she murmured.

"What?"

"That you'd be hard." His body jolted as she ran her exploring hands down his chest, over his abdomen. "And beautiful."

"Guys aren't beautiful."

"You are." When she pulled his black leather belt away and unbuttoned his pants, Cooper heard the nearby sea roaring in his ears. "When you walked out of the New Chance, you literally took my breath away."

He caught her hands as they moved to his zipper.

Patience.

Although it was the hardest thing he'd ever done, even harder than humping up Afghan mountains with a full pack on his back, Cooper continued to slow the pace, even when she would've speeded things up.

They undressed each other as their lips met and clung. Then separated. Then came together again. And again.

Finally, as they lay facing each other on the bed, Rachel's hands skimmed the planes and hollows of Cooper's body, her fingers tracing muscles that contracted under her exploring touch. In turn, Cooper's hands moved over her, caressing, claiming, drawing out a warm, smoldering pleasure that caused her breathing to grow heavy.

Her soft whimpers, when his teeth tugged at the rosy crest of her breasts, caused heat in his loins, but wanting to make this good for her, still even after he'd helmeted up with one of the condoms he'd bought specifically for this weekend, Cooper refused to rush.

"I love the way you feel in my arms." He lifted his head to give her a long, heartfelt look. "I love the way you feel in my arms. I love touching you here . . ." He cupped her breasts, kissed them, and nipped the taut nipples.

Gasping out soft little cries that had him throbbing, she arched her back off the mattress and reached for him. Knowing that if she touched him, she'd finish him off here and now, Cooper captured both her wrists and held them above her head. Even as she whimpered a complaint against his mouth, he felt her surrender.

Something he'd already determined she did not do often.

"And here . . ." He pressed his palm against her stomach, causing her to draw in a sharp breath before he moved lower. "And especially here . . ."

Rachel's mind was tumbling like a shell caught in the surf when Cooper spread her thighs wide and, oh, God, kissed her. She was so hot, so ready, that all it took was one quick stroke of his wildly wicked tongue to send her over the edge.

She was still trembling as he lifted his head. Although his expression was as serious as she'd ever seen it, there was a cocky male satisfaction in his deep green eyes.

"Stop gloating," she managed on a breathless laugh. Determine to shatter his rigid control once and for all, she took hold of him, shifted so she could wrap her legs around his waist and lifted her hips, taking him in.

Finally!

With a deep, guttural groan, he surged into her, fully, deeply, claiming her body as she'd begun to fear he'd already claimed her heart.

But that wasn't what tonight was about. Tonight was about living in the now. Which was glorious.

They held nothing back as they moved together. Sweat-slick flesh slapped against flesh, blood flowed hotly to where they were joined, storm waves built with each deep thrust until the powerful tsunami swept over them, engulfing them both.

Rachel had given herself to him, openly, eagerly. And, whether she was ready to admit it or not, she was his. All his.

Cooper's fingers played idly with the dark hair splayed across his damn chest. His body was satiated—for the time being—but his mind was not. Until tonight, while he'd given up meaningless sex, he'd forgotten the vast difference between having sex and making love.

Watching Rachel shatter in his arms the same way he had in hers, only confirmed what Cooper had admitted to his brother.

He loved her and wanted, more than anything, to shout that love from the rooftops.

The only problem with that idea, he considered as he brushed the hair away from her forehead and pressed a light kiss against her temple, was that Rachel wasn't ready for such a declaration. He'd just have to wait until after her Christmas opening. Which wasn't his first choice.

Still, there was a lot to be said for a midnight New Year's Eve proposal. Wouldn't that make for a story to tell their grandkids someday?

Latching on to that vastly appealing idea, Cooper wrapped her in his arms and drifted off to sleep.

36

RACHEL WAS FLOATING in a misty morning realm somewhere between sleep and awakening. Her body ached, not unpleasantly, bringing back erotic memories of waking up during the night to make love with Cooper again. And yet again, with a renewed passion that had the power to excite, even now.

Snuggling deeper into her pillow, she rolled over and reached for Cooper, her lazy feeling of pleasure disintegrating the moment she encountered empty space. Had he gone back to his room, taking that emotional distance she'd once thought she'd need herself?

But she'd only been wary of facing the dreaded morning after before coming here to Shelter Bay with him. After all they'd shared, the tender caresses, the murmured endearments, the absolute intimacy, surely last night hadn't been solely about sex?

Not that there was anything necessarily wrong with sex, she could practically hear Janet's brisk voice in her head. After all, she'd been attracted to Cooper from the beginning. What woman wouldn't be? He was a handsome, intelligent, virile, sexually compelling male. It wasn't surprising that after all the time they'd been spending together she'd end up in bed with the man.

As long as she managed to keep things in their proper perspective, remembering that what they'd shared had been merely highly enjoyable—okay, mind-blowing—recreational sex, everything would be all right.

Rachel was still trying to convince herself of that when Cooper walked in the door, carrying a breakfast tray and looking like every woman's hot, forbidden fantasy.

"I was hoping to get back before you woke up," he greeted her.

"I thought you'd left," she admitted with an honestly that would have proven difficult even yesterday.

"I called room service, but since we had more important things on our minds than putting out our order last night, they said it'd be a forty-five minute wait. Since I'm useless until after my second cup of coffee, I decided to go down and fetch breakfast myself."

His chestnut hair was tousled, as if he'd combed it by running those fingers that had driven her so insane last night through it. He was wearing a tight gray T-shirt, jeans, and those cowboy boots that gave him a mouth-watering male swagger.

Rachel tried to tell herself that it was chemistry that had her practically melting into the sheets.

But then, damn, he smiled at her—a slow grin gilded with intimate promise and sensual memories—and she knew she was sunk.

"Scott says you're not usually much of a breakfast eater, so I brought some yogurt, melon, and muffins," he said, his gaze on hers. "The server assured me that the muffins are made with fresh blueberries."

"I love blueberry muffins."

"I was hoping you did. But, just in case, I also got a couple of croissants."

They might be talking about breakfast, but Rachel's pulse quickened when his eyes turned darkly seductive. "Sounds like a veritable feast."

"I'm glad you approve."

As something warm and insistent curled through her, Rachel wondered if it were possible to turn into a nymphomaniac overnight. She didn't want muffins. What she wanted was Cooper. Hot. Naked. Now.

"Oh, I definitely approve Sheriff," she purred in a way in a way she hadn't even realized she had in her until he'd unleashed her hidden siren. She slowly, suggestively, drank him in, from his head down to the toes of those boots. "Of everything."

Setting the tray on the table, he came over to the bed to look down at her. "Exactly how hungry are you?"

"Do you have to ask?"

The mattress sighed as he sat down next to her and pulled off his boots.

"Confession time. I haven't been able to get you out of my mind since you first showed up at the New Chance, Rachel Hathaway." He skimmed his wickedly clever fingers over her face.

"It's the same for me," she admitted breathlessly. Her hands fisted in his T-shirt as she urged him down to her.

Needing no second invitation, Cooper went willingly.

37

"**Y**OU WERE WRONG."

Having retrieved the breakfast tray from the table, Cooper was stretched out on the bed, busily spreading butter onto his muffin. "About what?"

"About being useless until after your second cup of coffee."

He grinned. "Yeah. We should've high-fived. Or fist bumped."

She laughed. "At least." Her cheeks warmed at the memory. "You were amazing."

"I didn't do it myself."

True. She'd practically attacked him, riding him hard and fast to the finish line. "So," she said, brushing croissant crumbs from the sheet, "What's the plan for today?"

"I thought we'd have a leisurely breakfast in bed, drive along the coast for a while, have lunch at the Sea Mist restaurant overlooking the bay, and play the rest of the day by ear. How does that sound?"

What it sounded was wonderful even as she felt that now familiar spike of work-related anxiety.

No. She wasn't going to think about the New Chance.

At least not this weekend.

She was so close to the finish line. The wiring was done, the walls painted, and the wood floor had been buffed and sealed. Jake had finished the fireplace and not a pipe in the building leaked.

Mitzi's decorator friend, who'd insisted on working at cost, was delivering the recovered booths and chairs next week. Unless something totally unexpected happened, Cooper's promise that the New Chance would open by Christmas would turn out to be true.

"Perhaps we could drop into one of those galleries I saw across from the harbor," she suggested. "I still need paintings."

"I can take care of those."

"You?"

"Yes, me. How'd you like a couple Gideon Bond originals?"

Gideon Bond was a former professional bull rider turned western painter who'd hit the big time when designers discovered "Cowboy Highstyle" and started putting cowhide rugs on New York City apartment floors. Rachel had attended one of his showings at a SoHo gallery that had been one of Alan's clients.

The painter's scenery and ability to capture his cowboy and Native American roots had been exceptional, which had resulted in the prices of his work shooting sky-high.

"You know my budget. I could never afford a Gideon Bond original."

"What if I told you that he'd be willing to donate a painting? And let you hang some other canvases on the walls until they're sold?"

"You can't be serious."

"As a heart attack."

His smug, self-satisfied look had her narrowing her eyes. "Why would a famous artist give a painting to a woman he doesn't even know?" Okay, so they'd exchanged a few words, but there had been so many people crowded into the gallery that night, she doubted he'd remember her.

"Simple. I vouched for you."

"You know Gideon Bond?"

"Yeah. He lives in River's Bend."

"How did I not know that?" Rachel would have bet the deed to the New Chance that nothing in this town stayed secret.

"Gideon likes his privacy and people like Gideon, so gossip about him is pretty much off limits. But his family has a ranch here and he and I grew up together. He's gotten a lot more prolific since he quit traveling the bull riding circuit, but because he limits his shows to just a couple a year, he has a bunch of work stacked out at his place. You need paintings and he needs a place to store them."

"That print above your fireplace," she said as she thought back on that evening at his home. "That's an original?"

"A housewarming gift," he confirmed.

Rachel couldn't believe her good fortune. Not only was she thrilled to have such expressive work to display, just having the reclusive artist's paintings at the New Chance was bound to garner publicity.

"Thank you." Deeply moved by his gesture, she lifted her lips to his.

And then they were kissing again, and his body was on top of hers and her bare legs were wrapped around his and it was glorious.

38

AFTER RETURNING HOME from their weekend, which had turned out to be even more relaxing and special than Cooper had promised, they continued working nights at the café, after which they'd returned to Rachel's bungalow to make quiet, clandestine love while her son slept unawares in his own room across the hall.

She'd also discovered the wonders of quickies—in the new, empty cooler while the others were away for lunch, the bathroom at the house while Scott was over at Warren's playing video games and even in the backseat of the Jeep parked on a bluff overlooking the river on their way to pick up Scott, who'd begun taking horseback riding lessons from Dan.

One day at a time.

Sticking to the agreement she'd made with Cooper, their relationship remained sexually satisfying and emotionally unthreatening. So why, Rachel wondered as she watched him drive away in the pre-dawn hours to ensure he'd be gone before Scott woke up, did she suddenly feel sad?

One Sunday morning, after kissing Cooper goodbye,

she'd put on her flannel pajamas and returned to a cold and lonely bed only to be abruptly awakened some time later by Scott leaping onto the mattress. "Hey, Mom! Guess what?"

"Mmmmh." She rolled over and burrowed her face into the pillow.

Scott was not easily deterred. "It snowed last night."

"Good for it." She smelled coffee and decided she must still be dreaming.

"So let's go sledding. Like we used to."

She squeezed her eyes tightly shut, fighting against the rising awareness. "We don't have a sled."

"Cooper brought one over. He says he knows this really cool hill where he used to go when he was a kid."

"I've been known to go down it as a grownup," offered the unmistakable male voice.

Rachel's eyes flew open, and she sat up as Cooper walked into the bedroom.

"What are you doing here?"

"I'm bringing you your morning coffee," he said as he handed her the earthenware mug. "And Scott the sled."

"Well, that was certainly thoughtful of you." As she blew on the coffee to cool it, Scott appeared on the verge of exploding with anticipation. "Did you thank Cooper?"

"Sure. Well, can we?"

"Can we what?"

"Go sledding."

The coffee was rich, strong, and every bit as good as any she would have made.

"You should see all the snow, Mom! It's perfect!"

His tone was perilously close to a whine. He was dressed in his NFL pajamas, the cowboy hat perched on his head.

Rachel was in no mood to argue. Especially when she remembered her own youthful excitement at the first snow of the season. "All right. You can go."

"I told you she'd let me," Scott said to Cooper as he flung his arms around Rachel's neck. Coffee sloshed over the rim of the mug. "You're the greatest mom in the whole world!"

He was gone in a flash. A moment later she heard him rummaging in his closet as he searched out his snow clothing while Rachel began dabbing ineffectually at the coffee stains on the down comforter with a tissue.

Disappearing into the bathroom, Cooper returned with a dampened hand towel. "Here. Try this."

"Thanks." Rachel took the towel and continued her efforts. "Bringing Scott that sled and taking him out is very thoughtful."

"I'm looking forward to it. But we're not going alone."

"I can't go with you."

"Of course you can."

"The café—"

"Will still be there in a couple hours."

As she rubbed at her temple, where a headache threatened, he sat down on the bed and put his arm around her. "How long has it been since you've played in the snow?" he asked, nuzzling her neck. "Remember sledding, snowball fights, making snow angels? Tell me that doesn't sound the least bit appealing and I'll leave with Scott. Though I'd bet he'd have a lot more fun with his mom along."

Her flesh warmed where his lips touched, her heartbeat quickened as he nibbled lightly, possessively on her earlobe. Rachel closed her eyes and allowed herself to be tempted. "Why can't I ever say no to you?"

"You told me no this morning," Cooper reminded her. "When I wanted to stay in this bed." He trailed his lips up her cheek. "With you."

His fingers were stroking the base of her neck while his lips had moved on to create exquisite sensations at her temple.

"I didn't want to give Mrs. MacGregor any more grist for her gossip mill."

Personally, Cooper didn't give a damn about Mrs. MacGregor or her gossip mill.

But Rachel did. And that made all the difference.

"I know. That's the only reason I left." And had driven home in a blinding snowstorm at five this morning.

Rachel leaned against his chest, relaxing in the circle of his arms. "You were angry," she murmured.

"More frustrated." He kissed her hair, breathing in the scent of flowers. "But yeah, I was a little pissed. I didn't realize it showed."

"It did." For anyone who knew him as well as she'd come to. Rachel lifted her hand to his cheek. "But you came back."

Did she honestly believe he had any choice? "I came back." Cooper turned his head, burying his lips in her palm.

When his teeth closed on the fleshy part of her hand, Rachel gasped, almost spilling the rest of the cooling coffee. Taking the mug from her, Cooper put it on the table. Then gathered her more closely into his arms and gave her a deep, draining kiss.

"Hey, Mom."

At the sudden interruption, Rachel froze. Then struggling against Cooper's light hold, she tried to break away. But he refused to let her.

"Your mother's busy right now," he said over the top of her head.

"Yeah, I can see that," Scott responded. "But this is an emergency."

Rachel pushed against his chest. "Cooper . . ."

"Let me handle this," he told her. "What kind of emergency?" he asked Scott. "And it had better be good."

Scott considered Cooper's warning for a moment. "I guess it could wait," he decided. Cooper nodded approvingly. "That's more like it. Your mom will meet you in the kitchen in a few minutes, ready for a snow day of fun and frivolity."

"Okay." Scott turned in the doorway. "When you're finished with that mushy stuff, could you ask her if she knows where my boots are?

Cooper grinned. "I'll try to remember to bring it up," he promised.

39

SWATHED IN SNOW, River's Bend looked like an idyllic scene from a Currier and Ives print. The temperature had dropped dramatically during the night. Icicles hung like crystal ornaments from shaggy, snow-coated evergreens while lacy snowflakes danced on intermittent swirls of wind.

"I'd forgotten how much I enjoy winter," Rachel murmured as she and Cooper walked hand in hand toward the hill outside of town. Scott had run on ahead, dragging the sled behind him, accompanied by Hummer, who was happily plowing through drifts of snow. "It makes everything look so magical."

"If you overlook the brown slush that it'll turn into," Cooper said. "Not to mention road closures and chains, stranded tourists who have absolutely no idea how to drive in the stuff and have to be pulled out of drifts, and—"

"Hey." Rachel punched him lightly on his upper arm. "After dragging me out here, don't you dare spoil my fantasy with reality."

"I wouldn't dream of it."

Rachel smiled her approval. "That's better."

Cooper looked down at her. Her cheeks were already rosy, her laughing eyes as bright as diamonds. "Speaking of fantasies." Pulling her into a grove of pine trees, he framed her face in his gloved hands.

"Cooper." They were nearing the hill, and she could hear the gleeful shouts and laughter drifting on the crisp morning air. "Someone might see us."

Cooper doubted there was a person left in River's Bend who didn't know that the sheriff was keeping company with the widow Hathaway. "My sweet, lovely Rachel," he said patiently. "Don't you think everyone in the county has already figured out that I'm not spending all my spare time with you because you're in need of police protection?"

"We're friends."

"While I can always use another friend, our relationship is a helluva lot more intimate than just friendship."

She tried to move away only to find her escape impeded by a silver-white trunked aspen. "Even so, there's no reason to advertise that fact," she insisted. "And I'm not sure it was a good idea for Scott to see us together this morning."

Tired of skirting his way the barricades she continually set up, Cooper decided to crash through this one.

"If you're talking about me kissing his mother," he said, backing her against the trunk of the tree, "then he's just going to have to get used to it. Because I have every intention of kissing you whenever the opportunity presents itself."

To prove his intentions, Cooper covered her mouth with his. The kiss was hard, long, and wet and had her wrapping her arms around him as she returned his kiss with equal hunger.

The shouts and laughter of children echoed from the nearby hill, a blue jay scolded noisily from bare winter branches while dogs barked at fluffy-tailed squirrels who scampered to the tops of trees and chattered tauntingly back at them.

The woods were alive with joyful winter sounds, but Cooper and Rachel remained oblivious to them as he dragged her from the icy wonderland into a world of dazzling flames and dense smoke.

Much, much later he lifted his head. "Do you have any idea how much I want to drag you into the nearest snowdrift and have my wicked way with you?"

"In a snowdrift?" Her fingers were still linked behind his neck; Cooper was in no hurry to have her remove them. "People keep telling me that you Murphys are crazy. Perhaps they're right."

"Perhaps." He smiled as he skimmed his lips up her cheek. "This Murphy is definitely crazy about you."

"Still, wouldn't a snowdrift be awfully cold? And wet?"

He loved her rock solid practicality, which he suspected came from her Iowa farm roots, as much as he loved everything else about the woman. "A bed, then. A feather bed with thick, fluffy comforters and satin sheets."

"I've heard satin sheets are slippery."

"Maybe we should try them out. Like a scientific experiment." His mouth returned to hers. "Or, I've got a better idea."

"Oh?" She tilted her head, her lips plucking at his.

"On a fur rug, in front of a blazing fire, your ivory skin gleaming in the dancing glow of the flames."

"I don't have a fireplace."

"No problem. I do, remember?"

"Ah, but you don't have a fur rug."

"It just so happens Mitzi gave me a fake cheetah stadium blanket for my last birthday. Though she said animal prints are in, I stuck it in the back of a closet. But I can bring it out if you'd like to give it a try."

Rachel tilted her head as she considered that idea. He could see the temptation warming in her eyes. "I suppose, if we both used our imaginations, it might suffice."

Cooper's gaze held hers for several long, pulsating seconds. "Tonight."

Her exhaled breath formed a frosty ghost between them. "Tonight," she agreed. He hoped her breathlessness was as much from anticipation as the fact that it was getting cold enough to freeze his nuts off.

Tonight. Only twelve, maybe thirteen hours away. As he took her hand in his and began walking toward the hill again, Cooper wondered how he was going to wait.

40

S HE WAS HAVING an affair. Which shouldn't be that big of a deal. People did, after all, have affairs all the time, probably since the beginning of time. And Rachel was honestly loving every moment she and Cooper spent together. Not just the sex, but the snow day and working together at the New Chance, and something as simple as sharing a cup of cocoa in front of the fire after Scott had gone to bed.

Life was good. Scott was happy and loving his new school, her restaurant was nearly ready to open, she was making friends, including Layla, Austin and Jenna, who'd arrived with a gift certificate for a relaxation massage and mani-pedi they'd booked at a day spa in Klamath Falls for the day before the opening.

"Resistance is futile," Jenna insisted when Rachel protested she couldn't take the time. "It's not a full spa day. You'll only be away for a couple hours and think how much better things will go if you're all relaxed and spiffed up when you're greeting your first diners."

"And you really don't want to force me to lasso you and drag you there," Austin tacked on.

"Austin won the breakaway roping competition at last

Labor Day's Paulina Rodeo," Jenna said.

"There's nothing she can't rope," Layla said. "Including a runaway restaurant chef."

There was something to be said for looking her best, Rachel had considered. Especially if any of the press from all those releases Mitzi had sent out showed up.

So, adding in all that with a lover (and didn't she still warm at that word?) who had his own way of working out kinks from a long work day, why couldn't she just relax and stop looking ahead?

"Live in the now," she told herself as she dressed with more care than usual for a morning meeting with Gideon Bond. Knowing about her appointment with the artist, rather than returning for breakfast, he'd been doing since their weekend together in Shelter Bay, as Cooper left the bungalow before dawn, he told her he'd drop in around lunchtime to hear how things went.

Unfortunately, other than waking up in Cooper's arms, the day did not begin well.

The toaster seemed to have only two shades: black and blacker. She'd forgotten to buy milk, forcing Scott to eat his Cheerios dry, and the moaning noises coming from the heater made it sound as if something or someone was dying in the ductwork.

It was not, Rachel considered as she mopped up spilled orange juice, a propitious way to begin a new week.

"Are you going to marry Cooper?"

The question came from left field as Rachel scraped the worst of the char from the toast into the sink.

"What?"

Scott reached into the bright yellow box, pulling out a handful of the cereal that suddenly had Rachel thinking how she'd put Cheerios on the tray of his stroller on those rare Sundays she and Alan took him for walks in the woods behind the house.

"Of course not." The memory was bittersweet, but not painful as it once would have been. "Where on earth did you get that idea?"

"Mitzi's marrying Dan."

Rachel had given up trying to get her son to refer to Cooper's father as Mr. Murphy. Especially since Dan was no help by insisting formality had no place in River's Bend. "I know," she said. "And I'm very happy for them. But what does that have to do with Cooper and me?"

"Cooper says his dad's marrying Mitzi because they're in love." There was an obvious question in his tone.

"I'm sure that's the case." Rachel shot a pointed look at her watch. "Now, you really need to get moving." Most days he was able to walk, but adding to her challenging day, a storm had swept in off the mountain slopes and was blowing the snow sideways.

"Cooper's the same way with you."

The heater rattled ominously. With the forecast calling for more snow this afternoon, Rachel said a small, silent prayer that the ancient furnace wouldn't choose today, of all days, to die on her.

"What way?" she asked absently, wondering what appliance service calls cost in River's Bend.

"He kisses you like Dan kisses Mitzi," Scott explained. "So, are you going to get married?"

"No, we're not," Rachel said. "And if you don't hurry you're going to be late to school and I'll be late for my meeting with Gideon Bond." She was still amazed the artist was willing to let her hang his paintings, but when they'd spoken on the phone, he'd certainly sounded enthusiastic about the idea.

Scott was not to be so easily deterred. "But if Cooper loves you—"

"Cooper's feelings aren't up for discussion," Rachel said. "If you're finished with breakfast, gather up your boots and jacket."

Rachel shot her son her sternest, I'm-the-mom-and-I-said-so look and although he appeared inclined to argue further, he apparently thought better of it and left the kitchen. Minutes later, he'd returned, dressed for outdoors.

"Are you mad at me?"

Rachel sighed and went down on her knees and wrapped the red woolen scarf around his neck. "Me? Mad? Where did you get that idea?"

"Whenever I talk about you and Cooper you yell at me."

"I don't yell."

"Yes, you do. It's just kinda quiet yelling," Scott insisted.

"Perhaps I do," she admitted, feeling like the Grinch. "And I'm sorry."

A forgiving smile bloomed on his face. "That's okay, Mom. Cooper says everybody can have an off day once in a while."

Cooper again. There was no avoiding the man. "I suppose he's right."

"Sure he is. And he's real nice, too, huh, Mom?"

"Real nice," she agreed softly.

"Then you really do like him? At least a little bit?"

Having never believed in lying to her son, Rachel wasn't about to begin now. "I really do like him. A lot."

"If you like him a lot, and he likes you, then why don't you get married?"

"Scott . . ."

"Geez, look at the time!" Breaking free of her light embrace, he grabbed his books from the kitchen table. "We'd better get going or I'll get a tardy and have to stay after school."

He paused as he buckled up his seatbelt. "Would you at least think about marrying Cooper?"

"I've already told you—"

"Just think about it, okay, Mom?"

She was going to be late for her meeting and Scott was nearly late for school. Deciding this was not the time to continue arguing the matter, Rachel caved. For now. "Okay. I'll think about it."

Scott's answering grin could've lit up every Christmas tree in River's Bend through New Year's. "Sweet!"

Fortunately, her day picked up when Gideon Bond arrived at the café, looking even sexier than she remembered. Rachel decided if the rest of the country discovered that the appeal of western males wasn't some Hollywood movie exaggeration, they'd be flocking to River's Bend in droves.

"Cooper sang your praises," he said, as she gave him the tour, "but I had no idea of what an amazing transformation you've accomplished. Somehow you've managed to bring the place into this century without losing the appeal of its past."

"Coming from a painter who does exactly that on canvas, I'm flattered."

He waved off her statement with a wave of his dark, long fingered artist's hand that also bore scars she guessed were from his bull-riding days. "We're all creative in different ways. I hear your cooking is like edible art."

Even as the compliment warmed, she laughed. "Cooper sets a very low bar. The man considers sticking a pop tart in a toaster making breakfast."

They shared a laugh, then set about choosing the paintings from the portfolio he'd brought along. Two hours after he'd left, Rachel was having to pinch herself to believe that she could be so fortunate.

Pleased with how a day that had started so negatively could have turned around so well, she greeted Cooper with a huge smile as he walked into the restaurant. A smile that faded as she recognized the vertical lines between his brows. The brackets on either side of his lips were another sign that something had gone wrong.

"I've got to go back to Salem."

"Jake again?"

"Yeah. He left a message on Mel Skinner's voice mail, threatening to shoot him if he set a foot on his property. Not surprisingly, Mel's pressing charges of telephonic harassment."

"Do you think Jake would really do such a thing?"

"No. He's got a hot head, especially when he's drinking, but I've watched him get teary-eyed putting down a horse with a broken leg. He talks a tough game, but inside, he's a marshmallow.

"Plus, I confiscated all his guns when the situation began to get out of hand in September. The only weapons he currently owns are the ones he uses for the outlaw train ride. Still, he's got to learn that he can't go around threatening people. I've been telling him that the days of the Wild, Wild, West are long gone and River's Bend isn't

Dodge City, but it's not sinking in."

"Is leaving a threatening voice mail actually a crime?"

"It depends on the threat and the context. But threatening harm over a phone is definitely a Class B misdemeanor in Oregon."

"What's going to happen to him?"

"Under normal circumstances, he'd probably be hit with a stiff warning. Maybe community service. But given his recent behavior, and the fact that Skinner's a federal government employee, if you were the presiding judge, would you let him get away with a slap on the wrist?"

"No," Rachel answered, shaking her head sadly. "I suppose I wouldn't want to take the chance he might actually follow through on his threat."

"Exactly. There is one positive thing about this," Cooper said.

"What's that?"

"If he does get jail time, which I suspect he will, he'll still be locked up December twenty-third."

"The day the government auctions off his land."

"Unless something happens to stop them," Cooper confirmed.

"Do you think that's a possibility?"

"That's why I'm going back for one last try."

As Cooper kissed her goodbye and left for Salem, Rachel considered how Jake's very serious problems made her own remodeling frustrations seem trivial by comparison.

41

I T HAD BEEN THREE days and even longer nights since Cooper had left town in a last-ditch effort to extricate Jake Buchanan from his troubles with the government. Rachel missed him more and more with each passing day.

The good news was that the renovation on the New Chance was finally complete.

To Rachel's delight, River's Bend proved to be a treasure trove of artisans. People kept streaming in with pre-grand opening gifts—richly textured rugs woven on handmade looms, earthenware dishes thrown on potters' wheels in home studios and an intricately carved bear, an elk, and an antelope from Cooper's grandfather Mike.

Helen Masterson, from Masterson's Mercantile, brought a selection of woven baskets that were perfect for the lush green plants Cal Potter's wife, Lillian, had grown in her backyard greenhouse.

Along with the paintings Gideon Bond had loaned her, he'd created one especially for her, portraying the New Chance Café looking quaint and inviting with snow-capped Modoc Mountain looming in the background. Thankfully, he'd left off the cow. Steer.

Not wanting to be left out, artists from Klamath Falls, Lakeview, even Pendleton, up in the northeast corner of the state, offered paintings on consignment, which Rachel gladly accepted. By the time Rachel and Mitzi had hung them all, the formerly bare walls complemented Rachel's menu celebrating Oregon's western heritage.

Using her wide-ranging contacts, Mitzi had gotten the news of the café's re-opening published in the lifestyle and business sections of papers within the café's market area: the *River's Bend Register*, Klamath Falls *Herald and News*, Ashland's *Daily Tidings*, the *Lake County Examiner*, and the *Cascades Chronicle*. Even the popular statewide *Travel Oregon* magazine had highlighted the New Chance on its cover with an article chronicling both the café's colorful past and its revival.

The flood of reservations generated by the advance publicity would have warmed the heart of the most jaded New York restaurateur.

Although she'd had her doubts when she'd first seen the building, and her confidence had admittedly faltered from time to time, the New Chance had become a dream come true.

Everything was wonderful.

Perfect.

Except for one thing. Cooper wasn't here to share it with her.

Rachel sat alone in her empty café, drinking in the warm, inviting atmosphere as she studied the tan menu with the bold dark script that had been delivered from the Klamath Falls printer.

Tomorrow the truck from food wholesalers would begin to make their first deliveries. The next day she and the staff she'd been training would run through a trial service for friends. Invitations had gone out to Cooper, Ryan, Dan, Mitzi, Cal and Hal Potter and their wives, Fred and his wife, Hank Young, Layla, Jenna, Austin, Lu-LuBelle, and Mrs. MacGregor. Unfortunately, Jake was still in jail, but Rachel planned to send a meal back to the sheriff's office for him.

Then, finally, giving her time to make any necessary tweaks, two days after that, the New Chance would reopen.

Thinking back on the scene that had greeted her when she and Scott had arrived in town, it hardly seemed possible.

She was imagining her café filled with the hum of conversation, the rattle of cutlery, the aromas of hearty food wafting out of the kitchen, when Scott burst through the door.

"Hey, Mom! Guess what?"

"You got an A on your arithmetic test." They'd spent an hour last night unraveling the mysteries of long division.

"Nah. Well, that, too," he amended when she lifted a brow. "But this is something way cooler!" He was jumping up and down, looking as if he were about to burst.

"I give up."

"We're going to chop down a Christmas tree! Me and Cooper. And you, too," he tacked on as an afterthought.

"Cooper and I." So he was finally back. Rachel felt her heart quicken and wondered what it was about the man that had her behaving like a besotted, lovesick teenager.

"Yeah. All three of us," Scott agreed impatiently. "Cooper says he knows where the fattest, tallest, most perfect trees grow."

Rachel glanced outside. The light snow falling from a slate gray sky made the warm flames crackling in Jake's fireplace even more inviting. "I thought we'd buy a tree the way we do every year."

"In this part of the country, buying a tree when you can cut it yourself is viewed as heresy," Cooper said as he stomped snow off his boots on the tile floor of the entry.

Rachel felt something shift in her heart. He'd been gone three days. Seventy-two hours that had seemed like a lifetime. She was suddenly so very tired. Tired of trying to keep Cooper out of her thoughts. Out of her life.

Because she loved him. Truly. Madly. Deeply.

The revelation was thrilling. And terrifying.

Her legs were trembling as she stood up.

"It sounds wonderful. Just give me five minutes to pack a lunch for us to take along and I'll be ready."

Cooper had expected an argument. All the way back from Salem, he'd tried to think up an answer for every pale excuse Rachel might try to offer. That she acquiesced so quickly gave him hope that the rest of the day—and his carefully planned night—would go as well.

He looked down into that luminous face he hadn't been about to get out of his mind during those increasingly frustrating and lonely nights in Salem.

"Hey Scott," he said, not taking his eyes from Rachel's, "how about going out to the Jeep and keeping Hummer company while I help your mother fix lunch?"

Scott's answer proved that while he might be only nine years old, he was far from blind. "You're gonna kiss her, huh?"

"We're going to make sandwiches," Rachel answered

quickly.

"After I kiss your mother hello," Cooper corrected. "You see, sport, I've missed your mom while I was gone. Missed her a lot."

"Mom's missed you, too."

"Really?"

Rachel turned toward her son. "Scott—"

"Really," Scott insisted over her planned rebuke. "She yelled at me when I tracked mud into the house. And she was grumpy a lot and when I got up to go to the bathroom last night, she was watching television and crying. At three in the morning," he added significantly as he left the café.

Things were getting better and better, Cooper decided as he walked toward Rachel. "Crying?"

"I always cry when I watch Now, Voyager," she insisted.

"I'll accept that. My mom did, too. The question is, what were you doing watching old movies at three in the morning?" he asked as he continued moving toward her.

"I didn't have anything else to do."

"Ever try sleeping?"

"I couldn't." This time it was Rachel who moved closer. "You weren't there."

"Three days," he murmured. "But it seemed like freaking forever."

When she looked up at him, her emotions, no longer guarded, were in her eyes, on her smiling lips, in the trembling of her work-roughened hands as she framed his face between her palms.

"Forever," she agreed softly. "We'll have to make up for lost time."

Cooper ran his hands down her back, around her waist, over her hips as he pulled her even closer. "Lady, that's the best offer I've had all day."

He kissed her then, because it had been too long. "Tonight."

"Yes," she whispered against his mouth.

"I want to love you, Rachel. All night long."

"Yes."

"Until morning. After sunrise."

"Until morning." She smiled, her heart shining in her eyes. "Play your cards right, sheriff, and I'll even make you breakfast."

Cooper hadn't realized he'd been holding his breath, waiting for her answer, until he blew it out. "We'll make it together."

She wasn't agreeing to forever. It was, Cooper allowed as he kissed her again, slower, deeper, only one night. But it was enough.

For now.

Besides, if everything went as planned, by tomorrow morning, Rachel would be his.

Forever.

42

"I STILL CAN'T BELIEVE I hiked all over Modoc Mountain for a Christmas tree," Rachel complained several hours later.

"Not just any Christmas tree," Cooper corrected with a grin. "The best Christmas tree in the county."

"It's the best Christmas tree in the whole state," Scott insisted. "The whole country. Probably the best in the whole entire world!"

"I wouldn't doubt if for a minute," Cooper agreed.

"Well, all I know is that my feet turned blue hours ago, my nose is a block of ice and I can't even feel my ears."

Cooper looked over at her as he pulled up in front of her rental house. "I'm sorry. I didn't realize you were that uncomfortable. You should've said something, and we would've come home a long time ago."

The gentle concern in his gaze threatened to be her undoing. "It's not that bad. I was exaggerating."

"You'll probably feel better after a hot bath," he suggested.

"With bubbles," Scott said. "Mom likes bubble baths," he advised Cooper.

"Does she now?" Cooper's eyes were filled with wicked humor. It hadn't been that long ago that he and Rachel had heated up the water considerably in a bubble bath. Later, when he'd shown up at the office smelling like flowers, he'd taken some ribbing from Cal, but it had definitely been worth it.

Rachel felt the color rise in her chapped cheeks at the sensual memory. "A bath would be nice." Another bath with Cooper would be even better, but that would have to wait.

"Maybe you can wash her back, Cooper," Scott said helpfully. "Dad used to do that sometimes. It made her real happy."

A small pool of silence settled over them. Rachel, fearing that Cooper would resent the mention of Alan, pretended a sudden interest in a pair of neighborhood children's energetic effort to build a snowman.

"I'd like to make your mother happy," Cooper said. He kept his tone light, but Rachel could hear the wicked promise, along with a trace of laughter, in it as well.

"You do," she said softly.

Scott's gaze went from Rachel to Cooper, then back again. "Come on, Hummer," he said, tugging at the leash with one hand and opening the back door of the Jeep with the other. "Let's go help Warren and Jackie build that snowman."

"We'll be having dinner soon," Rachel warned.

Scott looked momentarily surprised. "But—"

"How about making it home by five-thirty," Cooper suggested. "That'll give you half an hour to finish up Frosty." He glanced over at Rachel. "Okay?"

For just an instant Rachel thought she detected something pass between Cooper and Scott. Something that seemed strangely like a secret shared. Then, deciding that she'd imagined it (she'd heard hypothermia caused delusions), she nodded.

"Five-thirty," she agreed.

HEAVEN. RACHEL LEANED back, luxuriating in the frothy bubbles, sipping on the Amaretto-laced coffee Cooper had prepared. The warm water soaked the chill out of her bones and the coffee spread a soothing warmth throughout her body, while Cooper's amazing gaze, as he leaned against the sink, looking down at her, created a slow, simmering heat all its own. A trio of fir and cinnamon scented candles added to the holiday mood she'd been too busy and distracted to enjoy until today's tree-hunting expedition.

"How did it really go in Salem?" she asked. When she'd brought it up earlier, Cooper had merely shrugged and said that things might not be as bad as they seemed.

"The situation may be looking up."

"I'm so glad." Putting the mug on the floor, she picked up the bath sponge and began soaping her arms.

Cooper knelt down beside the tub, took the sponge and ran it tantalizingly up her arm. "I finally found this woman, Karen Fairfield, in accounting, who's willing to dig a bit deeper into Jake's records."

"Do you think she'll be able to locate his missing payment?" Rachel asked as his slow, intimate touch warmed her blood.

"I sure as hell hope so." He squeezed the sponge, causing rivulets of warm, fragrant water to flow over her breasts. "Meanwhile, Cal tells me that the word has gone out about the foreclosure auction. There's not a rancher or farmer in the region will bid on Jake's land or any of his equipment."

Rachel wasn't as surprised by that as she would've been just a few months ago.

"Have I happened to mention that I love you?" he changed the topic with exaggerated casualness.

Cooper's quiet declaration should not have come as a surprise. Later Rachel would admit to herself that she'd been expecting it for days. Weeks.

At the moment, coming as it did out of a clear blue sky, it stunned.

She drew in a sharp breath. "Cooper . . ."

"No." Abandoning the bath sponge, he pressed his fingers against her lips. "It doesn't require an answer now, Rachel. I just wanted you to know." He leaned forward and caressed the side of her face with his fingertips. "After all, we've got all night to talk . . . and whatever."

He'd only touched her cheek, yet her heart felt as if it would burst out of her chest. "All night," she whispered, drowning in the depths of his gaze.

The sound of the screen door banging captured their unwilling attention. "I'd better get out there," Cooper said without enthusiasm.

Rachel nodded. "Yes."

"I could always tell him I was washing your back."

She loved the way he always seemed to be able to lighten a topic. But this was something that had concerned her and couldn't easily be teased away. "I'm sorry he brought up Alan."

"Hey, I've already told you that I've no problem with you having been married, Rachel. And since I hate the thought of you being unhappy, I'm glad your husband loved you. And that you loved him. Believe me, I know what a gift that is."

Although his expression had sobered, he grinned as they heard Scott banging around in the kitchen. "You're just going to have to get it through that hard head of yours, Rachel Hathaway, that I'm crazy about you. And that I'm also crazy about your kid."

With that he gave her a swift, brief kiss, then left the bathroom.

A moment later, Rachel heard Scott talking a mile a minute, something about Hummer and a snowball fight. When her son and Cooper shared a robust laugh, some small dark spot hidden deep inside her heart contracted.

Pressing her hand against her chest, Rachel wondered how something as wonderful as love could be so painful.

43

"YOU'RE JUST IN time," Cooper announced as Rachel entered the kitchen a few minutes later.

"In time for what?"

"Scott and I thought we'd take you out to dinner."

After spending the greater part of the day trudging through snow on Modoc Mountain's forested slopes, the idea of going back outside in a snowstorm was less than appealing. Especially when that drive meant going to Klamath Falls, which would be the nearest restaurant.

"Thanks guys," she said. "But I was planning on fixing something simple here. How does spaghetti Marinara sound?"

Cooper and Scott exchanged a brief look. Perhaps it was only her imagination, but Rachel thought her son's expression revealed a momentary panic. Cooper's expression was, as usual, calmly reassuring.

"It sounds great," he said. "But you'll have to save it for another time. Tonight's our treat."

Rachel didn't know whether it was Cooper's quiet insistence, or the fact that Scott seemed to be holding his breath, or that she was too tired to argue. Whatever, within minutes she found herself bundled into the front seat of the Jeep.

"Where are we going?"

"You'll see," Cooper said.

"It's a surprise," Scott added, doing that bouncing in his seat thing. At least as much as his seatbelt would allow.

Rachel was about to delve into this new mystery when Cooper pulled up in front of the New Chance. "What are we doing here?"

"I forgot something the other day," he said, cutting the ignition.

"What?"

Cooper didn't answer. Instead he said, "It may take me a few minutes to find it. So, why don't you and Scott come in with me so you won't freeze sitting out here?"

The snowstorm had picked up. Gusts of wind were blowing thick flakes against the windshield, making Rachel not eager to leave the warmth of the Jeep.

"That's okay. You can just leave the heater on."

"Sorry, but I can't do that."

"Why not?"

"I'm almost out of gas."

"You were going to drive out of town with an almost empty gas tank? In this weather?" That was not at all like him to be so careless.

"Come on, Mom," Scott complained. "We're wasting time and I'm starving!"

"All right." Rachel sighed. "But if I catch pneumonia after all my time running around in the snow today, you two are going to have to open the New Chance by yourselves."

"It's a deal," Cooper said.

"Totally," Scott agreed. "Cooper could make chili dogs. And I know how to cook frozen waffles in the toaster."

"Chili dogs and waffles. What a splendid Christmas menu," Rachel said dryly as she climbed down from the passenger seat. "I wonder why I didn't think of it?"

As she walked up to the building, Rachel experienced the now familiar burst of pride. It was really, truly hers. And she'd done it all by herself.

Well, not really by herself; everyone in town had helped out. But she'd been the driving force behind the renovation. She was the one who was now responsible for making a success of the restaurant, something she no longer had any doubts about doing.

In the beginning, after Alan's sudden death, faced with that mountain of debt, she'd acted on instinct, doing whatever was necessary to pay their many creditors. But the New Chance was something she'd planned. Something she'd worked hard for. Something she'd accomplished.

The run down, smoke-filled café in this small Southern Oregon town had given her a great deal more than a new chance. It had renewed her self-confidence. In fact, even as a sleety snow blasted her face, at this frozen moment in time, she felt downright invincible.

"Something funny?" Cooper asked.

Rachel glanced up at him. "Funny?"

"You were smiling."

"Was I?"

"Yep."

"You sure were, Mom," Scott agreed. "I saw you."

The smile she could now feel on her face widened. "I was thinking that I felt a bit like Wonder woman."

"Sounds good to me," Cooper said. As he followed her into the darkened restaurant, he leaned down and murmured in her ear. "You wouldn't happen to have the costume hidden away somewhere at home, would you?"

"Sorry," she said. "But that's another fantasy I'm not going to be able to fulfill."

"Don't worry." He took her hand, linking their fingers together. "You're all the fantasy I need."

Laughing, she turned on lights. Which was when the New Chance came to life with cheering people.

As her stunned gaze swept the room, Rachel guessed nearly everyone in town must be present. Grizzled Johnny Mott, New Chance's previous owner, was walking around, shaking his head in amazement, openly astounded by the transformation of the café he'd owned for so many decades. When she spotted Jake at the back of the room, Cooper assured her that he hadn't escaped, but had been released on temporary parole for the evening.

The restaurant was filled to its wide open rafters with colorful crepe-paper streamers and bright helium balloons. A *Good Luck!* banner hung over the hand-carved bar from an 1800s Gold Rush brothel Mitzi had unearthed in a Jacksonville antique shop, and the scents of pine and fir rose from the centerpieces gracing all the tables.

Rachel sank down onto a chair, staring blindly at an arrangement of pinecones, holly, and mistletoe branches. The holiday display blurred as tears welled up in her eyes and began to spill down her cheeks.

"I never imagined," she said. "All the time, you all were planning all this and I never knew."

"Speech!" Cal Potter shouted over the laughter and cheers. The idea spread, until everyone, including Scott, was calling for her to speak. When Cooper put his hands on her waist and lifted her up onto the bar, an expectant hush immediately fell over the café.

Taking a deep breath, Rachel scrubbed at her damp cheeks with the backs of her hands. For some reason, that gesture brought another long round of cheers and applause. She looked down at Cooper for encouragement, receiving it in the form of a reassuring wink.

"Only a few months ago," she began in a voice she wished were steadier, "my son Scott—" when she smiled over at him, he beamed back "—and I arrived in River's Bend. We were strangers, far away from home, and although I can't speak for Scott, I'll admit that I was scared to death. Especially when I found out that my long-awaited dream had nearly gone up in smoke."

An understanding murmur swept through the crowd. As Rachel looked down into the faces of those former strangers who'd become her friends, her nervousness drifted away.

"But Dan, Cal, Fred, and Cooper—" her gaze turned fond as it settled on each man in turn, lingering the longest on Cooper, "—assured me that River's Bend was a special place. A place where people care about one another. Where western hospitality isn't merely a cliché, but a way of life." Rachel smiled. "During these past months I've discovered they were telling the truth."

A new cheer arose as the group applauded themselves. The warmth of feeling in the room was palpable, and Rachel could feel the tears threatening again. "River's Bend is special because its people are so special," she said. "And I thank you all for allowing Scott and me to become part of your lives."

This time the cheers were deafening, lasting long after Cooper had helped Rachel down from the bar. He hadn't lied about taking her out to dinner. In the best tradition of a small-town potluck, everyone had brought a dish to contribute to the celebratory meal.

"Happy?" Cooper asked later that evening as they danced to the music of the River's Bend Volunteer Fire Department's country band.

The band, while enthusiastic, had a limited repertoire; they appeared to only know half a dozen tunes, a problem they got around by playing the songs over and over again. Dan's guitar broke its G string on a spirited rendition of *The Orange Blossom Special*; Cal Potter sang off key and Fred Wiley's foot-tapping consistently missed the beat. Rachel found them wonderful.

"Deliriously so." No longer caring what people might think about their relationship, she went up on her toes and lightly kissed Cooper. "This is definitely going to go down as one of the all-time best nights of my life."

Brushing her hair aside, Cooper skimmed his lips down her neck. "And just think," he said huskily, "the night's still young."

She looked up at him, drinking in the face of this very special man she'd fallen in love with. No words were spoken. None were needed.

44

THE SNOW HAD finally stopped falling. Moonlight streamed down from a midnight blue winter sky, lighting the bedroom with a silvery glow. Cooper had come to know Rachel's body well. His hands moved expertly over her, warming, pleasuring, kindling flashpoints.

His hands tempted; his lips seduced. His tongue, as it breached her parted lips, promised. The fragrance of her earlier bath oil mingled with the hot heady scent of desire. Her skin, gleaming with a pearly luminescence in the flickering light of the candles she'd lit, grew feverish, arousing them both.

Unable to remain passive while he was driving her mad, Rachel's touch grew greedy. The fluffy comforter slid unnoticed to the floor. The flower-sprigged sheets became hot as desire built, passion flared, needs escalated.

Like a man possessed, Cooper lost himself in the warm satin of her breasts. He buried his mouth in the heady fragrance of her neck, and when his exploring fingers dipped into her warm, slick moisture, raw desire tore through him, obliterating all but one thought: Mine.

He wanted to take her places she'd never been, uncover secrets she'd never imagined. The past vanished. The future dimmed. There was only now. Only Rachel.

Control disintegrated as the power swept them deeper and deeper into a hazy, smoldering world of their own making.

"DAMN," COOPER MURMURED much, much later, as Rachel, wrapped in his arms, still clung to him.

"Well, that's certainly romantic." She pressed her lips against his chest, making his vision, which had just begun to clear, blur again.

"Stop that," he groaned as her lips continued a downward trail. "How am I supposed to concentrate when you insist on seducing me?"

"Me? Seducing you?" When her tongue dipped into his navel, his body rebooted, coming instantly alive.

Although it wasn't his first choice, he wound her hair around his hand and lifted her head. "Don't play innocent with me, woman. If we keep this up, you're going to wear out my poor, abused body before I hit thirty-six."

Rachel sighed dramatically, braced her elbow on the mattress and cupped her chin in her palm. "I haven't heard you complaining. Until now."

Cooper ran his hand down her bare back, loving the way he could make her tremble beneath his touch. Even now. "It wasn't a complaint. It was just that your wild and wanton ways, which, for the record, I love, almost made me forget to give you your present."

"You bought me a present? Why?"

"Does there have to be a reason?"

"There usually is."

He shrugged. "Okay, I suppose we could call it a pre-grand opening present. Or an early Christmas present. Or a just-because present."

"Just because?"

"Just because I love you."

Apparently that wasn't the right choice because she sat up, pulling the sheet over her breasts, tucking them beneath her arms. The sudden sign of modesty after she'd been writhing beneath him only moments ago was not a good sign.

"Oh, Cooper . . ."

He pressed a finger against her lips. "Wait until you see what it is."

He felt her watching him as he left the bed and crossed the room to where his pants were draped over the arm of the wing chair. Although he'd never considered himself a coward, Cooper didn't watch her face as he pulled the square velvet box from his front pocket.

She took her time opening the box, reminding him of a demolitions guy he'd watched defuse an IED in Afghanistan. The tiny diamond solitaire was surrounded by a delicate white gold filigree setting.

"Oh, Cooper," she repeated on a soft sigh. "It's beautiful."

"It belonged to my great-grandmother Rose. Great-grandfather Niall sold his prize bull to get the money to buy it for his bride. Which, here in cattle country, contributed yet additional evidence to the Murphy's reputation for being crazy."

"Perhaps," she allowed. "But it was a wonderfully romantic gesture." She traced a fingertip over the lacey filigree. "Art-Deco was such an free-spirited period. Rose must have been a very liberated woman to wear such a modern style ring. Especially here in small town Oregon."

"All we Murphy men fall in love with spirited, liberated women." He watched her carefully. "After you told me about the antiques you used to collect and watching how excited you got about that banged-up old bar Mitzi found for the New Chance, I figured you preferred things with a history. A past."

"I do."

"That's why I thought you might like this."

"Oh, Cooper." This time her rippling sigh was filled with regret.

Cooper didn't need his cop detecting skills to know that wasn't a good sign. But along with calling the men in his family crazy, another thing people around these parts knew was that there was no quit woven into Murphy DNA. Which was why Cooper had no intention of giving up until she realized how good they were together.

"I love you, Rachel. And unless I've totally misread everything, you love me."

"I do."

It was only a whisper, but encouraged by the words he'd so wanted to hear, Cooper sat down on the edge of the bed and stroked her love-tousled hair.

"Then you'll marry me?"

Earlier, in the New Chance, her tears had been born of joy. The ones she was trying to blink away now were not. "I can't.

"Can't?" he asked quietly. "Or won't?"

"Does it really matter?"

Cooper tried to think calmly as he sought a way through this latest roadblock so they could salvage what was left of the night. It wasn't easy as pride warred with love, ego with need. For a moment, pride won out.

"I see."

When he would have backed away, Rachel grasped his arm, causing the velvet box to drop to the rumpled sheet.

"No, you don't understand," she insisted, her voice as strained as his.

"That's what I'm trying to do. What I've been trying to do from the beginning," he pointed out.

She took a deep breath that, dammit, since he was, after all, a guy, drew his attention momentarily to her breasts. Reminding himself that it would not only be totally wrong, but against the law to handcuff her to the bed and kiss her silly until she changed her mind, Cooper dragged his gaze back to hers and steeled himself against the pain he viewed in her damp eyes.

"I don't know where to begin," she said on a sad, trembling voice.

"Why don't you try at the beginning?" he suggested even he felt the punch to his gut.

His roughened tone had her suddenly studying him warily. *Cool move, Murphy.*

She dragged a trembling hand through her hair. "When I married Alan, I thought he was my Prince Charming. My knight in shining armor."

Although he could've done without the glowing description of her former husband right now, Cooper had accepted her feelings. "I thought we've already established that I don't have any problems with your having been in love with your husband," he reminded her.

"We did. And I appreciate that."

"Gee. Thanks."

He'd already determined that Rachel had her own fair share of pride. Which was why his regrettably sarcastic tone had her lifting her chin. "Do you want to hear this or not?"

"Do I have a choice?" Frustrated, he scrubbed his palms down his face. Patience. "Sorry. Please go on."

"I was brought up to believe in fairy tales. In happy endings."

"There's nothing wrong with believing in happy endings," he pointed out. "So long as you have a Plan B in case things don't work out exactly as planned."

"Don't you see?" Rachel dragged her hands through her hair again. "That's precisely what I'm talking about. I didn't have any plan. Because I left everything—every decision about my life, my son's life—to Alan.

"I was so thrilled to be his wife that I willingly gave up all my autonomy. I was totally unprepared to deal with the real world. It was as if, instead of living in the sunshine, the way I'd thought I'd been, I'd spent all those years in the dark, walking toward some unseen cliff.

"And when Alan died, leaving everything in ruins, I fell off that cliff and was left hanging from the edge by my fingertips."

"But you pulled yourself back up."

"Yes. But it wasn't easy and honestly, because of Scott, I didn't have a choice. Admittedly, once I got to River's Bend, I had a lot of help, which I'll always be grateful for. But I'm not sure I could do it again."

He wanted to assure her she wouldn't have to. But realized that at this moment, those words wouldn't mean a damn thing.

"You said you were young when you married."

She nodded. "Twenty-two."

"And Alan was what? Thirty? Thirty-three?" Rachel had mentioned that her husband had been older, but at the time Cooper hadn't grasped the significance of what she'd been trying to tell him.

"Thirty-nine."

Comprehension, when it finally dawned, allowed him to understood her continual insistence on independence, her almost obsessive drive to establish her own career, the frustrating way she'd struggled to keep him at arm's length.

"Hell, Rachel, that's nearly a twenty-year difference."

"Alan was good for me," she insisted. "For the girl I was."

"I believe that." Damn. Tears were beginning to silently flow. He ran his thumbs beneath her glistening eyes to wipe them away. "But you're not that vulnerable young woman any longer, honey. And what Alan never got to see, what he may have never thought to encourage, are some of the many things I love about you . . .

"Your strength, your drive, hell, even your stubbornness, which, at times, I have to admit, threatens to drive me up a wall. They're all part of who you are. Who you've become. I don't want to control your life, sweetheart. I'm only asking to share it."

"I know," she whispered.

Cooper decided that was a start. "Have I ever lied to you?"

"No, but—"

"Hey." He brushed her hair back, framing her too solemn face in his hands. "For your information, lady, I've always been wild about self-made women. Especially a certain successful, sexy as hell, beautiful self-made chef.

"And I can't wait for you to become a world-famous restaurateur so you can support me in the style to which I have every intention of becoming accustomed to. Hell, maybe I'll retire, turn my badge over to Cal, and become your own personal boy toy."

Her laugh was shaky. But, okay, it was still encouraging.

"You're so good for me," she said, love—oorah!—shining unguarded in her glistening eyes.

Definitely encouraging.

"I believe that's what I've been trying to point out."

"And I do love you."

"Ditto."

She arched a dark brow. "Ditto?"

Cooper looked at her with mock surprise. "Oh, did you want to hear those dreaded words again?"

"I don't think I could ever get tired of hearing them," Rachel admitted.

Cooper shrugged when he felt like singing hallelujahs to the heavens. "Well, since you put it that way . . ."

He gathered her into his arms and pressed his lips against her temple. "I love you." Kissed her eyelids, which fluttered shut. "Love you." Her cheeks. "Love you." Her adorably stubborn chin. "Love you."

"And I love you." Cooper wished Rachel sounded happy about that. "So much that I couldn't bear losing you."

"I'm not going anywhere." But this time he understood what she was talking about. "I've been there," he reminded her. "I understand losing the person you love and having your heart broken into pieces. I know how it feels to believe that you'll never be able to love anyone again. Thinking that no one will ever love you again.

"Or even worse, that you might fall in love with someone, only to have them die on you, too, throwing you back into that dark emotional pit again.

"But here's the thing, honey. After climbing out of that pit I'd wallowed in for a long time, although I'm not going to lie and say there weren't still dark moments, I managed to move on and became more or less content with my life. Hell, most days I was even happy.

"But then you arrived in River's Bend and reminded me what it felt like to be truly alive. And now, since I'm laying my heart out here on the line, I'll admit that just the idea of losing you and landing back in that pit, all alone again, is freaking terrifying."

"It is," she admitted, her ragged voice barely above a whisper.

He sat down on the edge of the bed again, took hold of her shoulders, and looked straight into her face. "But you, Rachel Hathaway, are worth it. I'm willing, no, make that aching to take the risk for the reward of spending the rest of our lives together.

"So, in case it's escaped your attention, I'm still waiting for your answer. About whether or not you're going to marry me."

"I want to. But . . ."

Oh, hell. Here came the waterworks again. Deciding that his heart had taken enough shredding for one night, Cooper pushed himself off the bed and began to dress.

Rachel stared up at him. "What are you doing?"

He pulled on a pair of gray knit boxer briefs. "Going home." His jeans were next, followed by the forest-green wool shirt Rachel had insisted on buying for him because she'd said the color reminded her of the color of his eyes when they made love.

"But I thought you were going to spend the night."

"I was." Which, once that barrier had tumbled, was why, instead of waiting for New Year's Eve, as he'd first planned, he'd brought along the ring. The mattress sagged beneath his weight as he sat down to put on his wool socks and boots. "But it turns out I'm a greedy man."

"Greedy?"

He stood up again, reminding himself to resist temptation. To stay firm and stick to the plan to win the long game.

"I love you. And I want more from you than just a few stolen hours, Rachel."

"But that's what tonight is all about. We agreed you were going to stay all night."

He shook his head. "Sorry. It's still not enough. I want all your nights. Every single long, love-filled night for the next fifty or sixty years." Despite the serious turn the conversation had taken, he found himself smiling broadly at that idea.

"Did you know that the sixtieth anniversary is diamonds? I learned that when I took great-grandmother Rose's ring to the jeweler's to get it cleaned. I figure if I start saving now, by the time I'm ninety-five, I should be able to afford a matching pair of earrings."

Rachel stared at him, as if searching for the joke. "You're crazy, Cooper Murphy."

"That's what they say," he agreed.

He bent down and gave her a quick, hard kiss that had her pressing her fingers against her lips as the brief flare ended all too soon. "I'll see you around, sweetheart. Give me a call when you change your mind."

It wasn't easier to walk away. Especially when she

called after him. "Cooper?"

He stopped in the doorway and closed his eyes, garnering strength before he turned around. Cooper knew what he'd see: Rachel, sitting amidst those love rumpled sheets, looking delightful, delicious, delectable, and most dangerous of all, vulnerable.

It was that soft trace of vulnerability, which she struggled so hard to conceal, that he found almost impossible to guard against. He glanced with feigned casualness over his shoulder. "Change your mind already?" he inquired pleasantly.

Her eyes were wide, lustrous, and eloquent in their need. It took every bit of self-restraint Cooper possessed not to surrender to their silent plea.

"What about the ring?"

Stifling a curse, he told himself that he shouldn't have expected Rachel to give in right away.

"Keep it," he suggested, with a careless wave of his hand. "Maybe after you get used to having it around, you won't feel so threatened by it."

With that he was gone.

Instead of running after him, Rachel stayed where she was, stunned, convinced his behavior had to be some sort of bizarre joke. He'd be back.

"After all, everyone knows the Murphys are crazy," she reminded herself as she heard the Jeep start up. Then drive away.

Somewhere in the distant hills, a lonesome coyote called out to the full moon. The sad song stimulated a similar response from neighborhood dogs. Next door, inside his heated doghouse, the Walker's German shepherd joined in mournfully to the chorus.

And still Rachel waited.

45

THE MIDNIGHT-BLUE OF the sky turned to pearly gray, then dusty rose as the sun crept over the horizon as a new day dawned. After tossing and turning and turning all night, Rachel was tangled in sheets that still carried the evocative scent of their earlier lovemaking.

And still Cooper hadn't returned.

Her method of working out difficult decisions had always been to cook. Which was what she did now. While Scott continued to sleep, blissfully oblivious of how their lives may have dramatically changed in a few short hours, Rachel dragged out every bowl, pot, pan, and kitchen utensil she owned to create mountains of food she had no intention of eating: wafer-thin crepes wrapped around plump strawberries and drenched in powdered sugar; buttermilk-almond biscuits; cinnamon pecan coffee cake and plump Belgian waffles.

"He's a sheriff," she said as she separated eggs into two bowls. "Some escaped criminal could shoot him." She tackled the yolks first, whisking them into a pale yellow froth in the larger blue bowl. "Or he could be out in the middle of the river fly fishing." He'd promised to teach her next summer. "And some drunken boater could run over him."

She was trying not to picture Cooper sliced into pieces by a boat propeller when there was a knock on the door. Her fingers tightened on the wire whisk.

Cooper!

She'd known he couldn't stay away!

She flung open the door open and felt her face falling as she viewed Mrs. MacGregor standing on the porch.

"Oh. Good morning."

"Morning'," the woman said, trying to look around Rachel. "Something sure smells good."

Belatedly remembering her manners, Rachel opened the door wider. "I was just making breakfast and I'm afraid I got carried away. Perhaps you'd like to share it with me."

"Well, that'd be right nice," the older woman said as she followed Rachel into the kitchen. "But the real reason I came over here was to . . ."

Her voice drifted off as she stared at the vast array of dishes covering the countertops. "Good gracious. I can't remember when I've seen so much food in one place."

"As I said, I got a bit carried away," Rachel admitted. "You're welcome to help yourself. I was, uh, just trying out recipes for the New Chance."

Mrs. MacGregor's eyes lit up like the town's Christmas tree in the park across from the courthouse as they settled on the coffee cake. Rachel could practically see her mouth begin to water.

"Well, if the food you plan to serve at the café is anything like this, you're going to be a real hit."

"Thank you." For the first time since she'd found

Mitzi's ad for the New Chance in that magazine, the success of her restaurant ranked way down on Rachel's list of concerns. "What can I do for you?" she asked as she took a plate from the cupboard and placed it on the table.

The elderly woman pinched off a corner of a golden-brown biscuit, rolling her eyes with ecstasy as she bit into it. "Do?"

"You said you came over here for a reason," Rachel reminded her as she placed a fork, knife, and napkin beside the plate. Although her heart was still aching from her argument with Cooper, she managed a slight smile. "Although, if you're here to borrow any eggs or butter, I'm afraid I'm all out."

"Glory be," Mrs. MacGregor exclaimed around a mouthful of corn fritter. "I nearly forgot. It's Cooper."

Rachel's blood turn as cold as the icicles hanging from the eaves outside the kitchen window. "Cooper? Is he all right?"

"Well, sure. Leastwise for now. But the way that Jake Buchanan's been actin' up lately, you just never know how things are going to turn out."

"Jake? Isn't he in jail?"

"He escaped last night after Cal took him back after your party. Seems they were playing poker when he just reached over and pulled Cal's gun from his holster with nary a *please* nor a *thank you*, demanded his phone, then locked him in the very same cell he'd been in. Then he took off.

"Nobody knew a thing about it 'til Cooper showed up this morning with some glazed packaged donuts he'd picked up at the mercantile." She eyed the abundance of dishes appraisingly. "I'll bet if Jake had been promised some of your cooking, he would've hung around at least until after breakfast."

Rachel's heart was beating a hundred miles a minute as thunder roared in her ears. "Did Cooper go after him?"

"Well, sure. After all, he's the sheriff. Chasing down escaped convicts is part of his job."

And wasn't that exactly what she'd just been worrying about?

Rachel pressed her fingertips against her temple. Her head was spinning. She had to think. "I have to go to him."

"I kinda figured you'd want to do just that." Mrs. MacGregor said pleasantly. "He's out at Jake's place, on the old river road just outside of town. You probably won't be able to miss it, since, from what they're saying on the radio, there are a lot of police, including ones from the State, and even a couple of feds out there.

"The F.B.I?"

"Don't know." She shrugged well-padded shoulders and cut into the coffee cake. "Maybe Homeland Security. Seems Jake's determined to have some sort of showdown with those government officials when they come to auction off his property."

"But the auction wasn't supposed to be held until the twenty-third."

"I wouldn't know about that." She shook her head and snorted as she slid a wedge-shaped piece of cake onto a second plate. "Word is that Jake's armed and dangerous. My guess is that he's taken that outlaw role playing he does on the train ride entirely too seriously and plans to reenact the shootout at the O.K. Corral."

"Oh. My. God!" Rachel had to remind herself how to

breathe.

"I wouldn't worry if I were you. It'll probably turn out okay. The radio's reporting that things have quieted considerably since Cooper went into the house."

"Cooper's in the house? With Jake? Alone?"

"Sure is. After all, it's—"

"Part of his job," Rachel said.

Damn. Hadn't she heard that enough times from the man himself? She glanced toward the stairway and thought about Scott. "Mrs. MacGregor would you mind—"

"I came over to sit with your boy," she confirmed. "While you go stand by your man."

Her man. Although it sounded a lot like a country song, Rachel still found the idea was wonderful. Cooper was her man. Just as she was his woman.

"I'll just check on him," she said, hurrying down the hall to his room, where she found him hugging the stuffed horse Mitzi had given him. He was sound asleep, innocently oblivious to the world. Taking another second, she dashed into her bedroom and retrieved the jewelry box from the tangle of sheets.

"Thank you," she said as she yanked her parka from its hook. "And please, help yourself to anything you want."

As Rachel raced out to her car, Mrs. MacGregor's gaze swept happily, hungrily, over the kitchen.

46

J AKE BRENNAN'S RANCH house, situated in a grove of trees and surrounded by serene white fields of snow, looked like something from Little House on the Prairie. The familiar Jeep Cherokee, the white Shelter Bay Sheriff's Department cruiser Cal usually drove, three Oregon State Police cars, a pair of unmarked black vehicles with federal plates, and a KOTI television news van from Klamath Falls revealed that the setting was not as peaceful as it appeared.

Then there were all the people standing behind the police barricade.

Spotting her, a grave-faced Dan Murphy, with an obviously distressed Mitzi by his side, made his way through the crowd to Rachel.

"He'll be all right, Rachel," he assured her. "Jake would never hurt Cooper."

"You can't know that," she insisted. "Not for sure. What was Cooper thinking of, going in there unarmed?" She'd learned that frightening detail on the car radio driving out to the ranch.

"He's trying to keep an old friend and former father-in-law from getting in even worse trouble," Dan said. "At times like this, if things escalate too fast and too far, innocent people could get hurt."

"What about him?" she asked, frustrated by the way first Mrs. MacGregor and now Dan were both taking Cooper's risky behavior so matter-of-factly. "Isn't he an innocent person?"

"He's the sheriff," Dan said, as if that explained everything. "It goes with the job."

"I swear, if I hear that one more time, I'll scream!"

Mitzi put her arm around Rachel's shoulder. "Cooper's one of the smoothest talkers I've ever met. Didn't he have me giving up my commission before we'd finished our coffee after dinner that first night? Believe me, that's the first time that's ever happened. He'll have Jake coming out of the house before all those cops' morning coffee gets cold back at the station."

"Why did the government move the date of the auction up?" she asked.

"They didn't. Since Jake took Cal's pistol, Cooper had no choice but to call in the State Police for backup, just in case. Things sort of snowballed from there once Mel Skinner picked up Jake's escape on his police scanner and called in the feds. Never would've pegged Mel as a scanner guy."

Rachel was furious Cooper would dare risk his life before she had a chance to accept his proposal. Before he could see her wearing Rose Murphy's pretty antique ring. "If Cooper gets out of there alive, I'm going to kill him."

"Spoken like a woman in love," Dan drawled with the same easy humor Rachel had come to love in Cooper. "Since Mitzi started planning our wedding, she doesn't always make sense, either."

"You're both damn lucky Rachel and I put up with the two of you," Mitzi shot back. "The entire town knows that the Murphy men have always been crazy, beginning with old Malachy."

"Guess that's what makes us so irresistible." Dan smiled encouragingly down at Rachel. "He'll be all right, honey." This time it was Cooper's unfailing optimism and confidence she heard in his father's voice.

As Rachel watched a SWAT team arrive in their armored vehicle, she could only hope he was right.

THREE HOURS. JAKE had sat there with that damn shotgun across his knees longer than Cooper ever would've thought possible. Even knowing that it wasn't capable of shooting a live round, didn't make Cooper less tired of looking at it. The only good news so far was that Cal's pistol remained on a side table. If Jake made a move for it, Cooper knew he'd have no choice but to stop him.

"Almost nine o'clock," he said conversationally, looking up at the mantle clock. "The federal offices will be open soon."

He'd told Jake about Karen Fairfield, the records the woman had pored over, the entries she'd found which had mistakenly credited Jake's payment to another account, and the lawyer who'd agreed to work all night, if necessary, preparing an injunction to stop the auction.

Unfortunately, having suffered too long in the tangled bureaucratic web, Jake refused to buy any of the story until he spoke with both Karen Fairfield and the judge himself.

The older man glanced out the window.

"I wouldn't do that, if I were you," Cooper said quietly.

"Do what?"

"Stick that bogus shotgun out the window again, like you're re-enacting the battle of the Alamo. In case you haven't noticed, they've brought in a SWAT team who might not realize the only thing it's good for is playing a train robber. You could end up getting us both killed."

Jake reached into his pocket with his free hand and pulled out a pack of Marlboros. Shaking one loose, he said, "So what?"

Cooper leaned back in the hard chair and forced himself to relax. Ten more minutes. His tailbone felt as if it were perched on a sharp rock.

"Well, maybe you don't have anything to live for," he said. "But once I get things buttoned up here, I intend to get married."

"To Rachel."

Cooper belatedly wondered if he'd made a tactical error, bringing up his plans to remarry. "She's a nice woman, Jake," he said with careful casualness.

His former father-in-law drew in on the cigarette, causing its red tip to flare. A cloud of blue smoke filled the air between them when he exhaled. "Can't argue with you there," he agreed gruffly. "Little skinny, though. She don't have much meat on her."

"Ah, but what the lady has is prime," Cooper pointed out with a grin.

Jake chuckled. "I always liked you, Cooper. You treated my Ellie real nice. Even if you weren't good enough for her."

"As far as you were concerned, there wasn't a man in the state good enough for Ellen Buchanan."

"True enough," Jake confirmed. "She was a sweet girl, wasn't she? And pretty as a picture."

"She was sweet," Cooper said. "And beautiful. And I loved her with my entire heart and soul."

Jake studied the ash at the end of his cigarette. "Never said you didn't . . . So, now you love Rachel."

"I do. Does that bother you?"

"Maybe a little," Jake admitted. "But only because I wish things could've turned out different. With you and Ellie."

"We can't always choose the way our life's going to turn out, Jake," Cooper said quietly. And weren't he and Rachel both living proof of that? "Although in this instance, I'd say you're holding both our futures in your hands." He reached over, picked up the cordless phone from the table and held it out to Jake. "Make your call."

47

TIME CRAWLED BY at a snail's pace as the crowd of spectators behind the police barricades increased. When there was still no action from the house, the television crew was forced to settle for a reporter doing standup reports from in front of the wooden gate leading to the ranch house.

Dan had, unsurprisingly, refused any interviews.

Meanwhile, the frighteningly well-armed SWAT team was poised for action, planning strategies, checking weapons.

After yesterday's winter blizzard, the day had dawned bright and clear and sunny. It was a day for laughing.

For loving.

Not for dying.

River's Bend's newest deputy, who didn't look old enough to drive, offered Rachel a cup of coffee in a cardboard cup. Rachel politely refused and kept her gaze riveted on the ranch house. Mitzi suggested she go wait in Dan's truck, where she could get out of the cold. Rachel wasn't about to move.

Cal Potter, looking twenty years older than he had while singing off-key at the party last night, muttered an abject apology for allowing Jake to escape. Putting a hand on his arm, Rachel offered reassuring words she wished she could fully believe.

Not once did she take her eyes from that front door.

Finally, after what seemed an eternity, it opened. Rachel had been unaware of holding her breath until she released it on a ragged, painful sob.

Then, ignoring the warnings of the various lawmen, shaking loose the deputy who tried to stop her, she leaped over the barricade, knocking it down, then burst through the gate, running across the soft white expanse of snow between them.

"You're all right!" she cried, flinging herself into Cooper's arms. "You're safe."

Cooper caught Rachel as she came hurtling toward him. "Of course," he said as she smothered his smiling face with kisses. "Don't tell me you had any doubts?"

"Doubts?" she shot back as he lowered her to the ground. "Damn you, Cooper Murphy, you had me frightened to death!"

She turned on Jake. "And you." She jabbed a finger into his chest. "How could you do something like this? To Cooper? To me? Don't you know how much he cares for you? How much we all care for you?"

A crimson flush rose from the collar of Jake's plaid snap-front shirt. "I guess I kinda found that out," he said sheepishly. "Turns out I was right about the government making a mistake, though."

"I always believed you," Rachel said. "Just as I always believed Cooper would find a way to prove that. Which was all the more reason not to hold your best friend hostage in a house surrounded by heavily armed law enforcement officers."

Jake rubbed his grizzled jaw as he gave Rachel a long, appraising look. Then glanced up at Cooper. "Your woman speaks her mind," he said finally.

"That she does," Cooper agreed.

"Probably going to be a handful."

Cooper grinned. "I'm counting on it."

Jake shook his head. "Everyone always said you Murphys are crazy."

"That's what they say, all right," Cooper acknowledged cheerfully.

"Takes all kinds," Jake muttered with another shake of his head. "You two take your time to work things out between you. Guess I'd best go turn myself in."

Cooper reached out and put a hand on the smaller man's shoulder. "I'll do what I can to get you a reduced sentence for this latest escapade," he said. "But you're definitely going to have to start going to *AA*."

"So long as I know my land's gonna be here when I get out, I don't mind giving up the bottle and spending some time in jail." He looked at Rachel. "You gonna be doing the cooking?"

"Yes. Although after what you put everyone through this morning, I'm not sure you're going to like it."

Jake's eyes narrowed suspiciously. "You wouldn't."

Rachel nodded. "I certainly would," she threatened. "We're talking bait."

"Mebee I can swing a deal to get sent to the State pen," he mumbled, shuffling through the snow toward the approaching cops.

"Bait?" Cooper asked, putting his arm around Rachel's waist.

"It's a long story."

"I've plenty of time."

"That's right. If I remember correctly, you said some-thing about fifty or sixty years," she said as they walked back toward the throng of onlookers.

"At least." He lifted her left hand. The stone sparkled in the bright winter sunshine. "I like this ring. It looks kind of familiar."

Rachel tilted her head back to smile up at him. "I like it, too. So much that I've decided to stick around for the matching earrings."

"Greedy," Cooper teased as he nibbled lightly on her smiling lips.

Rachel threw her arms around his neck. "Wait until I get you home alone," she promised. "And you'll find out exactly how greedy I can be."

A rousing cheer went up from the gathered spectators as their lips met and clung.

"Come on, Sheriff." She linked arms with him as they continued toward his Jeep. Mitzi had already assured her she'd drive Rachel's car back to her house. "I have breakfast waiting."

"Sounds great," Cooper said agreeably. "What are we having?"

Happy endings did exist after all, and not just in fairy tales. Rachel's answering laugh was free and breezy.

"It's a surprise."

The End

Continue reading for an excerpt from *A Sea Change* . . .

A Sea Change

A Shelter Bay/Castlelough novel

JoAnn Ross

1

Castlelough, Ireland

ALTHOUGH THE MICROBREWERY might be a new addition, Brennan's Microbrewery and Pub had been serving rebels and raiders, smugglers and sailors, poets and patriots since 1650.

And, Sedona Sullivan considered as she watched a young couple share a kiss inside one of the two snugs by the front door, lovers. The leaded glass window kept people's behavior reasonably sedate while the stained glass door allowed conversations to remain private.

Whiskey bottles gleamed like pirates' booty in the glow of brass-hooded lamps, a turf fire burned in a large open hearth at one end of the pub, warming against the chill of rain pelting on the slate roof, and heavy wooden tables were crowded onto the stone floor. Booths lined walls covered in football flags, vintage signs, old photographs, and, in the library extension, books and magazines filled shelves and wall racks.

The man murmured something in the woman's ear, causing her to laugh and toss hair as bright as the peat fire. As the woman lifted her smiling lips to his for a longer, more drawn-out kiss, Sedona felt a stir of envy.

How long had it been since a man had made her laugh with sexy abandon? How long since anyone had kissed her like that man was kissing the pretty Irish redhead?

Sedona did some quick mental math. Finding the sum impossible to believe, she recalculated. Twenty-two months, three weeks, and eight days? Seriously?

Unfortunately, given that she was, after all, a former CPA with excellent math skills and a near-photographic memory, Sedona knew her figures were right on the money. As where those additional sixteen hours she reluctantly tacked on to the initial subtotal.

How could that be possible?

Granted, she'd been busy. After leaving behind a high-powered accounting career in Portland, she'd opened a successful bakery in Shelter Bay, Castlelough's sister city on the Oregon coast.

But still . . . nearly two years?

That was just too depressing.

Unlike last evening, when Brennan's had been crowded to the ancient wooden rafters with family members and close friends enjoying Mary Joyce and J.T. Douchett's rehearsal dinner, tonight the pub was nearly deserted, save for the two lovers, three men watching a replay of a rugby match on the TV bolted to the stone wall, and an ancient man somewhere between eighty and a hundred years old who was nursing a foam-topped dark ale and singing sad Irish songs to himself.

And there was Patrick Brennan, owner, bartender and cook, whose smiling Irish eyes were as darkly brown as the fudge frosting she'd made for the chocolate groom's cake.

Which was what had brought Sedona to her ancestral homeland.

She'd met international movie star and award-winning screenwriter Mary Joyce when the Castlelough-born actress had visited Shelter Bay for a film festival featuring her movies. After Mary had gotten engaged to J.T., a former Marine who'd been pressed into service as the actress' bodyguard, Mary had asked Sedona to make both the groom's cake and the all-important wedding cake.

Happy to play a part in her friend's wedding, Sedona had jumped at the chance to revisit the land of her ancestors.

A cheer went up as a player dressed in a green jersey from the Ireland Wolfhounds scored against the England Saxons. After delivering her wine and taking her order, Patrick paused on his way back to the bar long enough to glance up at the screen and even the old man stopped singing long enough to raise his mug before switching to a ballad celebrating a victory in some ancient, but never to be forgotten war.

Sedona was thinking that watching a game when you already knew the final score must be a male thing, when the heavy oak door opened, bringing with it a wet, brisk wind that sent her paper napkin sailing onto the floor.

Before she could reach down and pick it up, her attention was captured by the arrival of a man she had already determined to be trouble on a hot, sexy stick.

His wind-mussed hair, which gave him the look of having just gotten out of bed, fell to a few inches above his broad shoulders and was as black as the sea on a moonless night. As he took off his leather jacket, revealing a lean hard, well-muscled body, testosterone radiated off him in bone-weakening waves that had her glad she was sitting down.

"Well, would you look at what the night gale blew in," Patrick greeted him from behind the bar. "I thought you were leaving town."

"I was. Am," Conn Brennan clarified in the roughened, gravely rocker's voice recognizable the world over. "I'm flying out of Shannon to catch up with the lads in Frankfurt. But I had a sudden craving for fish and chips and sure, everyone knows there's no finer food than the pub grub served up by my big brother at Brennan's."

Patrick laughed at that. "Sure, with talk like that, some would think you'd be from Blarney," he shot back on an exaggerated brogue. "So how did the party go? I assume the bride and groom enjoyed themselves?"

"The party was grand, in large part due to the music," Conn Brennan said. The infamous bad boy rocker known by the single name Conn to his legion of fans around the world had been dubbed "Conn of the Hundred Battles" by tabloids for his habit for getting into fights with the paparazzi.

"As for the bride and groom, I image they're shagging their brains out about now. The way they couldn't keep their hands off each other had the local band lads making bets on whether they'd make it to bed before consummating the nuptials."

The heels of his metal-buckled black boots rang out on the stone floor as he headed toward the bar, pausing when he almost stepped on Sedona's dropped napkin. He bent to pick it up, then when he straightened, his startlingly neon blue eyes clashed with hers.

And held for a long, humming moment.

"Well, fancy seeing you here. I would have guessed, after the busy day you've had, that you'd be all tucked away in your comfy bed at the inn, dreaming of wedding cakes, sugar plums, and all things sweet."

He placed the napkin on the table with a dangerously sexy smile he'd directed her way more than once as he'd rocked the reception from the bandstand. When an image of a bare-chested Conn sprawled on her four-poster bed at the inn flashed wickedly through Sedona's mind, something quivered deep in her stomach.

It was only hunger, she assured herself. Between putting the last touches on the towering wedding cake and working with the serving staff during the reception, she hadn't taken the time for a proper meal all day.

"I was in the mood for a glass of wine and a late bite." Her tone, cool as wintry mist over the Burren, was in direct contrast to the heat flooding her body.

He lifted an ebony brow. "Why would you be wanting to go out in this rain? The Copper Beech Inn has excellent room service, and surely your suite came with a mini-bar well stocked with adult beverages."

"You're correct on both counts," she acknowledged as the old man segued into "The Rare Auld Mountain Dew."

She took a sip of wine, hoping it would cool the heat rising inside her.

It didn't.

"But I chose to spend my last night in Ireland here at Brennan's instead of an impersonal hotel room. Besides, you're right about your brother's food. It's excellent." While the pub grub menu might be casual dining, Patrick Brennan had proven to be as skilled in the kitchen as he was at pulling pints. "There's also the fact that the mini bar is ridiculously expensive."

"Ah." He nodded his satisfaction. "Your parents

didn't merely pass down an Irish surname, Sedona Sullivan. It appears you've inherited our Irish frugality."

"And here I thought that was the Scots."

"It's true that they've been more than happy to advertise that reputation, despite having stolen the concept from us. Same as they did the pipes, which were if truth be told, were originally intended as an Irish joke on the Scots, who, being dour people without any sense of humor, failed to get it."

"And didn't I recognize your famed Irish frugality the moment you roared into town in that fire-engine red Ferrari?"

He threw back his head and laughed, a rich, deep, sound that flowed over her and reminded her yet again exactly how much time had passed since she'd been with a man.

Your choice.

"And wouldn't you be a prime example of appearances being deceiving?" he countered.

"Don't be disturbing my guests, Conn," Patrick called out.

"We're just having a friendly conversation." Conn's eyes hadn't left Sedona's since he'd stopped at the table. "Am I disturbing you, a stór?"

Yes.

"Not at all," she lied.

The truth was that she'd been feeling wired and edgy from the moment he strode into the hall for a sound check before the reception.

"Though you do force me to point out that I'm no one's darling," she tacked on. He'd undoubtedly used the generic Irish endearment the way American men used "babe" or "sweetheart."

Even without having read about all the rich and famous women the rocker was reported to have been involved with, any sensible woman would keep her distance from Conn Brennan. Despite having grown up on a commune of former hippies and flower children, Sedona had always considered herself unwaveringly sensible.

Her knowledge of the endearment failed to put a dent in his oversized male ego. Instead, amusement danced in his electric blue eyes.

"Would you have learned that bit of Irish from some local lad attracted by your charms?" he asked as he rubbed a jaw darkened with a day-old stubble that added machismo to his beautiful face. "Which, may I say, despite your short time in our fair village, would not surprise me in the least."

"My parents believe everyone should speak at least two languages," she responded mildly. "I'm fluent in Spanish, know enough French to order a baguette and wine in Paris, and thanks to a year studying abroad at Trinity College Dublin, along with the past few days having an opportunity to practice, I can carry on a bit of a conversation in Irish."

Raindrops glistened in his black hair as he tilted his head. "Mary wasn't exaggerating when she was going on about your charms," he said finally. "And aren't brains and beauty an enticing combination? As for you not being my darling, Sedona Sullivan, the night's still young."

"Perhaps not for those in Dublin or Cork," she said, struggling against the seductive pull of that smile. The rugby game ended with a score by the redshirted Saxons. The men who'd been watching the TV shuffled out, muttering curses about allegedly blind referees. "But if you don't leave soon, you won't be able to drive your fancy 'frugal' import to the airport because Castlelough's cobblestone streets will have been rolled up."

He gave her a longer, considering look, his intense blue eyes narrowing as he scrutinized her in silence for what seemed like forever, even as some part of her brain still managing to function told her must have only been a few seconds.

"Your order's up," he said, without having even glanced toward the bar. "Since Patrick's occupied with my fish and chips, I'll bring your late bite back with my ale."

He smelled so amazing, like night rain darkened with the scent of leather and the tang of sweat from having played as energetically for his home town crowd of a hundred wedding guests as he had to his recent sell-out crowd of ninety thousand in London's Wembley Stadium.

Tamping down a reckless urge to lick his dark neck, Sedona forced a faint smile.

"Thank you. We certainly wouldn't want your fish to burn while your brother's distracted delivering my meal."

Assuring herself that there wasn't a woman on the planet who'd be capable of not checking out the very fine butt in those dark jeans, she watched his long, lose-hipped outlaw's stride to the bar.

Not wanting to be caught staring as he returned with his dark ale and her plate, she turned her gaze back to the couple in the snug. The woman was now sitting on the man's lap as they tangled tonsils.

Why didn't they just get a damn room?

"Now there's a pair who know how to make the most of a rainy night," Conn said as he sat down across from her.

There was no way she was going to respond to that.

Instead, she turned her attention to the small white plate of deep fried cheese served on a bed of salad greens with a side of dark port and berry sauce. The triangular piece of cheese that had been fried in a light-as-a-feather beer batter nearly made her swoon.

As she'd discovered when making her cakes, Irish dairy farmers seemed to possess a magic that churned milk into pure gold. "This is amazingly delicious."

"The French claim to make the best cream and butter, but I'd put ours against theirs any day. That St. Brigid's cheese you're eating is a local Camembert from Michael Joyce's farm."

Michael was Mary Joyce's older brother. Sedona had met the former war correspondent turned farmer and his American wife at a dinner at the Joyce family home her first night in Castlelough.

"And speaking of delicious," he said, "I'm remiss in not telling you that your cake had me tempted to lick my plate."

"Thank you." When his words brought back her earlier fantasy of licking his neck, she felt color rising in her cheeks.

"Of course, I wouldn't have," he continued, thankfully seemingly unaware of her wicked, too tempting thoughts. "Because I promised Mary."

"You promised Mary you wouldn't lick your dessert plate?"

"No, despite being an international movie star, Mary can be a bit of a stickler for propriety. So I promised to behave myself."

He waited a beat, just long enough to let her know something else was coming. "Which was the only reason I didn't leave a set to the lads and dance with you at the reception."

"Well, no one can fault you for your confidence."

"Would you be saying you wouldn't have given me a dance? If I hadn't been performing and had asked?"

Dance with this man? From the way he'd watched her from the bandstand, his eyes like blue flames, Sedona had a feeling that dancing wasn't precisely what he'd had in mind.

"I came here to work," she said. "Not dance." Nor hook up with a hot Irish musician.

"It was a grand cake," he said. "Even better than the one I was served at the White House." Where he'd received a presidential medal for his social activism, Sedona remembered. "And one of the few that tasted as good as it looked. Most cakes these days seem to have Spackle spread over them."

She laughed at the too true description. "That's fondant, which creates a smoother surface to decorate."

"It's shite is what it is. When I was growing up, my mam's carrot cake always won first prize at the county fair. With six children in the family, we'd all have to wait our turn to lick the bowl or she'd never have ended up with enough frosting to cover it, but I always believed that cream cheese frosting was the best part."

Sedona was relieved when Patrick arrived at the table with his brother's fish and chips, interrupting a conversation that had returned to licking.

"Something we can agree on," she said, dipping the cheese into a currant sauce brightened with flavors of ginger, orange, and lemon. "Which is why I used buttercream on the cakes for the wedding."

He bit into the battered cod. Heaven help her, somehow the man managed to make chewing sexy.

"So," he said, after taking a drink of the dark Rebel Red microbrew. "Mary tells me you make cupcakes back in America."

"My bakery, Take the Cake, specializes in cupcakes, but I've also added pies."

"Good business move," he said with a nod. "Who wouldn't be liking a nice warm piece of pie? Cakes are well enough, but pies are sexy."

Said the man who obviously had sex on the mind. Unfortunately, he wasn't alone. As she watched him bite into a chip, she found herself wondering how that black face scruff would feel on her breasts. Her stomach. And lower still.

"Well, they've proven popular," she said as her pulse kicked up. "Which was rewarding, given that it proved the validity of months of research."

He cocked his head. "You researched whether or not people like pie?"

"Well, of course I already knew they like pie. I merely did a survey and analysis to calculate the cost and profit margins."

"Which told you lots of people like pie."

He was laughing at her. She could see it in his eyes. "Yes. Do you realize how many businesses fail in any given year? Especially these days?" They were finally in a conversational territory she knew well.

"Probably about as many people who don't succeed in the music business," he guessed. "Though I've never done a sales analysis before writing a song."

"That's different."

"Is it, now?"

She tried again. "What if you wrote a song that didn't

connect with your fans?"

He shrugged and took another bite of battered cod. "I'd write it off as a mistake and move on. No risk, no reward. I tend to go with my gut, then don't look back."

"My father's the same way," she murmured, more to herself than to him.

He leaned back in the wooden chair and eyed her over the rim of his glass. "And how has that worked out for him?"

"Very well, actually."

He lifted the glass. "Point made."

"Different strokes," she argued.

"You know what they say about opposites." His gaze moved slowly over her face, his eyes darkening to a stormy, deep sea blue as they settled on her lips, which had parts of her body tingling that Sedona had forgotten could tingle.

"I have a spreadsheet," she said.

"I suspect you have quite a few." When he flashed her a slow, badass grin she suspected had panties dropping across several continent, Sedona sternly reminded herself that she'd never—ever—been attracted to bad boys.

So why had she forgotten how to breathe?

As that fantasy of him sprawled in her bed next door in the Copper Beech Inn came crashing to the forefront of her mind, Sedona reminded herself of those twenty-two months, three weeks, eight days and sixteen, going on seventeen hours.

Even if she hadn't been coming off a very long dry spell, every instinct Sedona possessed told her that not only was Conn Brennan trouble, he was way out of her league.

"They're not all business related. I also have one for

men."

Putting his ale down, he leaned across the small round table and tucked a strand of blond hair, which had fallen from the tidy French twist she'd created for the reception, behind her ear. The brush of fingertips roughened from steel guitar strings caused heat to rise beneath his touch.

"You put us men in boxes." His eyes somehow managed to look both hot and amused at the same time.

It was not a question. But Sedona answered it anyway. "Not men. Attributes," she corrected. "What I'd require, and expect, in a mate."

Oh, God. Why did she have to use that word? While technically accurate, it had taken on an entirely different, impossibly sexy meaning. Desperately wanting to bury her flaming face in her palms, she remained frozen in place as his treacherous finger traced a trail of sparks around her lips, which, despite Ireland's damp weather, had gone desert dry.

"And where do I fit in your tidy little boxes, Sedona Sullivan?"

Although she was vaguely aware of the couple leaving the snug, and the pub, his steady male gaze was holding her hostage. She could not look away.

"You don't."

"I'm glad to hear that," he said in that deep, gravely voice that set off vibrations like a tuning fork inside her.

Conn ran his hand down her throat, his thumb skimming over her pulse, which leaped beneath his touch, before cupping her jaw. "Because I've never been comfortable fenced into boundaries."

And growing up in a world of near-absolute freedom, Sedona had never been comfortable without them. "There's something you need to know."

"And that would be?"

"I'm not into casual sex."

"And isn't that good to know." He lowered his mouth to within a whisper of hers. "Since there'd be nothing casual about how you affect me."

She drew in a sharp breath, feeling as if she were standing on the edge of the towering cliff where J.T. and Mary's wedding had taken place in a circle of ancient stones.

"I'm taking you back to your room."

Somehow, her hand had lifted to his face. "Your flight . . ."

He parted her lips with the pad of his thumb. "It's my plane. It takes off when I'm ready." His other hand was on her leg, his fingers stroking the inside of her thigh through the denim of the jeans she'd put on after returning to her room after the reception. "I'll ring up the pilot and tell him I'll be leaving in the morning."

Then his mouth came down on hers and Conn was kissing her, hard and deep, setting off a mind-blinding supernova inside Sedona.

They left the pub, running through the soft Irish rain into the inn next door. As the old-fashioned gilt cage elevator cranked its way up to her floor, he continued to kiss her breathless, making Sedona forgot that she'd never, ever, been attracted to bad boys.

Check out more books in the Castlelough Series:

A Woman's Heart

Fair Haven

Legends Lake

About The Author

When *New York Times* bestselling contemporary romance author JoAnn Ross was seven-years-old, she had no doubt whatsoever that she'd grow up to play center field for the New York Yankees. Writing would be her backup occupation, something she planned to do after retiring from baseball. Those were, in her mind, her only options. While waiting for the Yankees management to call, she wrote her first novella—a tragic romance about two star-crossed Mallard ducks—for a second grade writing assignment.

The paper earned a gold star. And JoAnn kept writing.

She's now written around one hundred novels (she quit keeping track long ago) and has been published in twenty-six countries. Two of her titles have been excerpted in *Cosmopolitan* magazine and her books have also been published by the *Doubleday*, *Rhapsody*, *Literary Guild*, and *Mystery Guild* book clubs. A member of the Romance Writers of America's Honor Roll of best-selling authors, she's won several awards.

Although the Yankees have yet to call her to New York to platoon center field, JoAnn figures making one out of two life goals isn't bad.

Currently writing her Shelter Bay and River's Bend series set in Oregon, where she and her husband grew up, and her Castlelough Irish series—from where her grandparents emigrated and one of her favorite places to visit—JoAnn lives with her husband and three rescued dogs (who pretty much rule the house) in the Pacific Northwest.

Sign up to receive the latest news from JoAnn
http://www.joannross.com/Page.asp?Navid=117

Visit JoAnn's Website
http://www.joannross.com/

Friend JoAnn on Facebook
https://www.facebook.com/JoAnnRossbooks

Follow JoAnn on Twitter
https://twitter.com/JoAnnRoss

Follow JoAnn on Goodreads
https://www.goodreads.com/author/show/31311.JoAnn_Ross

Check out more books in the Shelter Bay Series:

The Homecoming
One Summer
On Lavender Lane
Moonshell Beach
Sea Glass Winter
Castaway Cove
Christmas on Main Street

Made in the USA
San Bernardino, CA
28 May 2014